Shadows of the Game

Penned by:
Askari
AKA
The King of Philly Street-Lit

Lock Down Publications
Presents
Shadows of The Game
A Novel by: *Askari*

Askari

Lock Down Publications
P.O. Box 870494
Mesquite, Tx 75187

Visit our website
www.lockdownpublications.com

Lock Down Publications
Like our page on Facebook: Lock Down Publications @
www.facebook.com/lockdownpublications.ldp
Cover design and layout by: **Dynasty Cover Me**
Book interior design by: **Shawn Walker**
Edited by: **Shawn Walker**

Stay Connected with Us!

Text LOCKDOWN to 22828 to stay up-to-date with new releases, sneak peaks, contests and more...

Thank you!

A Note from The Author

As an author of urban fiction, my ultimate goal is to write about the streets in its purest form, while at the same time entertaining and captivating the minds of the readers. Now, in order to reach that goal, it's imperative that I write about "The Game" from both sides.

In my *Blood of a Boss* series, I brought y'all the raw and uncut. But this time around, I had to dig a little deeper and bring y'all the *real*. It's easy to focus on the money and drugs, and the glitz and glamour that comes along with being in "The Game". But what about the *Shadows of the Game*? The hardships and struggles, and the stories that are rarely told? For every gangsta in the street, there's a bullet with his name on it; and for every hustler pushing weight, there's a prison sentence with a state number attached. There's a big mama crying at the cemetery, and a baby mama crying in the courtroom. So, this story is dedicated to them.

Respectfully Yours,
Rayshon "Askari" Farmer

Dedications

This book is dedicated to the little brothas feeling hopeless and trapped. I know things are hard on you, and you feel like saying "Fuck it". But trust me, lil' bro, if you work hard, believe in yourself and stay the course, things can and will get better. Your current situation doesn't define you. Your *environment* doesn't define you. So, move like a champ and keep your eyes on tomorrow, because tomorrow has the potential to be so much brighter. Your current struggle is only for a moment, but the wrong decisions could affect you for a lifetime. So, be intelligent. *Think!* You have to analyze your struggle from each and every angle, and then think of a way to turn what's negative into a positive. And if you need someone to holla at, just hit up big bro, and I'ma hit right back.

Bulletproof Love,
Big Brotha, Askari

Rayshon Farmer GE—4161
Smart Communications/PA DOC
SCI Coal Township
PO Box 33028
St. Petersburg, FL. 33733

7

Askari

CHAPTER ONE

EBONY
Friday, November 20th, 2015
9:06 am

I was pissed the hell off when I pulled into the parking lot of the Abington Junior High School. It was the second time in three weeks that I received an email from my son's principal, informing me that he'd been suspended. It was cool, though, because the last time he pulled this shit I let him off the hook with a warning. But this time around, I had a surprise for that ass. I was taking that shit back to the old school, straight up Big Mama style.

And y'all *know* what I'm talking about!

Don't try to act like I'm the only one who grew up with a Big Mama—titties so big they reminded you of watermelons, freely swinging under a nightgown that smelled like Ben Gay and fried chicken. The undisputed Queen of a three-bedroom project; the same place where three of her grandchildren called home. Come on, now, y'all remember the backbone of the family. The beautiful black woman with the pastel painting of The Last Supper? The black-and-white television propped up on the broken-down floor model?

Umm-hmm, that's right. *Big Mama*!

Now, *my* Big Mama, *Miss Sadie-Mae Johnson*, ol' girl wasn't playing any games. So, to hell with Compton, Sadie-Mae was straight outta Kick-A-Kids-Ass. And with me and my siblings ripping and running through the projects of North Philly, there wasn't a day that went by where Sadie-Mae wasn't homesick. Step outta line if you wanted to, she would have stared you down, placed her hands on them Georgia-bred hips and said, *"Go outsiiiiiide, fetch me a switch, and then hop yo' black ass in that shower. And you bet' not dry off!"*

So, if you ask me, that's the problem with the kids these days. They're missing out on that good old fashion Big Mama act right. And if you call ya'self try'na give it to 'em, the DHS will be knocking on your front door bright and early like a Jehovah's Witnesses.

But on the flip side, when we *don't* discipline these babies and allow 'em to run wild in the streets, the same folks that'll condemn us for whipping a little ass will be the same ones calling us unfit parent because we can't control our children. And the police? Humph, y'all been watching the news. They're killing our young black men without a care in the world. So, as parents, especially a single black mother such as myself, what are we supposed to do? Just sit back and watch our babies fall victim to these trigger-happy, racist ass cops? Or what? Just kick our feet up and watch 'em fall victim to a corrupt and unjust legal system? Oh no, not all; not this beautiful Queen here. My name's Ebony Beatrice Johnson, and I'ma geek about mines.

Any who, back to my thirteen-year-old son, Kenyatta. A little over a year ago, me, him, and my eighteen-year-old, Jabari, left the streets of North Philly and moved into a townhouse on the outskirts of the city. The transition from the city life to the 'burbs was like a much-needed breath of fresh air. But even then, Kenyatta just couldn't seem to keep himself out of trouble. He was just suspended three weeks earlier for sticking chewing gum in a little girl's hair, and now his little ass had the nerve to be fighting.

I swear I'ma have to do something about that boy.

After climbing out of my Lincoln Navigator, I tossed my Chanel clutch over my shoulder and casually made my way toward the school's entrance. The first thing that grabbed my attention when I stepped in the building was the Blue-Ribbon banner that hung from the ceiling. It proudly displayed the fact that its students had the highest academic test scores in the state of Pennsylvania. I was extremely proud that Kenyatta was part of that student body, but still it broke my heart to see him squandering away the opportunity to receive such a stellar education. It made no sense to me whatsoever.

Now, when it came to my oldest son, Jabari, ol' money grip was doing the damn thang. Aside from having a 3.0 GPA, he was the number one ranked high school basketball player in the nation. He had a full-ride scholarship to Duke University, and was projected to be the number one, overall pick in the 2017 NBA Draft.

So, basically, that was one down and one to go. Jabari was situated, but little Mr. Kenyatta? Oh, homeboy must'a thought I was sweet. It was cool, though, because just like Kevin Hart's daddy used to say, that ass was gon' learn today.

Aw-right. Aw-right. Aw-riiiiiiiight!

As I approached the principal's office, I spotted Kenyatta through the window. He was sitting on the wooden bench beside the door. His little ass had the nerve to be looking just like me. His smooth, honey brown complexion was the same as mines. He also had my thick lips, my cute little button nose, and my slanted Asian-like eyes. He was dressed in a Polo sweat suit and the brand-new Kobe's that I bought him a few days earlier. Thinking about it now, I shouldn't have bought his little ass shit; cutting up in school two times in a dag-gone month.

I didn't even get a chance to step into the office before he turned his head to look at me. He attempted to speak, but I shut his ass down, giving him a look that said, *"Not now, but trust and believe I'll be dealing with that ass later."*

Kenyatta shook his head and leaned back against the wall.

Now, keep in mind I'm totally embarrassed because I was just there a couple of weeks earlier for the same exact shit. So, when I approached the secretary's desk and stated my business, the only thing on my mind was strangling Kenyatta.

I swear, I wanted to kill that boy.

The secretary was a freckled face, white woman with curly red hair. The artificial suntan she sported was the same color as cantaloupe. Her skinny fingers were jabbing at her keyboard, scribing out the paper she was looking at. She knew I was standing there, but instead of speaking she just kept on typing.

"Excuse me, but I'm here to speak with Principal Weaver," I announced.

Now, don't you know this heifer had the nerve to scoff. Still typing, she looked up and rolled her eyes at me.

"Principal Weaver's busy at the moment. So, go over to the bench and have a seat next to your son."

Say whaaaahhh?

I started to check her ass, but I didn't. Instead, I just backed away from the desk and took a seat on the bench beside Kenyatta.

I sat quiet for close to five minutes, periodically glancing at Kenyatta and giving him the look of death. Then a few minutes after that, I heard the click clacking of high heeled shoes moving down the hall. It was Principal Weaver. We locked eyes as she waltzed passed the window and stepped inside of her office.

Well, damnit if she didn't remind me of Thelma Harper from the 80's sitcom Mama's Family.

Her stringy, gray hair was scraggly and loose, and pulled back into a bun. Her wrinkled face was smothered in makeup, and the lenses in her Coke bottle glasses were so thick that her eyeballs were five times larger than normal. The blue blouse with the butterfly collar she wore was fresh out the 70's and her corduroy suit had the stale aroma of cigarette smoke and moth balls.

Yuck!

"Good morning, Ms. Johnson," she greeted me with a wide smile, showing off her coffee stained teeth. "I absolutely hate it that we have to meet again under such circumstances, but here at Abington Junior, we have a zero tolerance for fighting." She cut her eyes at Kenyatta. Her words were more directed at him than me.

"I totally agree," I replied, while standing up to shake her hand. The tone of my voice and my choice of words were proper, the way Big Mama would do whenever speaking to white folks. "Now, Principal Weaver, can you please tell me exactly what happened?" I flashed her an incredulous smile.

"Well, according to my hall monitor, Kenyatta, here," she pointed at my son, "for no reason at all, punched another little boy in the face. This was immediately prior to first period."

"But, Ma!" Kenyatta interjected. He was leaning forward and looking up at me with bright, wide eyes. "He—"

"Kenyatta, be quiet!" I lashed out, completely cutting him off. "You know better than to be talking in grown folks' conversations. As a matter of fact, here." I handed him my car keys. "Go outside and wait for me in the car."

Kenyatta sulked. He accepted the keys from my hand and walked away mumbling.

"So, back to the little boy." I returned my attention to Principal Weaver. "How is he? Is he doing okay?"

I was hoping like hell he was, because I definitely wasn't trying to pay for some dag-gone medical bills.

"Well, he *does* have a black eye," she slowly replied, being more dramatic than what was necessary. "But other than that, he should be just fine. His mother came to pick him up less than an hour ago, and that's the last I heard. So, I'm assuming he's okay."

Still thinking about the medical bills, I would potentially be responsible for, I adjusted my purse and sucked in a deep breath.

"Well, you're absolutely right, Principal Weaver. Fighting is most definitely intolerably, and I can assure you that something like this will never happen again."

"I hope you're right, Ms. Johnson. Because if something like this *were* to happen again, Kenyatta's going to be suspended indefinitely, meaning he will no longer be permitted to attend any schools in the Abington School District."

The undertone of her voice was condescending, talking to me as though I were a goddamned child, like I didn't know the meaning of the word *indefinitely*. Hell, I graduated from college with a bachelor's degree. This chick must'a her lost her mind.

"Clearly, Abington Junior is a far cry from the inner-city charters that you all are accustomed to," she continued speaking snobbishly. "So, I'd strongly suggest that you talk to Kenyatta, and the two of you get with the program. Because this is the last time I'm going to say it, I have a zero tolerance for violence of any kind at my school. I thought about this long and hard, and the only reason I'm giving Kenyatta another chance is because he's proven to be one of our brightest students. So, because of that, he'll only be suspended for a total of three days. It's the Thanksgiving weekend, so he can return to school on the thirtieth with the rest of the children."

Everything inside of me wanted to smack this bitch with the dark-skinned part of my hand. But instead, I just nodded my head and smiled. Kenyatta's education was far more important than my pride.

"Well, thank you, Principal Weaver, we truly appreciate it. And from here on out, I can assure you that Kenyatta won't be causing any more problems."

"Well, we'll see about that." She looked at me skeptically.

We briefly shook hands and then went our separate ways.

CHAPTER TWO

EBONY

When I returned to my Navigator, the first thing I noticed were the sounds of Meek Mill bumping from my stereo system. The second thing I noticed was Kenyatta's silhouette through my tinted windows. He was nodding his head and grooving to the music. I snatched open the door and gave his ass an earful.

"Boy, you better turn that music off, 'fore I knock them waves out of your goddamned head! Got me looking like a fool in front of these dag-gone people. You must'a lost your rabbid-ass mind."

Irritated without justification, Kenyatta turned the music down and sucked his teeth.

"Suck your teeth again, and I'll rip 'em out of your fucking mouth! Ain't got no business sucking your teeth any ol' damn way. That's a female trait."

I climbed my little self up in the driver's seat and started the engine. I wanted so bad to pop his ass, I swear I did. But the understanding I had with my boys was that whenever they did something wrong, I would first give them the opportunity to explain themselves before bringing down judgement. This time was no different. So, after backing out the parking space and pulling off slow, I gave Kenyatta his one chance to speak.

"Go 'head. I'm listening."

"Ma, that white boy called Bianca the 'B' word," he stated like it was the best shit to come up with.

"Bianca? Isn't she the same little girl you stuck chewing gum in her hair?"

"Yeah, that's her." Kenyatta nodded his head. "We was—"

"We *were*," I corrected his grammar, cutting him off mid-sentence.

"Alright," he began his story for the second time. "We were chilling in the cafeteria waiting on first period, and that's when I noticed the white boy, Todd. He was yelling at Bianca and pointing his finger in her face. Bianca told him to stop, and that's when he called her a bitch."

"Boy, you better watch your mouth." I reached over and popped him upside the head.

"Alright, Ma, dang. I was only telling you what happened."

"So, what! You didn't have to repeat it verbatim. Now, finish telling your story."

"Alright. So, after he called Bianca the 'B' word, I stepped to him and demanded that he apologize. But when he wouldn't do it, I got mad and socked him in the eye. And the only reason I did it, was because of what you said the last time I got in trouble. You said that little black girls were beautiful, black Queens, and that because I'm a young black King, I was obligated to respect and protect them. So, how could I just stand there and let this corny, little, white boy disrespect a beautiful black Queen? Come on, Ma, you know I wasn't going for that."

Hold up. *Is his little ass try'na kick game?*

I stopped at a red light on Easton Road and looked at Kenyatta skeptically, searching for any signs of deception. Knowing my child like the back of my hand, I was looking for that guilty ass smirk of his. I squinted my eyes and studied him closely, but I didn't see it. My baby was telling the truth, he was really sticking up for that girl. So, how can I be mad at him after hearing what he just said?

The traffic light turned green and I continued southbound, headed back to Philly.

"Now, Yatta, you know I was about to put them paws on you, right? But I'ma give you a pass this time because I understand the reason you did what you did. I still have to punish you, though. 'Cause at the end of the day, you can't just go around punching on people. There are better ways to resolve your problems than resorting to violence."

"Aw come on, Ma," Kenyatta complained. "I was only sticking up for Bianca. If a dude was disrespecting you, calling you the 'B' word and pointing his finger in your face, wouldn't you want a young, handsome King, such as myself, to step up and get it rocking for you?"

I knew exactly what Kenyatta was up to, he was setting me up to prove his point.

A few years ago, he and Jabari were forced to witness the physical abuse that I suffered at the hands of my ex-boyfriend, Terry. That man used to beat my ass to no avail. And because Kenyatta knew this, he also knew that I'd relate to everything that happened to that little girl, Bianca. There was also the possibility that his subconscious, thirteen-year-old mind characterized Bianca as me and that white boy as Terry. Maybe that's the *real* reason he did what he did, sticking up for Bianca for all the times he wasn't big enough to stuck up for me.

"Come on, Ma, keep it real," Kenyatta persisted. "You know if that was you, you would have wanted somebody to step in and defend your honor."

Slowly, I shook my head and sighed. My baby was right, and I was forced to admit it.

"Yes, Yatta, of course I would have wanted someone to step up and defend my honor. But that still doesn't justify you punching that little boy in his face. What if Principal Weaver would have expelled you from school? Or even worse, what if you would have really hurt that boy? Did you even consider that?"

"Dang, Ma, you're acting like I shot him. It was only a punch."

"*Kenyatta.* That's not that point. What I'm trying to get you to see is that for every action there's a reaction, and that there's no room for error; especially for young black men in America. The deck has already been stacked against you. The first time you slip up and give these people a reason to hold you back, they're gonna make your life ten times harder than what it already is. So, you have to *think*, Kenyatta. You have to seriously slow down and think. Do you understand what I'm telling you?"

"I kinda understand, but then again I don't," Kenyatta replied. He was leaned back in the passenger's seat and gazing out the window. "Everybody makes mistakes, Ma. Nobody's perfect."

"You're absolutely correct," I agreed with him. "Nobody's perfect, and yes, we all make mistakes. The key, however, is that we don't make the *big ones*. Because the big ones are the mistakes that

Askari

warrant no redemption. There's some things you just can't return
from."

Stopping at another red light, I reached over and caressed the
side of my baby's face.

"So, *now* do you understand what I'm saying?"

Kenyatta nodded his head and smiled at me.

"Good." I stroked his face once more, then continued driving
when the light turned green.

"Hey, Ma?" Kenyatta perked up in is seat. "So, now that we
came to an understanding, are you still going to punish me?"

"Boy, you've gotta be kidding. That ass is on lock. Barred. B-
A-R-R-E-D. *Barred*!"

"Aw, man, come on, Ma. For the entire Thanksgiving break?"

"Hmmmmm, well, now let me think." I rubbed my chin. "Sticking chewing gum in a little girl's hair...Fighting in school...Sus-
pended twice. Yeah, I'd pretty much say the entire break."

"Aye, yoooooo! Come on, Ma, don't do me like that."

"Alright. Well, maybe not the entire break." I cracked a smile.
"I'm willing to make deal."

"A deal?" He shot me a leery look. "A deal like what?"

"You remember what I taught you about Dr. King?"

"Of course, I remember. You know I'ma swagged out geek on
the low."

"And what about Brotha Malcolm? Do you remember what I
taught you about him?"

"Most definitely, I love Brotha Malcolm, also known as El-Hajj
Malik Shabazz." He flashed me another smile, showing off the fact
he remembered the name Brotha Malcolm adopted when returning
from his pilgrimage to Mecca.

"By any means necessary!" Kenyatta exclaimed. I laughed at
his silliness.

"Alright, so this is the deal, instead of being locked down for
the entire weekend, I've got a particular book that I want you to
read. It's pertaining to the histories of Dr. King and Brotha Malcolm. The faster you read it, the faster I'll release you from punishment."

18

"I'm cool with that." Kenyatta nodded in agreement. "You know I love to read books. So, what's the title, and who's the author?"

"The title of the book is *To Kill A Black Man*, and the author is Louis Lomax. The deal is that you read the book, then after that provide me with a written report addressing the theory of nonviolence. Is that a deal?" I extended my right hand.

Kenyatta smiled at me and accepted my proposal. "Deal."

Askari

CHAPTER THREE

EBONY

It was a quarter after ten when Kenyatta and me stepped inside of the The *Afrikan Arts* book store on Chelten Avenue. The entire layout was peaceful and serene. The chocolate, brown book shelves that sat against the were fully stocked, and perched on the walls, high above the shelves were African artifacts that appeared to be straight from the Mother Land. There were war masks and shields, clay baked pottery and different little tools and trinkets. They were all so unique, and each artifact was just as elegant as the next.

Looking at the book shelf to my left, I noticed the names of some of our most renowned black scholars; my two favorites being Maya Angelou and Molefi Asante. There were also works by Chinua Achebe, Na'im Akbar, Toni Morrison, and James Weldon Johnson to name a few.

It was my first time visiting the store, and I must say, I was quite impressed. The kindling burn from the sweetest Frankincense made love to my nasal, as the sounds of Jill Scott set my mood on ease. But what struck me the most was the life-sized mural of Chaka Zulu and Queen Nzinga that was painted on the back wall. King Chaka was painted on the left, and Queen Nzinga was painted on the right. A large, golden Ankh was painted on the wall between them.

King Chaka, looking powerful and determined, had an intense look in his eyes. A gold crown was resting on his head, and a leopard skinned loin cloth was covering his waist. A stone-edged spear was gripped in his right hand, while a zebra skinned shield was clutched in his left.

Queen Nzinga, looking beautiful and fierce, was also dressed in a leopard skin cloth. The look in her eyes was proud and defiant. Gold bangles decorated her neck and wrist, and the crown she wore was similar to Chaka's; just a more soft and feminine version.

Once again looking around the store, it dawned on me the store was empty. There were no employees working the counter, and from what I could see, Kenyatta and me were the only two customers.

Ding! Ding! Ding!

I gently tapped the bell on the counter beside the register, and that's when it happened. He emerged from his office in the back and approached the register.

Umm-mmm-mmm! Good Lawd, this brotha's fine!

About six-foot-three of chocolate godliness. Fresh wife-beater. Jeans. Chest and shoulders rippled with muscles. Neatly manicured, shoulder length dreads. A thin mustache connected to an inch-long goatee. Prominent cheek bones. Light brown eyes. Pearly white smile. Thick, juicy lips. Dimples. My kitty kat? *Tingling!*

"Good morning," he greeted Kenyatta and me. His voice was deep and masculine, yet soothing at the same time. "My name's Zion Tumojawa, and I'm the owner of Afrikan Arts. How may I help you?"

How can you help me? From the back, from the front, from the side.

That's what I thinking, but obviously couldn't say, especially in the presence of my son. But I couldn't even front, this brotha had me stuck, completely incapable of formulating the right words. Hell, any words for that matter. So, instead of speaking, I just stood there staring at him.

He seemed to be in his late thirties, or maybe even his early forties judging by the specks of gray in his goatee. But even then, his boyish face made him appear to be much younger. A youthful face suspended in time? A man preserved? Prison?

Did I mention this brotha was fine?

An awkward silence filled the air between us, as we stood there staring at one another. Kenyatta had to snap us out of our trance.

"Earth to Ma. Earth to Zion. Snap out of it," he giggled.

Equally embarrassed, Zion and me laughed it off, playing as though our mutual attraction was nonexistent.

"Excuse my manners," I finally spoke while extending my right hand. He accepted my hand with a soft, warm squeeze and then slowly released me.

Whooh! Is it getting hot in here, or is it just me?
"And umm, my name's Ebony Johnson and this is my son, Kenyatta." I gestured towards my little man, who was four inches taller than me. "We're looking for a book on Dr. King and Malcolm X. The title is *To Kill A Black Man*, and it was written by—"

"Louis Lomax," Zion finished my sentence as he and Kenyatta shook hands. "That's a great book. It's actually one of my favorites." He moved from behind the counter and began walking towards the bookshelf on the front left wall. "Come on, y'all, follow me. I've got a few copies on the top shelf."

"King, I would follow you to Jupiter and back," my eyes would have said had the good Lord designed them for speaking. *Did I mention this brotha was fine?*

As we followed him to the bookshelf, I couldn't help but to wonder if Zion was the man that I'd been praying for to come into my life. My beautiful onyx in the midst of debris, the ying to my yang, the King to my Queen, my handsome black man created in the image of the *ONE*.

When we approached the bookshelf, Zion reached up and pulled down the book that I asked him for. It was a purple and yellow paperback, and had a picture of Dr. King and Brotha Malcolm printed on the front.

"Here you go, Sis." Zion handed me the book. "Now, answer this question for me. Out of all the books that were written about Dr. King and Brotha Malcolm, what made you guys want to read this one?"

My response was a simple one. "It was the book I had to read for my final exam a few years ago."

"Oh, yeah?" Zion smiled while caressing his goatee. "So, which college did you attend, and what was your major?"

"Temple University. I graduated with a bachelor's degree in psychology. African American studies was one of my minors."

"Okay." Zion nodded his head and smiled. "And that's when you were first introduced to the book?"

"Yup. And for our final exam, we had to read it and present the class with an oral report."

23

"So, why the interest now?"

"*Him.*" I pointed at Kenyatta. "He was just suspended from school for fighting. So, reading this book is his punishment. He has to read it, and then draft me a written report on the theory of nonviolence."

"Dang, Ma, just like that?" Kenyatta put up a protest. "You just gon' put me on blast and tell all my business?"

"First of all, *young man,*" I playfully rolled my eyes and snapped my neck, "you're little thirteen-year-old butt doesn't have any business. And secondly, if you're embarrassed by something you've done, then you shouldn't have done it in the first place."

Zion chuckled when I said it.

Kenyatta looked away, embarrassed.

"You know, your mom *is* right." Zion smiled at him, showing off the dimples. "But if you don't mind me asking, what happened that you felt the need to fight?"

Kenyatta looked at me, then he set his sights on Zion.

"This white boy at my school was talking crazy to one of the sistas, so I went upstairs on him."

Zion's facial expression caught me off guard. It seemed as though what Kenyatta said amazed him. I started to say something, but Zion beat me to it.

"So, tell me something." He placed his hand on Kenyatta's left shoulder. "What is it that makes a man or a woman a warrior?"

Zion looked at me, and I smiled. I knew exactly where he was going.

"I mean, I'm really not sure," Kenyatta answered. "I didn't even know a woman could be a warrior."

"Well, she was a warrior." Zion pointed at the portrait of Queen Nzinga.

"And who was she?" Kenyatta asked.

"That's Queen Nzinga," Zion replied. "But to her people, she was known as *King* Nzinga."

"A woman being referred to as a king?" Kenyatta questioned, looking back and forth between Zion and the mural. "*And* she was a warrior?"

"Absolutely," Zion confirmed. "And do you know where she was from?

"Ughn-ughn." Kenyatta shook his head.

"Well, she was from Angola. Do you know where Angola is?"

"Of course, I know where Angola is, it's a country in West Africa. Its right next to Nambia."

Zion smiled at me, thrilled to know that I'd taught my son more about Africa than just King Tut and the Egyptian empire.

"Okay," he said as he returned his gaze to Kenyatta. "So, in the seventeenth century, Queen Nzinga's brother, the King of Angola, was doing business with the King of Portugal."

"Business?" Kenyatta asked. "What kind of business."

"Trading," Zion answered.

"Trading what?"

"He was trading his own people in exchange for alcohol and guns. You see, the Queen's brother was what you would call a *sell-out*. He was selling off his own people, committing them to a lifetime of slavery. But Queen Nzinga," he pointed at the wall once more, "the Queen wasn't having it."

"So, what did she do?" Kenyatta's eyes grew wide.

"She assembled a band of warriors, and together they killed her brother."

"So, that's how she became the king? She killed her brother and inherited her brother's crown?"

"Umm, well, I guess you could say that," Zion reasoned with him. "But what's more important is that she stood up for her people. She even took it a step further and waged war on the King of Portugal."

Zion's depiction was a tad bit watered down, but he made his point, nonetheless.

Kenyatta looked at me, amazed.

"Yo, Ma? Did you know about Queen Nzinga?"

"Yes, Yatta. I learned about the Queen in my sophomore year."

"Alright," Zion interjected, "let's get back to what it means to be a warrior. There're three elements. The first," he held up his right index finger, "is that he or she has a clear understanding that the act

25

of waging war is always the last resort. Secondly," he held up his middle finger, "he or she has to be a student of peace, as well as a student of war. And third," he held up his ring finger, "he or she has to be disciplined and determined, never becoming too comfortable. Even during the times of peace, they prepare for war."

"Dang!" Kenyatta smiled at him. "I never even looked at it from that perspective. I just always assumed that a warrior's purpose was to wage war, not peace."

"Nah, lil' man, it's much deeper than that. And I'm pretty sure that's the reason your mom's making you to read this book."

"And that's an actual fact," I consigned, while handing Kenyatta his new book. He flipped through the pages, then lifted his gaze back to Zion.

"Alright, Zion, so tell me this. How is a warrior supposed to know when it's time to wage war?"

"Well, that's something each warrior must determine on his own. But I'll tell you what, when you finish reading the book, how 'bout you ask your mom if she can bring you back to the store, and then the three of us can sit down and talk about it?"

Kenyatta smiled at him. "Yeah, I'm cool with that."

I removed a piece of lint from Kenyatta's hair, and then softly caressed his back. Looking up at Zion, I said, "Thanks for the help. And by the way, I absolutely love the layout of your store. Did you decorate it yourself?"

"Actually, I did," Zion confirmed while slightly nodding his head. "It was a vision I had for almost ten years now. I'm just thankful I had the chance to materialize it."

"Oh, okay," I said, while digging down inside of my purse. "So, how much do I owe you for the book?"

"Don't even sweat it." Zion shook his head and waved me off. "Hopefully, it'll give Kenyatta a better understanding of everything we were just talking about. To me, that alone is worth way more than money."

Say whaaahhh? Now, didn't I tell y'all this brotha was a King?

"Well, thanks again, Zion. And I'll definitely be telling all of my family and friends about your store. Hopefully, they'll support you. Lord knows we need more book stores in the hood."

"I appreciate that," Zion sincerely replied. "And here," he handed me a beige card with chocolate-brown print, "take my business card. So, if you ever need my assistance," he paused for a brief second and stared into my eyes, "please, don't hesitate to call. All of my information is listed."

"I most definitely won't." I cracked a smile.

I was just about to place the card in my purse, but couldn't escape the urge to take a peek at it. Right away, I noticed his last name. It was quite peculiar and appeared to be African.

"How do you pronounce this? Your last name?"

"Too-mo-ja-wa. *Tumojawa,*" he sounded out the syllables for me.

"Is that an African name? Swahili, maybe?"

"It is," he confirmed. "In the Swahili language, it means a part of this one family."

"Oh, okay, that's nice. Actually, it's beautiful. Wow."

Zion just smiled.

I thanked him once again before stepping out the store, and Kenyatta did the same. The entire ride home I could only think of one thing, *Zion.*

Askari

CHAPTER FOUR

ZION

As Ebony and Kenyatta left my store and pulled off in a champagne Navigator, I found myself biting down on my bottom lip. Talk about a Queen! One who's just my size. About five-five, sexy as hell and thick in all the right places. A beautiful sista with the prettiest skin I had ever seen—a smooth, honey brown with a natural glow, no makeup needed. Umm mmm mmm! From her eyes to her lips, to the thickness of her hips, this sista's the shit! I was fascinated by her prince, as well.

Kenyatta's a fly lil' dude, and I can tell from our brief interaction that's he's sharper than your average. I wonder if Ebony's married to his father, or any other brotha who was fortunate enough to be blessed by the love of a woman so beautiful. I didn't see a ring, but a sista like her, she's *gotta* have a man. I mean, why wouldn't she?

I moved away from the door and returned to the counter. Stepping behind the register, I reached in my pocket and pulled out my ones, fives, and tens that I brought along to add to the register. But the second I opened the cash tray, the thumping sounds of Beanie Sigel's new mixtape echoed throughout the store. The bass was so strong, the artifacts on the walls were beginning to shake. Irritated, I stepped from behind the counter and looked out of the window.

"Come on with the bullshit," I mumbled under breath, looking at my younger brother, Dawood. I kept telling that fool to stop bringing his heat around my store, but what did he do? He did the shit anyway. He was parked out front in a cherry-red Audi A8. The too loud music was thumping from his sound system.

"Aye, yo, Uzi?" I called him by his nickname when I stepped outside on the stoop. My arms were folded across my chest, and the look on my face was serious. "Aye, yo, *Uzi!*" I boomed at him much louder, causing him to turn his head my way. "Yo, turn that loud ass music down, fam. What the fuck is wrong wit'chu?"

Askari

Uzi popped open the door and stepped out slowly. I'm assuming he told the brown skinned sista who was seated in the passenger's side to turn down the music. Because she looked at me and rolled her eyes like *I* was the one killing *her* groove, and then turned the music down to a level where I couldn't hear it.

Now, don't get me wrong, I'ma die-hard rap fan and Beanie Sigel's a hometown legend. He'd been dropping heat for damn near twenty years, but my little brother, Dawood, was hot for a completely different reason.

Eleven years ago, me and Dawood were the biggest hustlas in Uptown Philly. But in 2004, the cops raided my spot and caught me with a brick of raw. I was thirty years old and wouldn't see the streets again for another ten years. My daughter, Dominique, had just turned five, and her mother, my ex, Felicia, was running through my dough like a field mouse in a Wonder Bread factory. The one good thing she *did do*, was dropping off the fifty racks that was set aside for my lawyer. But after that, Felicia went straight up crazy, spending all my money. The first thing she copped was a brand-new house in Fox Chase. Then after that, a new Lexus and a hair salon in North Philly. I even heard stories about the clothes she wore. She was dressing so exquisite that Versace, himself, would have crawled out of his grave just to give her a modeling deal.

Now, ask me if Felicia had the decency to send me any of my money. *Hell no*! And to make matters worse, she cut off all communication between me, and my daughter.

So, there I was, dead broke and frustrated and sentenced to ten years in an upstate pen. I hate to say it, but it wasn't long before I turned into a beast, terrorizing and running down on my fellow inmates. On commissary days, I would go cell to cell with a pushrod toilet sword collecting what I felt was due. I had a crew of young wolves from Uptown who were riding with me. They either knew or heard about me from the streets, so because I was considered a *major nigga* they basically did whatever I said. My jailhouse capers only lasted for three years, because after that the craziness happened.

In the spring of '07, this old head named Chester moved on my tier. He was twenty-three years into a Life Sentence, and had just finished a twelve year stretch in the hole. The word throughout the jail was that Chester was a straight up killer, the type of man who was not to be fucked with. Yeah, right! His old ass was living on *my tier*, and on *my tier*, I was the nigga who wasn't to be fucked with. So as far as I was concerned, Chester was just another victim.

The day of our next commissary, I was prepared to make my move. It was time for the old lion to know and recognize that a younger and much hungrier lion was the new King of the pride. However, as fate would have it, the CERT team raided my cell. They found three shanks, a cell phone, ten grams of heroin and two ounces of Loud. I was sanctioned to the hole for the next two years.

On May 12th, 2009, I was finally released from the RHU. And guess whose cell the prison administration decided to stick me in. *Chester's*! There wasn't a soul on the compound who didn't know that I was plotting on Chester the day I went to the hole. So, now that I was back out in population, everybody was standing around waiting to see the box office flick that was sure to be Old School versus New School.

Slowly, I strolled the tier, prowling like the true savage the system conditioned me to be. My war face was on full display, and the ten inched shank I had gripped in my hand was more than enough to turn Chester's Life bit into a ten-to-twenty; meaning ten-to-twenty stabs and his old ass was outta there. Everybody was lined up on the tier—inmates and prison guards alike. Not a single person said a word.

When I finally reached Chester's cell, I was amped up and ready to pop. But when I looked inside, I was completely thrown off balance. I was expecting to see him standing against the wall with his shank out ready to rock. But instead, he was sitting at his desk reading a book. His goose-neck lamp was beaming down on the book, and beside the lamp was a flipped open notepad.

Is this a joke? I remember thinking to myself, as I stood there staring at him thinking he was crazy. He *had* to know that I was coming for him, everybody else did.

"Aye, yo, ol' head? What the fuck is up?" I hissed at him, making the first move. *"Niggas saying you try'na holla me. Well,* let's holla then."

Chester didn't even look my way. He just jotted something down in his notepad and continued reading.

"Fuck is you deaf?" I adjusted the grip on my shank. *"You try'na holla, I'm right here."*

Calm, cool and collected, Chester closed his book. He removed his wire framed glasses and stood to his feet. His salt-and-pepper dreds nearly hung to the floor. At six-foot-six, one hundred and eighty-five pounds, Chester was tall and lanky. He looked at the shank in my hands and then looked me square in the eyes.

"Young brotha," he stated in a steady, masculine voice, *"I'm not your enemy. So, you can put that little shank of yours away. There's no need for that here."*

His words carried no aggression, nor did they embody any fear. I didn't realize it at the time, but in my thirty-five years of living, that was the first time I had ever encountered a real man. Not a *grown male,* but a man. My bloodline was a thousand percent gangsta, but the energy exuding his cell was like nothing I had ever experienced. And for reasons that defied my logic, I carefully slid my shank in my back pocket. I didn't know it then, but what I realize now is that my ancestors were talking to me. The core of my essence was saying, *"Zion, be patient. Be cautious. Measure twice and cut once."*

Sensing a change in my demeanor, Chester returned to his seat and continued reading his book.

Still standing at the door, I glanced around the cell knowing that easiest way to peep a man's steeze was to take an account of his personal surroundings.

On the back wall, I saw a black-and-white poster of Dr. King and Brotha Malcolm. They were dressed in black suits, shaking hands and smiling for the camera. On the wall above his desk, I saw sketches of the African continent. There were also pictures of The Honorable Elijah Muhammad, Minister Farrakhan, George Jackson, Huey P. Newton, and Bobby Seale. On another wall, were pictures of Assata Shakur, Angela Davis, Michelle Brown, Stokely Carmichael, and Dick Gregory. I also noticed a poster of Marcus Garvey that was hanging on the wall beside his bunk.

Piles of books were scattered throughout the cell, and on the top bunk, in my designated space, was a tan paperback with a picture of a little girl's face on the front. I approached the bunk and picked up the book.

"*The Miseducation of The Negro*," I read the title out loud. "*By Carter G. Woodson*."

I returned my sights to Chester.

"*Hey, umm, Old Head? Where do you want me put your book?*"

"*My name isn't Old Head*," he quickly corrected, with his nose still buried in his book. "*It's Seekumbuzu, and that book belongs to you now.*"

"*It belongs to me?*" I was taken aback. "What's that *supposed to mean?*"

Chester removed his reading glasses and returned to his feet. His face was pleasant, and his deep-set eyes were full of wisdom. The energy of his essence demanded my respect.

"*Young Brotha*," he spoke in a slow, steady rhythm, "*that book belongs to you now. It's a gift, from me to you. You're going to accept it ...and you're going to read it.*"

With that being said, he sat back down and continued reading his book.

From that day forward, Seekumbuzu was like the father I never had, the missing link between me and my higher self. He introduced me to a crew of young brothas who embraced his energy the same as I had. Their names were Masomakali, Zuberi, Donkur, Omowali, and Atiba. Together, we dedicated our time to nourishing our intellects. We worked out together and spent endless hours studying. We also made plans for a new organization we would start when we returned to society.

The name of the organization was *BTS*, the acronym for *Back To Society*. We realized that in order to have positive impact on our communities, we had to first start with bettering ourselves. Then after that, doing everything we could to nourish the minds of our youth.

Now, back to my younger brother, Uzi.

In the wake of my incarceration, he continued making money hand over fist. But not once did he ever reach out to help me financially. In hindsight, I should have expected as much. Because if he wasn't true to himself and his community, then how could he be true to me?

When I was released from prison about a year ago, Uzi expected me to reclaim half of my drug empire, but I declined. I flat out refused to accept the brand-new Benz, the jewelry, and the twenty keys of raw he attempted to *bless* me with.

Uzi looked at me like I was crazy. He couldn't accept the fact that I no longer glamorized, nor had the desire to live such a destructive lifestyle. I was focused on doing something so much better. And besides, I was far from broke when I left the penitentiary. Our grandfather died on the eighth year of my bit, and he left me and Uzi an insurance policy worth about a half of a million dollars. Wisely, I took my half of the money and put it to good use. After setting aside sixty racks for Dominique's college fund, I spent another seventy racks on my book store, and another eighty to purchase the building for my BTS rec center.

As I stood there looking at my younger brother, it was easy to see how his life would eventually end, a jail cell or a casket. I was afraid to see him in either one.

"Yo, didn't I tell you to stop coming around me like this?"

"Coming around you like what?" Uzi asked with a devilish grin, knowing damn well what I was talking about. He looked down at his iced-out necklace and watch, and then brushed away the imaginary dust on his waist length mink. "Come on, Zi, you know what it is. You know how a nigga get down."

"And that's the whole point. So, how many times I gotta tell you? Stop bringing your heat around my fucking store."

"Nigga, you a'ight," Uzi came back at me. "And stop bitching," he chuckled. "That's not a good look for you."

"Ain't nothing funny, Uz, I'm serious. For all I know, the feds are watching, thinking that I'm back in the game. And then here you go, looking like the million-dollar fucking baby. They're probably watching us right now, thinking we're still partners. Or even worse, that I'm moving weight from the store."

Uzi burst out laughing. For some reason, he thought shit was funny.

"Yo, that's crazy, bro. Them crackas done brainwashed you. You done went upstate and got soft on a nigga. At one point in time, you was the flyest nigga in Uptown. *But now?*" he paused for a second and pointed at my book store. "You just a fucking librarian! Yo, where the fuck they be doin' that?"

"Yo, Uzi, who the fuck is you laughing at?" I stepped towards him, ready to prove that my get down was still official.

"*You, nigga!* That's what the fuck I'm laughing at!" he called himself try'na check me. "All those years I was waiting on you to come home, so we could get back to how it was. Fucking up the city in back-to-back foreigns. But nawl, you had to come on some weirdo shit. Driving around in that old ass Range Rover, and talking all this Farrakhan, black power, save the hood shit. Niggas ain't try'na hear that shit, bro. You ain't doing nothing but wasting ya time."

I swear if this boy wasn't my brother, I'd smash him.

"So, what? What'chu mad at me now?" He tried to laugh it off with his arms stretched wide. "I'm just giving you the real, bro. The Christians only care about the Bible. The Muslims only care about the Qur'an. The hustlas and stickup boys? If it ain't about the bag, them niggas don't give a fuck. And these *bitches*? These *stanking-ass skally wagz*?" He pointed at the sista who was watching us from the car. "These bitches don't want nothing but a dick to suck, and a muh'fucking welfare check. And half of 'em don't even spend that shit on they fucking kids. So, how the *fuck* is you supposed to fix some shit like that?"

Irritated beyond words, I shook my head and scowled at him.

"That's the reality, bro. It is what it is."

"Not at all. That's *your* reality, not mines."

"Nigga, that's the reality of the hood. Fuck is you talking 'bout?"

The more I listened to my brother's logic, the more I realized he was a lost cause. He was the victim of a typecast system that was strategically set to keep us in place. The sad part was that he didn't even dig it. He was too caught up in the imagery that was propagated through the media; images that depicted black people as nothing more than criminals and freeloaders.

"You know what, Uzi? The real waste of time is me standing here arguing with you. 'Cause at the end of the day, no matter what I tell you, you're gonna do you anyway. All I'm asking is that you respect my wishes, and stop bringing that negative energy around me and my store."

"Say less," Uzi replied as he extended his right hand to shake mines. He laughed when he realized I wouldn't shake it. "Damn, Zi, it's like that?"

"Like you said." I folded my arms across my chest. "It is what it is."

"Well, fuck it, then." He shrugged his shoulders. "You're still my big brother, and I still got'cha back. So, whenever you ready to get'cha head out the clouds, just let me know. I got a duffle bag wit'cha name on it."

After shaking his head, Uzi climbed back in his car and pulled off.

As I spun around to head back in the store, I noticed that Mrs. Pinckney, the elderly woman who lived on the second floor, was standing in her doorway looking at me. The pink rollers she wore were sticking out the bottom of her headscarf. Her gray bathrobe was tied tight.

"Good morning, Mrs. Pinckney." I waved at her and smiled.

I was expecting her to do the same. But instead, she rolled her eyes at me and slammed the door. It didn't bother me because I knew the reason she was upset. It was Uzi and his loud ass music. That, and all the shouting he was doing as we stood there arguing. It was then, a valuable jewel I learned from Seekumbuzu popped

inside of my head. He said, *"Men of wisdom never argue with fools. 'Cause from a distance, the people watching can't tell who is who."*
This fucking Uzi!

Askari

Empty content.

CHAPTER FIVE

JABARI

"Yo, stop playing and suck my shit right," I told my young jawn, Shameeka. She was under the sheets sucking my dick, but wasn't doing it the way I taught her. Instead of topping me off, she was only licking around the sides.

"Shut up, boy, dang. Lemme do what I'm doing." Shameeka giggled. "I didn't say anything to you when you were eating my pussy."

Before I knew it, Shameeka sopped me up in one big gulp. Her bottom lip was pressed against my sack, and my eight inches of steel was stretching out the back of her throat. Shorty was a straight up beast! No gag reflexes or none of that shit.

"Umm," Shameeka groaned while slurping the head of my pistol. She twirled her tongue around the neck of my shit, and then brought me back to the depths of her tonsils.

Yo, these county chicks are freakier than a muthafucka. Ever since me and my folks left the city and moved to Willow Grove, my life was like a Burger King commercial. *I was having it my way*! Pussy action on whole 'nother level. I'm talking about five or six times a week, sometimes twice a day.

"Damn, Meek, you done turned into a pro wit'cha head game, huh?"

Slurp!

Shameeka pulled me out of her mouth and stroked me up and down with both hands. After that, she popped her head out from underneath the sheets and cracked up laughing when she saw the look on my face. My mouth was wide open, and I was looking at her cross-eyed. Shorty had a young nigga going crazy!

"Yeah, nigga!" Shameeka smiled at me and stuck her tongue out. "I told your ass to stop talking shit, acting like a bitch ain't know what she was doing."

Ignoring Shameeka's outburst, I placed my hands on her head and guided her mouth back down to my pistol. Talking like a robot, I said, "Shut—up. Deep— throat."

Shameeka laughed at me, then went right back to sucking my dick.

I rested my head on the pillow and looked over at my mom's nightstand. The alarm clock read 11:17.

Ma' Dukes wasn't getting off of work for another six hours, and my little brother, Kenyatta, wasn't getting outta school until 2:30. I was supposed to had been in school my damn self, me and Shameeka, both. But a few hours ago, I had Shameeka call the school acting like she was Ma' Dukes, telling 'em I had a doctor's appointment. I did the same thing for her, acting like I was her stuck-up ass pops. So basically, I had another three hours to bust Shameeka's ass, wash my mom's bed sheets, and then jet back to school to get ready for my season opener, the first game of my senior year.

Yo, I was killing these turkeys on the ball court, straight up. I was the number one ranked, high school baller in the nation, and at 6'11, 268 pounds, they were calling me the next Shaq Diesel.

Last summer, me and all the top recruits from around the country were invited to the Nike Basketball Camp in Atlanta. I hate to be one to brag, but *I was ballin' on they punk asses*! After averaging 29 points, 18 rebounds and 9 blocks a game, every NCAA coach in the country wanted to recruit me. They would fly me out to their universities and meet me at the airport with four or five white girls that were willing to do whatever. I couldn't even front, I was tearing them snow bunnies to shreds.

Unfortunately, none of that was enough to persuade me. Because no matter how hard those coaches tried to recruit me, I had already decided way back in the ninth grade that I was going to Duke University. I wanted to play for Coach K and the Blue Devils, and hopefully win a national title. I wish that I could go straight to the NBA, but the NCAA would never allow that, they gotta get a piece of this money, too. So, after one year of playing for Coach K, my next step is the 2017 NBA Draft. I'm projected to be the number one, overall pick.

Now, back to the issue at hand. Shameeka must'a lost her god-damned mind.

"Aye, yo, Meek? What the fuck is you doing?" I pushed her away from my body and scooted my back against the headboard. "Yo, I *know* you ain't just try to lick my ass!"

Shameeka giggled, but I was far from amused. She knew a nigga wasn't down with none of that freaky shit.

"A'ight, so you just gon' lay there looking stupid?" I nodded my head and looked at her mischievously. "You wanna be playing games? Cool. Now, I'ma bust ya ass!"

Shameeka laughed at me and rolled over on her back. Her head was hanging off the edge of the bed, and her silky long hair was flowed down to the floor.

"Bae, can I suck it like this? Upside down?"

I chuckled at her request. "Yo, what's up wit' all this freaky shit?"

"Stop asking so many questions. Dang."

"Nizzaw. I'm done playing brain games."

I hopped off the bed and stood to my feet.

"Bend ya ass over, so I can bust it from the back."

Shameeka assumed the position, face down with her ass in the air. I stood behind her, then I reached over and grabbed my phone from the nightstand. I activate my video app and pressed *record*.

"Ahn-ahn, Bae, I told you about that," Shameeka whined, looking back at the phone in my hand. "The last time we made a video, you put it on Facebook for all of your friends to see. And then your stupid ass friends shared the video with their friends, and their friends shared the video with their friends. The situation got way out of hand. Then worst of all, them little dirty-ass bitches at school were try'na play me."

"Man, fuck them bitches. Them bitches be on the Book, too, face down wit' they yams in the air. And to top it off, they be fuck-ing wit' a bunch of broke niggas. Now, me on the other hand, I'm 'bout to be a superstar in the league. So, look on the bright side, if the video goes viral, you could fuck around and be the next Kim K."

Shameeka pouted. "I don't know, Bae. These hating ass bitches gon' make me hurt something."

"Come on, Meek, chill. I said, I got'chu."

Before she could utter another word, I slipped inside of her cream pie and she cried out in ecstasy.

"Umm, Bae. Shit!"

I was monkey stomping that thang to death. My left hand was tugging at her hair, and my right hand was clutched around my iPhone.

"You love this big dick, don't you?"

"Yes, Bae! Yes!" She threw her phat ass against my pelvis, then reached between her thighs to massage her clit. "Fuck, yes!"

"Umm-hmm, I know."

I aimed the phone at my hamma and watched it on the screen. It was covered in Shameeka's cream, plunging in and out of her every time our bodies separated and came back together. I released Shameeka's hair and roughly smacked her on the ass, making her butt cheeks wiggle.

"Damn, y'all see this shit? My baby got that tidal wave pussy," I stated for the camera.

Ja—bar—i!" Shameeka screamed my name, causing me to pump harder. "Hit it, Bae, hit it! Fuck this pussy! Fuck me nice and deep. Just like that, Bae. Just like that. *Eeeeeeeeewwwwwwww!*"

The sexy tone of her voice was driving me crazy. Eager to handle my biz, I bit down on my bottom lip and went straight up *ham!* Shameeka was going crazy, clawing at the bed sheets and crying out to holy heaven.

The stereo on my mom's dresser was playing *Love Faces* by Trey Songz, and damnit Shameeka ain't have a nigga making 'em. I was zoned out, smashing the pussy like I'd lost my mind. I smacked Shameeka's ass once more, and she cried out even louder.

"What the fuck was that?" I panted, still stroking the coochie. I wasn't sure, but it sounded like somebody was standing outside in the hallway. "Yo, Meek, you heard that?"

Instead of replying, Shameeka tightened her walls, and started shaking like she was having a seizure.

"Ewwww! Ewwww! I cumming, Bae. *Shit!*"

***

EBONY

After stopping at KFC to pick up an early lunch, I drove back to the house to drop off Kenyatta. I had a ton of paperwork that still needed to be processed back at the office, so the plan was to drop off Kenyatta and get back to work as soon as possible. I didn't like the idea of leaving my baby home alone, but it was almost a quarter after eleven and Jabari would be home from school in a few more hours.

As I turned the corner and cruised up the block, I noticed Jabari's Camaro. The silver, tinted-out coupe was parked in our driveway, right beside a burgundy BMW that I'd never seen before.

"Hey, Ma? What's Jabby doing home from school so early?" Kenyatta asked from the passenger's seat. He was leaned forward and pointing at Jabari's car through the windshield. "Doesn't he have a game tonight?"

"I don't know, Yatta. Maybe they let him out early," I surmised. "That better be the reason."

I parked along the curb and killed the engine.

"Bring that food in the house," I told Kenyatta, while staring at the unfamiliar car in my driveway. "And don't forget to grab your book."

When we stepped inside the house, I immediately noticed that Jabari's book bag and Polo jacket were laying at the foot of the stairs. The living room was empty, but the sounds of Trey Songz were blasting from the second floor. I could also hear the distinctive sounds of a female moaning.

"What's that noise?" Kenyatta asked with a goofy look on his face.

"Boy, take that food in the kitchen."

43

Kenyatta giggled and walked away with a smirk on his face.

Slowly, I crept up the stairs and made my way to Jabari's bedroom. But the closer I got, the more I realized he wasn't in there.

Oh, hell to the muthafuckin' nawl!

Can you believe this boy had the nerve to be fucking some girl in my goddamned bed? Fuming mad, I ran down the hallway towards my bedroom and snatched open the door.

"Jabari Maleek James, Junior? Are you fuckin' crazy?"

CHAPTER SIX

JABARI

I jumped out the pussy and spun around quickly, surprised to see Ma Dukes and Kenyatta standing in the hallway. Ma' Dukes was looking at me like she wanted to body a nigga. Kenyatta was crouched down behind her, licking his lips and rubbing his hands together. His lust filled eyes were looking at Shameeka's phat ass tooted in the air.

"Boy, you must have lost your rabid-ass mind!" Ma' Dukes shouted at me. She was taking off her earrings and slowly moving towards the bed.

Scared as hell, my hands shot up in the air like a bank robber caught red handed. Although I was two and a half feet taller, and a hundred and thirty pounds heavier, I knew better than to sleep on Ma' Dukes. She was a straight up pit bull when tested.

Shameeka jumped off the bed with the sheets wrapped around her. Looking back and forth between me and Ma' Dukes, she nervously backed herself into the corner. Her flustered, light skinned face was red with embarrassment.

"Dang, Jabby, shorty thicker than a Snickers!" Kenyatta blurted, then flinched when Ma' Dukes clonked him upside the head.

"Yatta, didn't I tell you to take your ass in the kitchen?" She looked at him crazy.

"Yeah, but—"

"But nothing!" she cut him off. "Go in your room and close the door."

Shameeka was looking at me like she wanted me to save her. The look that I gave back was saying, *"Bitch, is you crazy? I'm try'na think of a way to save my muthafuckin' self."*

Looking down at Ma' Dukes, I was still thinking of something to say. I thought as hard as I could, but nothing came to mind.

Whack!

Yo, I know she ain't—

45

Whack!

Damn, she did it again. Ma' Dukes jumped up and smacked the shit outta me. She jumped up and took another swing, but I caught her in the air and gently sat her back down.

"Come on, Ma. Chill."

"Muthafucka, you raising your hands to me?"

"Not at all," I quickly explained. "I'm just try'na get you to calm down. I would never raise my hands to you."

"You know what?" She scowled at Shameeka, then swung that shit back to me. "You get this little heifer out of my house, 'fore I catch a body up in this piece."

Shameeka wasted no time. She quickly made her way towards the door, but before she could roll out, Ma' Dukes snatched her by the hair and slung her to the floor.

"Oww!" Shameeka squealed.

"Fuck is you going with my goddamned sheets?" Ma' Dukes snarled at her, pulling the sheet so hard that it ripped down the middle.

I reached down and grab Shameeka's clothes from the floor. But before I could hand them to her, she hopped up and hauled ass, running through the hallway butt naked.

"Yo, Shameeka?" I called out behind her. "What about your clothes?"

Shameeka just kept on running. She shot past Kenyatta, who was peeking out of his bedroom door. The smile on his face was like a fat kid's in a cheesecake factory.

Whack!

Ma' Dukes cracked me upside the head once again, only this time she used her pocketbook.

"Come on, Ma. Stop hitting me."

"Get'cha ass out of my goddamned house!" She pushed me in the back. "And don't come back until you learn how to respect me!"

"But, Ma?"

"Get!" she shouted like a woman possessed. "Got the nerve to be freaking off with some girl in my goddamned bed! Fuck you think this is?"

Her right hand was gripping the strap on her pocketbook, and her left hand was pointing down the hallway towards the door.

"I'm not playing with you, Jabari. I want you out of my fucking house."

I looked at my little brother, and he lowered his head.

"A'ight," I said, as I looked back down at Ma' Dukes. "If you want me to leave, I'm out."

I dipped inside of my room, got dressed and gathered a few bags of clothes. The last thing I wanted to do was leave my mom and my little brother. But if that's what she wanted, then that's what I was gonna give her.

After stepping out of my bedroom, I stood back in front of hers.

"I'm sorry, Ma. I know I was wrong for doing what I did. But since you want me to leave, I'm out. If you need me, I'll be at Auntie Elisha's with Uncle Tony and Reeko."

Ma' Dukes didn't even look in my direction. She was too busy changing her bed sheets.

"Fuck it, I'm out."

Askari

CHAPTER SEVEN

REEKO

12:07 p.m.

"Stop making all that goddamned noise!" Pops yelled down the stairs from the second-floor hallway.

He was talking to me and my two homies, Uno and Boo-Boo. We were chilling in my living room smoking Loud and playing NBA 2K. I guess we must'a been too loud because Pops brought his ass down the stairs drawin'.

"I got a double shift tonight, Reeko, and I just finished doing one from yesterday. Now, shut up all this goddamned noise, so I can get a little rest. Ain't got no business being here no damn way. *None of y'all.* 'Posed to have ya black asses in school."

Embarrassed by Pops' appearance, I pressed the *pause* button and shook my head.

"A'ight, Pops, we gon' keep it down," I told him, praying that he hurry up and take his ass upstairs.

"I'm not playing with you, Reeko. You better get it together. Ya ass don't wanna go to school, you *don't* wanna work. The only thing ya lazy ass wanna do is hang out with these...with these god-damned hoodlums." He pointed at Boo-Boo and Uno. "Boy, I'm getting sick of this shit."

"A'ight, Pops, damn. I told you we gon' keep it down."

When Pops dipped back up the stairs, Uno and Boo-Boo started laughing at me and going in on Pops.

"Damn, Reek, how ya pops gon' come down the stairs wit' the zebra-striped Speedos?"

"I know, right?" Boo-Boo instigated. "And on top of that, he got the nerve to have his taco meat out. Tell that nigga to shave his nappy-ass chest. Fuck a Chia-Pet, that nigga got a *Chia-Chest*!"

Uno was laughing so hard, that his eyes began to water.

"Aye, yo, Reek, dawg, real shit," he said, looking at me with a stupid grin on his face. "How this nigga got a baldie up top wit' them long-ass dreds on the side? Nigga, look like he wearing a Kufi!"

"Fuck outta here," I laughed it off, and then took another pull on the Dutch before passing it to Boo-Boo.

"Nah, Reek, this some real-ass shit," Boo-Boo said while puffing on the Dutch. "Ya pop's name is Tony, ya mom's name is Elisha, and the last time I checked, ya name was still Reeko. So, why the *fuck* he got a choker chain wit' a silver 'S' hanging from it? Who the fuck is 'S'?"

Awwwww, shit. Here come Pops again.

"That's it!" Pops shouted, still wearing them tight-ass Speedos. His "taco meat" was on full display, and his sweaty, brown "Kufi" was glistening like a mah'fucka.

"I'm sick of this shit! Y'all get'cha lil' asses outta my house wit' all that goddamned noise!"

"Aw, come on, Mr. Tony. We was only playing," Uno said with a smile.

"Umm-hmm," Pops grunted. "Uno, I *know* you ain't the one that was down here talking shit? Not wit' that ugly-ass momma of yours? The bitch got a Michael Jordan baldie wit' a crusty-ass plait sticking out the top. Looking like a cupcake wit' a candle stuck in the middle!"

Uno was mad as hell, but me and Boo-Boo was laughing like a mah'fucka. Pops tore his ass up with that one.

"And *you*." Pops pointed at Boo-Boo. "Fuck is you laughing at? I heard you down here talking about the 'S' on my necklace. So, just for the record, what's yo' momma's name?"

"Sonia," Boo-Boo answered real slow, knowing that Pops was about to hit him with some slick shit.

Pops smiled at him, then he pointed at the 'S' on his necklace.

"Umm-hmm, that's right. *Sonia!*"

Boo-Boo shook his head and threw his hands up in defeat.

Me and Uno laughed at him and pointed.

"Now, y'all get'cha asses outside wit' all that goddamned ruckus. I need to get me some rest, 'fore I go back to work. And you." Pops pointed at Boo-Boo, as we headed towards the door.

"Gimmie that ganja y'all smoking on. Fucking wit' y'all, I'ma need me a sedative."

Boo-Boo looked at Pops, then he looked at the Dutch in his hand.

"Come on, little nigga." Pops gestured for him to hand it over. "Pass de Dutchie pon de left-hand side."

After Boo-Boo handed Pops the smoke, we stepped outside and posted up on the stoop. The block was deader than a door knob. My early morning flow of dope fiends done came and went, and my late afternoon flow wasn't coming for another few hours; somewhere around four o'clock. That's when most of my custies would be getting off of work, dope sick and fiending to get the monkey off they backs.

Reaching down in my pants pocket, I pulled out a sandwich bag of Loud and a pack of Backwoods. I handed them to Uno so he could twist sum'n up.

"Look at this nigga, here." I pointed up the street where Quiet Storm, a neighborhood smokah, was cruising down on his ten-speed bike.

"Reeky Raw, you still got summa that Danger?" Quiet Storm asked me when he stopped in front of my stoop. *Danger* was the stamp on the wax bags of heroin I sold. But I'd never known Quiet Storm to snort or shoot dope, so I looked at him skeptically.

"Yeah, I got it on deck. Why, what's up?"

Quiet Storm dug down in his sweatpants pocket and pulled out a crumbled fifty.

"Man, I got me this lil' snow bunny from out the county. She's looking for a fifty spot of that Danger."

He pointed up the street where a skinny white girl, who looked to be about nineteen, was standing at the light pole looking stupid. Her skintight jeans were showing off the gap in her thighs, and her gumdrop nipples were showing through the fabric of her pullover hoody. She scratched the side of her face and then looked around nervously.

"So, how you know this bitch?" I looked back at Quiet Storm.

"I just met her around 10th Street."

"So, how you know this bitch ain't a cop?"

"Say what, now?" Quiet Storm scratched his head.

"I said, how you know this bitch ain't a cop?"

"How I know who ain't a cop?"

"*Gramala Anderson*!" I pointed at the snow bunny. "How you know this bitch ain't a cop?"

"Man, that bitch ain't the po'. Look at her. You see she got the monkey on her back."

I looked at Gramala, who was smoking a cig and anxiously tapping her foot. After scoping her for a few more seconds, I looked back at Quiet Storm.

"A'ight. So, why I ain't never seen her before? And how the fuck she knows about my Danger stamp?"

"*Nigga,*" Quiet Storm spoke in a slow, animated voice. "You know how the game go. Well, then again, maybe ya young ass don't. So, listen up, 'cause I'm about to learn ya. When a nigga put a stamp on his dope and the shit is fiyah, word travels fast, lil' nigga. Dope fiends from all around gon' be breaking they necks to come get it. Especially, if they hear about it killing a muthafucka. That's the shadows of the game, baby. That's just the shadows of the muthafuckin' game."

Me and my crew nodded our heads in agreement; the shit made sense. So, I accepted the fifty from Quiet Storm and handed him the five bags of Danger that I dug out of my left sock.

"Now, Quiet Storm," I stared him in the eyes as he stuffed the dope in his sweatpants pocket, "if I hear about this bitch being a cop, I'ma shoot you in the ass."

Quiet Storm laughed. "Nigga, you ain't shot nuffin' since the day ya daddy shot you."

"Yeah, a'ight." I nodded my head, as Quiet Storm turned his bike around pedaled up the street. "Fuck around if you want."

"So, Reek?" Uno said, as he handed back my sandwich bag of Loud and my pack of Woods. "We still rolling out to Jabby's game tonight?"

"Why wouldn't we?" I replied, thinking about my cousin, Jabari. "This his first game of the season, so you know he going in his bag. I bet'chu he have a triple double—thirty points, twenty re-bounds, and ten blocks."

"Hell nawl." Uno shook his head, then fired up the spliff he rolled. "I ain't fucking wit' Jabby's big ass. That nigga fuck around and score a hunnid points."

Jabari was my first cousin on my mom's side. His mom, my Auntie Eb, was the second oldest of my mom's two sisters. My mom's the oldest, my Auntie Eb's the second oldest, and my Auntie Erica's the youngest.

We were all born and raised in the Richard Allen projects. Me, my pops and my moms were living in on Poplar Street at my Big Mama's crib. Jabby and them used to stay around the corner on Brown Street; him, his little brother, Kenyatta, his dad, Big Jabby, and my Auntie Eb. My Auntie Erica was living with us at Big Mama's crib, but was never home. Most of the time, she was staying with her boyfriend, Uzi.

From what I heard, Jabari's dad, Big Jabby, was a major nigga from the projects. Niggas be saying he had the hood on lock. I was too young back then to really remember. But what I *do* remember is the day he bought 'em that big-ass house down in Delaware. My Auntie Eb was happier than a mah'fucka leaving the projects. Un-fortunately, just a few months later, her and my cousins was right back down that mah'fucka. Big Jabby got his wig pushed back, and she ain't have enough money to keep the crib. That was a bad time for the fam. And to make shit worst, it was the same year that Big Mama died.

The city tore the projects down, and we were all forced to go our separate ways. Me and my folks moved into a three-bedroom house on 12th and Huntingdon; My Auntie Eb, Jabby and Yatta moved into a Section 8 crib on 16th and Diamond; and my Auntie Erica moved into a condo with her boyfriend, Uzi.

Even after leaving the projects, me and Jabby was still close. We was more like brothers than cousins. We would get together on the weekends, chill out and smoke Loud, and fuck every lil' bitch in the hood that was giving up the yams. It wasn't until high school, that me and my nigga started drifting apart. My main focus was fucking with the block, while Jabby was doing his thing on the b-ball court. I wasn't mad at him, though. 'Cause like I said, I loved him like a brother. He chose to follow his dreams, and I supported him a thousand percent. Besides, my big cuz was something special on the basketball court. Ever since the eighth grade, he would always tell me that one day he'd make it to the NBA and take care of our entire family.

"Bentleys for everybody!" That's what he promised us last year when the fam had Christmas dinner at their new house in Montgomery County. We believed him, too. Not only was he the #1 ranked, high school baller in the nation, he had already graced the covers of *Sports Illustrated* and *Slam* magazines. They were calling him the next best thing since Lebron James. And to keep it a hunnid, that's the reason I stopped going to school. Get an education for what? My big cuz about to be swimming in millions like Scrooge McDuck and breaking bread like Jesus was sitting at the table. So, fuck school.

"Aye, yo, speaking of Jabby," Boo-Boo said, puffing on the spliff that Uno just passed him. "Ain't that his car cruising down the block?" He pointed up the street where a silver Camaro was slowly creeping towards us.

"Hell, yeah, that's my nigga's car," I confirmed with a smile. "But what the fuck is he doing back down the way? He's supposed to have his ass in school."

Now, I know what y'all are prob'bly thinking: how the fuck was Reeko worried about Jabari skipping school, when his ass didn't even go? Simple answer: my black ass ain't the one who was destined for the NBA.

You feel me?

Uno shrugged his shoulders and sparked up a Newty.

"They prob'bly let him out early," he spoke through a cloud of smoke. "You know they be treating him like he King Joffy Joe, just to keep him playing for they school.

When the silver Camaro pulled up in front of my house, the tinted-out passenger's side window rolled down slow, and the music that was bumping on the inside went mute. Jabby was sitting behind the steering wheel in a black hoody. His Brooklyn Nets fitted hat was pulled down low.

"What's up wit' it?" Jabby said to Uno and Boo-Boo. Looking at me, he said: "Yo, cuzzo, lemma holla at'chu."

"Big Cuzzo, what it do?" I smiled at him and gave him some dap through the window. "Fuck is you doing down the way? Ain't you 'posed to be at school?"

"Ma' Dukes on some other shit," he replied, deliberately side stepping my question. "She even kicked me out the house."

"*Auntie Eb?*" I looked at him skeptically. "Trippin' on *you*? Her pride and joy? Nigga, what the fuck you done did?"

"You remember my young jawn, Shameeka? The one I brought through the block a couple of weeks ago?"

"Yeah." I nodded my head. "The lil' redbone chick wit' the super phat ass. Aye, yo, hold the fuck up." I looked at him sideways. "Yo, I know you ain't got lil' buddy on prego?"

"Me? Get Shameeka pregnant? Nigga, you buggin'." He reached inside of his glove compartment and pulled out a box of XL Magnums. "Nigga, I stay strapped. And if for any reason I *do* happen to go raw, I pull out the second I feel my nuts tingling."

"TMI, my nigga. TMI." I smiled at him, relieved to know that none of these lil' smutt buckets trapped my nigga wit' a seed. "So, what happened? Why is Auntie Eb buggin' out on you?"

Just as Jabby was about to give me the rundown, Uno shouted out behind me, "*Po-po! They raiding the block!*"

I looked up and the first I saw was Uno and Boo-Boo running. They jetted towards the ally in the middle of the block, dipped inside and got ghost.

The paddy-wagon Uno must'a spotted was speeding up the street in the wrong direction. Two black Chevy Impalas were zooming down from the top of the block, and out of nowhere, a ghetto bird swooped in, looming over the street. Them pussies was try'na box me in.

"Fuck!" I shouted, thinking about the two bundles of Danger that was stuffed down inside of my sock. I took off running towards the house, but it was too late. The two detectives that hopped out the first Impala was already on me. They tackled me to the ground to the second I reached the stoop. One of 'em was white, and the other one was black. The white detective reminded me of Al Bundy, and the black detective reminded me of Big Worm from the movie *Friday*. They placed me in handcuffs and snatched me off the ground like a ragdoll.

"Get'cha punk-ass up!" The black detective shouted from behind me. He gripped the back of my Polo sweater and forcefully slammed my face against the front of my house. The white detective was roughing me up, too. His forearm was pressed against the back of my neck, grinding my face into the cool, red bricks. I wasn't even resisting, yet still they were fucking me up. The black detective hit me with a body shot that damn near made me shit on myself, and the white detective followed up with a karate chop to the side of my head.

"Fuck is y'all doing?" I snapped out, hoping all the noise would wake up Pops. My right eye was beginning to swell shut, and I could taste the warm blood that was gushing out my nose.

"Yo, this some straight up Eric Garner shit! What, y'all gon' kill me too? I wasn't even doing nuffin'!"

"Say something else, and I'ma blow ya fucking head off!" the black detective threatened. He was standing so close, that his stank-ass breath was making me nauseous; it smelled like raw onions dipped in shit.

"You think I'm playing wit'chu?" He placed his .45 to the side of my dome. The shit was so big that I could see the barrel sticking out the corner of my left eye.

Wham!

The white detective hit me with a rib shot that buckled my knees. I fell forward and slid down the wall. As I struggled to catch my breath, the black detective snatched me up and pinned me back against the wall. He kicked the insides of my ankles, forcing me to spread my legs apart. Then immediately after that, the white detective began searching me. His pale hands traveled around my waist, and then patted me on my chest and back. After searching my pockets, he groped my balls and then his hand down the crack of my ass.

Still not satisfied, he snatched off my Timbs. He searched my boots one at a time, and then pulled my socks off.

"Jackpot!" he gloated when he came across the two dope bundles.

"So, you weren't out here doing nothing, huh?" Big Worm said, as he laced me with another body shot. He pulled me away from the wall and drug me towards the paddy-wagon. It was then, I noticed the third detective, a young black dude who was playing the role of a street nigga. His black Phillies hat was cocked to the side, and his Monclear variety jacked was hanging open, showing off his iced-out chain. A black nine millie was clutched in his right hand, and the barrel was aimed at Jabby through his windshield.

I looked through the window at Jabby, who was sitting there shaking his head. I could tell from the look on his face, he was ready to pop off. He was huffing and puffing, and had tears welling at the rims of his eyes. The only good thing was that his hands was in the air, showing he was unarmed. That alone, kinda put me at ease. Because one thing about the cops in Philly, is that they'll kill a nigga quick. Black cop or white cop, it really didn't matter. They both represented a racist-ass system that was known for treating blacks and Latinos far harsher than they treated the whites in the city. With the whites, it was, "*Good evening, sir. I pulled you over because...*" But with the blacks and Latinos, it was, "*Get your ass outta the fucking car!*"

"Come on, man, loosen up these tight-ass handcuffs," I complained. "They're tearing into my fuckin' skin."

"So, the fuck what," the white detective replied, then he kicked me square in the ass. "You shouldn't have been out here selling dope."

My right eye was completely closed, and the blood from my nose was all over the front of my sweater. Still looking at Jabby, I was afraid he might do sum'n stupid.

"*Nah, Jabby,*" I mouthed the words, still staring at him through the windshield. "*Don't do it, Cuz. Chill.*"

I knew my nigga like the back of my hand, so when he closed his eyes and bit down on his bottom lip, I knew my words hit a mark. He was calming himself down.

When we finally reached the back of the paddy-wagon, the white detective opened the double doors, and guess who the fuck I saw...yup, you guessed it, ol' stupid-ass Quiet Storm. Come to find out, I was right about Gramala Anderson. She wasn't a cop, but she was damn sure working for 'em. A few hours earlier, she was arrested in Kensington for buying dope from an undercover cop. But instead of taking her to jail, the narcs cut her a deal. They gave the bitch a tatted-up fifty and had her going around the hood setting niggas up.

Ain't that a bitch?

CHAPTER EIGHT

JABARI

"Nah, Jabby. Don't do it, Cuz. Chill."

Those were the words Reeko mouthed to me right before they tossed him in the back of the paddy-wagon. Them pussies ain't have to fuck him up like that—punching him in the ribs and banging his face against the wall. He wasn't even resisting, and they *still* felt the need to beat him up. As I sat there watching the whole shit, the only person I could think about was Freddy Gray. I was hoping the cops didn't do to Reeko what they did to him. Because the last time Freddy Gray was ever seen alive, was right before the cops threw him in the back of a paddy-wagon; the same way they just did Reeko.

"Driver!" the detective who was aiming his toolie at my windshield shouted. "Get'cha ass up outta the car! *Slowly!*" he cautioned with a vicious mean mug. "'Cause if you make any sudden moves, I'ma toss ya brains in the back seat."

Back seat.

Back seat.

Back seat.

Shit about to get real mah'fuckin' goofy. On the floor of my back seat, wrapped in a towel, was the Glock .45 that I got from my Auntie Erica's boyfriend, Uzi.

Now, keep in mind I'm far from a thug, and I'm definitely not a gangsta. But ever since my face was on the cover of *Sports Illustrated* and I did an interview with Steven A. Smith on his sports show *First Take*, niggas in the hood was thinking I had a whole bunch of money. From where, I had the slightest idea. Because other than the fact I dressed nice and drove a brand-new Camaro, I was broker than a joker. And to keep it a hunnid, I didn't even own the mah'fucka. It belonged to an alumni of the high school I played for, the same dude who owned the house where me and my family lived. But niggas in the hood wasn't hearing that shit. According to them,

I was already sitting on millions. So, whenever I was back in the hood, to keep myself protected I packed the fo' fifth. I wish that wasn't the case, but it's the shadows of the game. Jealousy breeds envy, and niggas that's starving will do whatever to eat. That's something I learned from when my pops got killed. It was basically over jealously.

"Driver!" the detective continued shouting. "If you make me say it again, I'ma throw some of this hot shit at you!"

By then, the other two detectives were positioned around my car. Their burners were aimed at my wig, and from the way they were looking at me, I could tell they wanted me to give 'em a reason.

I cracked open the door and climbed out slow with my hands raised high. I was so nervous, that my brow began to sweat. I was thinking about Mike Brown, and how the cops killed him even though he had his hands up.

Damn, I hope these mah'fuckas don't shoot me.

The first detective, the fake-ass street nigga, was looking at me like he wanted to start blasting. From the crease in his brow, to the hate in his eyes, there was no doubt he was thinking about smoking me. His nostrils were flaring, his chest was heaving up and down, and he was anxiously biting down on his bottom lip. Then, all of a sudden, he changed his demeanor. He squinted his eyes and leaned his head slightly.

"Jabari? Jabari James Junior?" he asked me in a much calmer voice, clearly recognizing my face.

That's when reality sat in, and I really began bitching. In the back of my mind, as clear as day, I could see the top story on every sports blog from Philly to LA:, *High School Basketball Star, Jabari James Junior, Arrested In Drug Bust, In Possession Of A Stolen Firearm.*

Goodbye, Duke University. So long, 76ers. The hood, I'm yours forever.

"You know what?" the white detective said, as he holstered his weapon. "That *is* Jabari James Junior!"

"Jabari James Junior?" the Big Worm lookalike asked his partner. "Who the fuck is that?"

"Are you shitting me, or are you kidding me?" the fake-ass street nigga looked at him like he'd been living under a rock for the past two years. "He's only the number one ranked, high school basketball player in the nation. —Mr. Twenty-Eight Points A Goddamned Game! Ain't that right, big man?" His astonishment returned to me.

Everything inside of me wanted to smack this nigga's face off, or at least say something slick, but I didn't. The best thing to do was play my part. 'Cause if the three stooges searched my car and found the burner in my back seat, my NBA career would be over before it even started.

"Naw," I flashed him a forced smile, "that's Mr. *Twenty-Nine* Points A Goddamned Game. Come on, bro, you had me thinking you was a fan."

The three detectives burst out laughing, and I exhaled a sigh of relief. But I was still praying they didn't search my ride. You never know with these mah'fuckas. You see how they be doing Meek Mill.

The white detective reached inside of his pocket and pulled out a pen and a notepad. He walked up on me and asked me for my autograph. The nerve of this nigga. Not even five minutes ago, him and his partners were beating the shit out of my cousin, and now he wanted an autograph?

"Loosen up, big guy." He looked up at me with a silly grin on his face. "And put your hands down, you're not in any trouble."

I slowly lowered my hands, but was sure to keep them in plain view, just in case Big Worm tried to go Doc Holiday on a nigga. I noticed that he never put his gun away, and his super cop ass was still giving me the side eye. I was praying like hell he didn't search my car.

"Just make it out to Andy," the white detective said as he handed me the notepad and pen. "Andy's my twelve-year-old kid, and he's completely nuts about you. He swears to hell and back you're the next coming of Shaquille O'Neil."

Reluctantly, I wrote down exactly what he told me. I did the same thing for the other two detectives, and after talking about basketball for the next couple of minutes they let me go without searching my car.

Talk about a close one!

***

A half an hour later, I was parked in front of my girlfriend, Tonya's, house on 23rd and Diamond. She wasn't home from school yet, but a nigga ain't have nowhere else to go. I probably should have just drove around and waited for Tonya to come home, but there I was parked in the middle of the projects. The niggas around there was grimy as hell, so you best believe I had the fo' fifth laying across my lap.

That situation with the cops had a nigga shook. And even though I got away without catching a burner case, I was still worried about my cousin, Reeko. For all I knew, they had him locked in a cell damn near dead. I knew that I needed to do something to get him out of there, but I didn't have any money to pay his bail. The only person I knew who had that type of money and would do whatever to get him out, was our Auntie Erica, my mom's baby sister. My Auntie E was clocking mad paper as a dancer at Club Onyx, and her boyfriend, Uzi, was one of the biggest hustlas in Uptown. So, if anybody had the money to pay Reeko's bail, it was Auntie E.

I reached inside of my hoody pocket and pulled out my iPhone. After thumbing in my security code, I went to my call log and pressed down on Auntie E's number.

CHAPTER NINE

ERICA

"Nigga, where the fuck ya ass was at?" I snapped at my boyfriend, Uzi, when he walked through the door after running the streets all night. His ass wasn't home when I came in from work this morning, and I could tell by the goofy look on his face that he'd been laying up with the next bitch.

"Nigga, answer my goddamned question!"

"Cut the bullshit, Erica, you already know what was I doing," he replied with an agitated voice.

He was wearing the fox fur coat that I bought him last Christmas, some PRP jeans, and a fresh pair of butterscotch Timbs. A duffle bag was draped over his right shoulder, and a Foot Locker bag was clutched in his left hand. He tried to brush past me, but I quickly stepped in front of him blocking his path.

"Come on, Erica, stop playing all the time."

"Ain't nobody playing with you, Dawood. Where the fuck ya ass was at last night?" I demanded to know.

Uzi looked at me like I was crazy, then he held the Foot Locker bag that I already knew was full of money. I wasn't impressed, far from it.

Sniff.

Irish Spring?

"Ooohhhh, so that's where ya ass was at." I squinted my eyes and folded my arms across my chest. "You was laying up with one of them cheap-soap-dollar-store-bitches."

"Cheap soap, what?" Uzi frowned at me. He gently moved me aside, then continued walking down the hallway towards the kitchen. I popped his ass in the back of his head, and then took off in the opposite direction.

A devious smile was plastered across my honey-brown face. Reverse psychology, it worked every time. Because little did Uzi know, while he was running around the city like a pit bull with his pink rocket sticking out, a bitch was getting her pussy ate and her back blown out by this boss nigga named, *Rahmello Moreno,* from the Bad Landz. So, it's just like Big Mama used to always say, *"What's good for the goose, is good for the gander."*

So, basically, what was good for Uzi was good for my black ass too.

Ha!

After jogging up the spiral staircase and stepping inside of our bedroom, I heard a strange noise coming from the walk-in closet.

What the hell?

I tiptoed toward the closet and snatched the door wide open.

"Gucci!" I shouted at my miniature Yorkie, who was rolling around on the floor chewing on my brand-new pumps. "Not my Emilio Puccis! You stop that, right now!"

Gucci released my pump from her sharp little teeth, then looked up at me as though she hadn't done anything wrong. The red bow that was tied around her head was slightly cocked to the left, and her diamond studded choker was glistening bright. I wanted to kick her little ass outta the house, but I couldn't. She was just too damn cute.

As I looked back and forth between Gucci and my chewed-up pump, she stood up on her hind legs and extended her left paw. Completely disregarding my shoe, I scooped my baby off the floor and carried her over to the bed. It was a California King sitting on a small platform with a one-step drop.

After laying Gucci down on the bed, I peeled out of my bathrobe and plopped down beside her in nothing but a G-string. Gucci licked the side of my face and wasted no time burying her head beneath my left arm. I was dead tired from a long night of shaking my ass and throwing this pussy on my side nigga. So, all I wanted to do was put some Loud in the air, and then take my black ass to sleep.

I gently moved my baby from underneath my arm, then rolled over and reached in the top drawer of my nightstand. That's where I kept my goodies. Without looking, I felt around the drawer to fish out my smoke and one of my blunt wraps.

"Umm!" My kitty kat tingled when my fingers brushed across the life-sized dildo that was molded into the image of my favorite porn star's dick. I had plans to deal with that monster later.

Ha!

As I continued fishing around the drawer, I finally found exactly what I was looking for.

"Blunt wraps, check. Jar of Loud, check."

I pulled my goodies from the drawer, but before I could twist up and get my chief on, my Hello Kitty iPhone began vibrating on the nightstand.

Vrrrrm! Vrrrrm! Vrrrrm!

My crazy ass was so freaky, that my *other* Hello Kitty came to life thinking that Mr. Marcus was coming out to play. I know, I know, I know... I'ma bona fide nympho and I need to see a psychologist. But so what! Y'alls asses is some freaks, too. A bitch ain't the only one.

Picking up my iPhone, I saw the caller was my nephew, Jabari. I looked at my Rolex and wondered why he was calling me so early.

Shouldn't he still be at school?

"Yes, Jabari," I said after accepting his call.

"Yo, Auntie E, where you at?"

"Where am *I* at?" I replied with a voice full of sarcasm. "Where is *yo'* ass at? And you better say school."

Although I'm only sixteen years older than Jabari, who's my oldest nephew, I was hella protective when it came to him, Reeko and Kenyatta. And that's because I knew firsthand how the streets of Philly could devastate the lives of young black men. My daddy went to prison for killing the man who raped and murdered my mother. Then, when I was seventeen, my boyfriend, AJ, received a Life Sentence for shooting up a house party in West Philly. And being as though I was born and raised in the infamous Richard Allen projects, you can only imagine the countless number of young black men that I've seen fall victim to the streets. So, naturally, I had a healthy fear when it came to the safety and the wellbeing of my nephews; especially Jabari, who was one step away from changing the lives of our entire family. For as long as I could remember, our family's been plagued with poverty, prison, drug abuse, and death. So now that Jabari was so close to playing in the NBA, a lot of our hopes and dreams were wrapped up in him and his talent.

"Nah," Jabari answered my question. "I'm not at school. I'm in the projects on 23rd and Diamond, parked outside of Tonya's house."

"*On 23rd and Diamond*?" I raised my voice. "Parked in front of Tonya's house? Where the hell is Tonya? Did that girl have you skipping school, just to come see her?"

That lil' girlfriend of his was a piece of work, and deep down I had the feeling the bitch was up to no good. Just the other day he brought her lil' fast ass over here, talking about the heifer was seven weeks pregnant. Then he had the nerve to turn around and make me promise not to tell Ebony.

"Nah, it wasn't Tonya," Jabari spoke in his deep voice, "she ain't have nothing to do with this shit. I was chilling with my side jawn, Shameeka."

Now, that *Shameeka*, I liked her a lot. She came from a good family, and I could tell that she really loved Jabari. But for some reason, his ass didn't see it.

"Well, obviously, Shameeka's not with you being as though you're parked outside of Tonya's. So, how did you go from chilling with Shameeka to being parked in the projects?"

"Mommy kicked me out the house."

"*Ebony did what*?" There was so much fire in my voice, that Gucci wiggled away and scampered toward the edge of the bed. From the way she was looking, I could tell that she didn't know whether or not to run away or console me.

"She kicked me outta the house," Jabari repeated.

"She kicked you outta the house for what? You told her about Tonya being pregnant?"

I knew there had to be a good reason for Ebony to do something so drastic. She loved Jabari to death, and was more over protective of my nephews than I was.

Clearly, there was something that Jabari wasn't telling.

"Nah, she doesn't know about Tonya."

"Well, what happened then, Jabari? Because I know she didn't kick you outta the house for no reason. So, what happened? What did you do?"

The phone went silent for a few seconds, then he finally confessed what he did.

"She came home from work early and caught me fucking Shameeka in her bed."

"*Jabari!*"

I wanted to laugh so bad, but I didn't want Jabari thinking I condoned his actions. But, boy oh boy! Talk about a scandalous bitch named *Karma*! If my memory served me correct, Ebony's little hot ass did the same exact thing back in the day. I was sick at school, and Big Mama had to leave work early to pick me up. And wouldn't you know that when we got home, Ebony's lil' fresh ass was up in Big Mama's room getting her freak on! Big Jabby had her pinned against the headboard with her legs in the air, digging them guts out. I remember that shit like it was yesterday.

"I didn't mean for Mommy to catch us," Jabari continued in a somber voice. "Had I known she was coming home from work early, I wouldn't have done it. So, it wasn't like I was blatantly try'na disrespect her. The shit just happened."

"Alright, Jabari, don't worry about it. I'll call Ebony and straighten everything out. And why are you just now calling me? You should have come to me before you went to that, to that *girl*."

I couldn't stand Tonya's ass, and Jabari knew it.

"I went over to Auntie Elisha's house first, and that's the reason I'm calling. Reeko got locked up, and we gotta go bail him out."

"Reeko got locked up?" I sat up and listened more attentively. "Locked up for what?"

"I guess he was out there hustling," Jabari said. "When I pulled up in front of the house, he was standing outside with Uno and Boo-Boo. I waved him over to the car, and then the next thing I knew, the cops was pulling up from everywhere. Uno and Boo-Boo got away, but the cops got Reeko. They fucked him up for try'na run, and when they searched him, they found some dope in his sock."

I was mad as hell; not only because the cops beat up my nephew, but because deep down in my heart I knew that Uzi was the one who gave Reeko the dope he was selling. I *been* told his ass to stop giving my nephew them goddamned drugs!

"The cops, they didn't beat him up too bad, did they?"

"Not *too* bad, but they definitely fucked him up. They were banging his face against the wall and lacing him with body shots. His right eye was completely swollen and his nose was bleeding down the front of his sweater. I wanted to hop out and help him, but the last thing I needed was the cops finding the gun that was stashed in my back seat."

I wasn't naive to the streets, so I didn't flinch when Jabari mentioned that he had a gun. If it were up to me, I would rather that he be caught with it than be caught without it. Yeah, I know that sounds kinda crazy, but really, it's not. Just take a look at the murder rate in my city, and you'll understand why. It's a fucked-up position to take, but that's the way it is around here. It's the shadows of the game.

"Alright, Jabari, I'm gonna call my lawyer. Then after that, I'm gonna throw on some clothes and drive down to the precinct."

"Say less? I'ma meet you down there."

After disconnecting the call, I hopped off the bed and ran out the door, ready to give Uzi a piece of my mind. This nigga knew full fucking well that I didn't want Reeko selling any goddamned drugs. And his fuckin' ass gonna give him the shit *anyway*? This nigga got me fucked up.

"*Uzi!*"

CHAPTER TEN

SHAMEEKA

Well, at least I was able to grab my cell phone, that's all I could think about when I pulled into my driveway a little over an hour ago. Luckily for me, I had an extra pair of clothes in my trunk when Jabari's mom kicked me out of their house. That woman was crazy as hell. I honestly thought she was going to kill me. So, that was the reason I took off running just as naked as the day I was born. I snatched those clothes from my trunk, threw them on quick, and then got my little yellow self out of there. Can you imagine how awkward it would have been driving home completely naked? And what about the police? What if they would have pulled me over and asked me to step out of my car? Aww man, that ish would have been ug-a-ly!

I lived about fifteen minutes away from Jabari in a small town called Elkins Park. My family's estate is right around the corner from Bill Cosby's. And speaking of Mr. Cosby, I've been seeing him on the news lately for some very horrible things. But just like Kermit sipping on his teacup, *that ain't none of my business, though.*

I guess you could say I had a privileged life. I was rough around the edges, but privileged, nonetheless. My mother was the Montgomery County District Attorney, and my father was a gynecologist. They both attended and graduated from the University of Pennsylvania. They met, fell in love, and had me a few years later. I was an only child, so basically I got whatever I wanted.

My entire life, I lived in this ginormous estate about five miles north of Philadelphia. It was so boring in my neighborhood. I mean, like, literally, there was nothing to do in Elkins Park. As I kid, I really didn't know any better, so I honestly didn't care. But the second I grew me some hips and a perky pair of b-cups, I was yearning for a little action, and by action, I mean boys. Not these corny-ass boys from Elkins Park, but the boys from the city.

Askari

When I was thirteen, my best friend, Lauren, and me, would go to the Cheltenham Mall where we got our first taste of the city life. Technically, we were still in Montgomery County, but right across the street from the mall was Uptown Philly. On Saturday afternoons, my mother would drop us off at the mall and we would hook up with Lauren's cousins, Ashley and Asia, who at the time lived in Uptown. Specifically, they lived in Mt. Airy, which was more suburban than urban. But even then, to Lauren and me, two girls from Elkins Park, Mt. Airy was most definitely the city.

Anyway, Ashley and Asia would take us across city limits and show us around their neighborhood. It was so much liver than Elkins Park. There were corner stores, barbershops, hair salons, and most importantly an endless supply of swagged out city boys, cute as hell with that Uptown flavor.

Lauren and me had been best friends since the first grade, so being as though Ashley and Asia were Lauren's first cousins, my parents got to know them pretty well over the years. In fact, even their parents became close with mine, and by the time I was fifteen my parents didn't think twice about allowing me to spend the weekends at their house. Now, that's when the fun really began!

Ashley and Asia's parents were divorced, and they lived with their mom, Ms. Angie, who was always at church. Whether it was Bible study or choir rehearsal, Ms. Angie was there. It was during those weekends that I smoked my first blunt, got drunk for the first time, lost my virginity, and had my pussy ate by another girl for the first and only time. Everything was cool, all the way up until last summer. That's when shit got crazy, and my life changed forever.

During one of our weekend escapades, Lauren met and fell in love with this Jamaican dude named Gavin from West Philly. Well, actually, he was born and raised in Kingston, Jamaica, but was living in West Philly.

At first glance, I didn't know what my girl saw in this dude, but it didn't take long for me to figure it out. Gavin was one of them ugly-ass, Shabba Ranks looking Jamaicans. But he was caked up with mad money and he loved to spend it on Lauren. He even copped my girl a drop-top Benz for her seventeenth birthday. It was cherry-red with butter leather seats and had chromed-out rims. Mannnnnn, when I tell you my girl was hype! And it wasn't because of the car, because had she wanted a Benz, her parents would have bought her a Benz. It was the fact that she snagged herself a baller, one who was willing to give her any and everything she desired.

That entire summer, Lauren, Ashley, Asia, and me were balling out something serious. On Saturday nights, we would rock the latest fashions, throw on our best jewelry, and cruise around Philly in my girl's drop-top Benz. My girl behind the steering wheel, me in the passenger's seat, with Ashley and Asia flexing hard in the back. Top down, chrome rims gleaming—the four of us looking like money.

Then one morning, about two weeks before school started, I was awakened by the soul piercing sound of my mother screaming. I jumped out of bed and ran down the stairs, where I found her sitting at the dining room table. Her cell phone was laying on the floor, and she was crying uncontrollably. The person on the other end of the phone was Lauren's mother, Ms. Paula. She'd just finishing telling my mother that was Lauren was murdered the night before. Apparently, Gavin had a jealous baby mama who wasn't feeling the fact that her baby daddy was stepping out with another female. The Benz that Gavin gave Lauren for her birthday used to belong to his baby mama, and because she still had the code to its GPS system, she'd been keeping tabs on my girl's every move.

According to Ms. Paula, Lauren and Gavin were leaving some reggae club in Southwest Philly when his baby mama ran up on the car and began shooting. She shot Lauren three times in the face, and then stood over top of her and filled her body with eight more bullets. Gavin's coward-ass escaped unharmed. Supposedly, he took off running when the shooting erupted, leaving my girl to deal with the consequences of *his* actions.

Devastation.

Anger.

Pain.

Regret.

Those were the four words, better yet feelings, that entrenched my mind, body, and spirit; similar to a genie that was trapped inside

of a bottle, desperate to break free and wreak havoc on any and everything that opposed him. I couldn't eat. I couldn't sleep. I couldn't
even cry. My sister was gone; gone forever, and there was nothing
that I, nor anyone else could ever do to bring her back. No more
smiles, no more joy, no more tears, no more pain. I was completely
numb, utterly emotionless.

A few days after my girl was laid to rest, I had to report back to
school for the beginning of my senior year. I was far from excited,
and was basically going through the motions. To me, my senior year
was just the first thing on a long list of life experiences that I would
to go through without my sister being there to tag along for the ride.
But what I didn't see coming, was that a week after my first day of
school, God would bless my life with the best thing that could have
ever happened to me.

I was leaving third period heading to my next class when this
tall, handsome brotha slid up beside me. He was so tall, that when I
turned my head to tell him to fuck off, I was eye level with his broad,
muscular chest. Looking up at his handsome face, I was instantly
mesmerized by his soft, hazel eyes. He had a smooth, peanut butter
complexion, a neatly trimmed goatee, and a razor-sharp hairline that
complemented his thick, dark, wavy hair. He smiled at me, and I
couldn't help it; I didn't want to, but before I knew it, I was smiling
back at him. He didn't even try to kick game, or say anything slick.
He just reached down and calmly removed the chemistry book that
was I holding in my left hand. As he walked me to my next class,
he told me how beautiful my smile was and encouraged me to smile
more often. When we arrived at my next class, he returned my
chemistry book and then walked away without saying another word.

Later the night, I laid in my bed thinking about the handsome
giant who managed to put a smile on my face when nothing or no
one else could, and I realized that I didn't even know his name. I
never asked him, and he never offered to tell me. I kind of had an
idea who he was, because last year everybody was talking about the
new kid from North Philly. He was supposed to had been this big
shot basketball star who was destined for the NBA, but none of that
mattered to me. The only thing I cared about was getting to know

the handsome giant who was able to bring a sliver of sunshine into my dark, cloudy existence. So, for the next two hours I searched the internet and discovered that his name was Jabari James.

The next day at school, I noticed how all the girls were sweating him constantly. But dang, if y'all could have only seen their faces when Jabari ignored them and went out of his way to carry my books to home room.

For two weeks straight, Jabari and me were like two peas in a pod. We spent all of our free time together, and would talk about any and everything. I told him about the situation with Lauren, and he told me about his father being murdered when he was seven years old. Eventually, we made love for the very first time and it amazed me how patient, loving, and passionate he was. He took his time and did everything right; everything to make sure that I was comfortable. It was then, that I fell in love with Jabari. He *was* and still *is* my everything. There's absolutely nothing I wouldn't do for my special guy. But deep down in my heart, I wonder if he even knows.

Askari

CHAPTER ELEVEN

JABARI

After talking to Auntie E, I received a text message from Shameeka.

1:18pm: Meek: *Hey, Bae, just thinking about you. I hope you're safe and okay, and that your cray-cray mom didn't kill you. LMFAO!!*

I sent her a text right back.

1:19pm: Jabari: *I'm good, lil' buddy. Thnx 4 axn, tho.*

1:20pm: Meek: *Okay, Bae. I'll see you tonight at the game. Love ya.*

1:21pm: Jabari: *Fa'sho.*

Shameeka was good peoples, but'cha boy wasn't really checking for her like that. We'd definitely grown close over the past few months, but that was only because I was living out of town away from my girl, Tonya. I couldn't even front, though, me and Shameeka were clicking on a whole different level, and at times I found myself really starting to feel shorty. But the second them feelings popped up, thoughts of Tonya would snap me back to reality.

Me and Tonya had been kicking it since the seventh grade, and now that she was carrying my seed, I could honestly see myself putting a ring on her finger. My only problem was Ma' Dukes and Auntie E; they straight up couldn't stand Tonya. They said she only cared about the money I was about to be making. At first, I didn't agree, but lately I was starting to see a new side to Tonya. She was always talking about the diamonds and furs I'ma lace her with, and the brand-new Bentley I'ma have her pushing. That was one of the many differences between her and Shameeka. Tonya was born and raised in the projects, just like me. But Shameeka's been around money her entire life and could care less about the material shit. The only thing she cared about was the way I maked her feel. I took Shameeka to meet Auntie E, and Auntie E was feeling lil' buddy. She even had the nerve to pull me aside and tell me that Shameeka was the one. I wouldn't go that far, Auntie E, but for the time being I'ma keep shorty around. You never know.

After stuffing my iPhone back inside of my hoody pocket, I started the engine and threw the car in gear. I was just about to pull away from the curb, but was blocked in when a black Benz coupe pulled up beside me. I looked over to tell the driver that I need some room to murk out, and guess who the fuck I saw sitting in the passenger's seat...*Tonya*! She was nodding her head to the *Power of Money* by Yo Gotti, and looking at her reflection in a hot pink Mac-Book. She must'a felt me staring at her, because she turned in my direction and then quickly crouched down in the seat.

The dude who was sitting behind the steering wheel looked at Tonya and started laughing. He was a light-skinned, curly head, August Alsina looking ass nigga. He looked at me on some cocky shit, shrugged his shoulders and then said something to Tonya. The music was too loud for me to hear what he was saying. But whatever he said, he must'a embarrassed Tonya because sat up straight and started shaking her head. When she looked back at me and saw that I was climbing out the car, she waved her hands and mouthed the word, "*No.*"

I wasn't hearing none of that shit. I was flaming mad, so you damn right I wanted answers. I pushed open the door and hopped out the car in one motion. But what I didn't realize was that my Glock .45 was still laying across in my lap. So, the second I touched the pavement, it tumbled to the ground and left off a single shot.

Boca!

"Aw, shit!" The loud sound scared me, as I hopped back to avoid the stray bullet. I looked around praying I didn't see any cops, then I reached down and scooped it back up.

August Alsina was quicker than a mah'fucka. I didn't even see him when he climbed out the Benz. But there he was, just a few feet away with his .44 bulldog aimed at the front of my grill.

Damn, I hope this nigga don't blast me.

"Pussy, you was dumping at me?" the nigga said with his finger on the trigger. He was every bit of five-foot-seven, and from the looks of his tight-ass Gucci shirt, I pegged him to be about a hunnid and twenty pounds.

Looking down the barrel's black hole, I could feel the sweat trickling down my forehead. I was completely frozen and didn't know what to say. My fo' pound was clutched in my right hand, but like I said before, I was far from a gangsta. And even if I was a gangsta, there was clearly nothing I could do to defend myself. The nigga had the drop on me.

Tonya hopped out the Benz and positioned herself between me and the fake-ass August Alsina. Her back was to me, as she stood there facing him.

"Come on, Trey, chill the fuck out," Tonya pleaded with him. "This is my boo, Jabari. The one I was telling you about."

"Fuck I care about this nigga being ya boo?" Trey snarled at her with his bird chest puffed out. "Especially when this nigga was just shooting at my fuckin' car,"

Tonya began crying. I didn't know this nigga from a can of paint, but obviously Tonya did. So, now I'm really bitching. Because based on how scared she was, I couldn't help but to wonder if "August" was the type of nigga that wouldn't think twice about killing us both.

"Trey, *please*?" Tonya sobbed. "It's not that deep, so can you please put your gun away?"

"Bitch, is you crazy?" Trey looked at her with the most vicious ice-grill. "You don't see that big-ass gun in homeboy's hand? Got the nerve to ask me to put my shit away, but ain't gon' say nothing to him? Bitch, you trippin'! Matter of fact," he looked up at me with his gun still aimed at my face, "nigga, give this bitch ya burner. And Tonya," he returned his gaze to her, "you throw that muthafucka inside of my car."

"Here, Tonya, take this shit." I handed her my fo' pound. Tonya grabbed the gun from my hand and quickly tossed it inside the Benz.

"Listen, bro," I spoke in a calm voice, praying I could talk some sense into this nigga. "I don't want no trouble, and I apologize if I offended you. And just for the record, I wasn't try'na shoot at you or your car."

"Umm-hmm, that's what I thought," Trey said as he lowered his gun. "Ya bitch-ass better had apologized. I'ma let it slide this

time, but if we ever bump heads again, I'm killing you and I'm killing this stankin-ass bitch."

When he hopped back in his Benz and pupped off, Tonya tried
to explain that dude was just a friend from school who was giving
her a ride home. I wasn't try'na hear it, though. The bitch was lying.

"Jabari, don't leave!" Tonya whined, as I hopped back inside of
my car and slammed the door. "At least, let me tell you my side of
the story," she continued whining, as she ran around the front of the
car and hopped in on the passenger's side. "Just hear me out, baby,
please?"

"Get the fuck out of my car, Tonya." I was so done with shorty
that I couldn't even stand the sight of her.

"Nope, I'm not doing it." She folded her arms across her chest.
"I'm not going anywhere, not until you tell me that you're not mad
at me."

I took a deep breath and sighed.

"Listen, Tonya, I'm going through a lot right now, and I really
don't feel like arguing with you. Reeko got locked up, and I need to
go down to the precinct to see what's up wit' him. So, just go in the
house, and I'ma holla at you later."

Tonya didn't respond. She just looked at me with puppy dog
eyes and stuck out her bottom lip.

"Fuck it, then." I threw the transmission in *drive* and then took
off down Diamond Street, headed towards the 26th District.

CHAPTER TWELVE

DOMINIQUE

5:48 pm

"What the Ellen Degeneres?!"

That's what my mommy's best friend, Mimi, blurted out as she placed her hands on her wide spread hips. She was glaring out the front window of Mommy's hair salon, looking at the pretty dark-skinned woman who had just finished getting her hair done. The woman was standing in front of the salon hugging and kissing on a slim, brown skinned woman who reminded me of the rapper Fabolous.

"Jesus take the whe-el!" Mimi continued, still looking at the two women loving on one another. "Now, they asses know they wrong, going against God and the Bible like that. Don't make no dag-gone sense."

Mimi was a trip. She was always in the next person's business, and quick to have an opinion about any and everything around her. I'd known her my entire life, and loved her as though she were a second mother.

"Mimi, if you don't sit ya black ass down somewhere," D'Lovely told her. He was applying a new perm to his client's hair and shaking his head at Mimi. "Always try'na judge some damn body. Gurl, bye!"

"Excuse me?" Mimi whipped her head in D'Lovely's direction. "First of all, wasn't nobody talking to no Caitlyn-motherfucking-Jenner."

"Child, puh-lease!" D'Lovely smacked his lips and spun around before striking a pose. "That deep voice, Sylvester Stallone sounding heifer ain't gots not a damned thang on Miss D'Lovely, bitch. So, get it the fuck straight."

"That's right, gurl, you tell her," said Simone, one of my mommy's hair stylist. Her salon chair was placed in the center, between Mimi and D'Lovely's. And just like me and everyone else who frequented the salon, she loved it when the two of them went for the other's jugular. She gave D'Lovely a high-five, and then stuck her tongue out at Mimi.

D'Lovely was looking immaculate as usual. His black Versace dress shirt was unbuttoned at the top, showing off his muscular chest, and his leopard print Versace slacks were skintight, showing off the bulge in his crotch and his tight lil' buns in the back. He had a dark, chocolate complexion, a clean shaved face, and a head full of finger-waves that he religiously kept lined up to perfection.

"Bitch, I am *fierce!*" D'Lovely boasted. "That Caitlyn bitch wish she had a swag like mines."

"Boy, bye," Mimi said as she washed her hands in the small sink beside her work station. Mimi was a big one. She was pretty in the face, super thick in the waist, and had a light caramel complexion. Her navy-blue Polo shirt was hanging down just below the top of her thighs, and her skintight jeans were clinging on for dear life, twisting and turning with her every curve and crevice.

"Nique-Nique, you better tell her something," D'Lovely threw me in the mix. "Because *obviously*, Miss Mimi didn't get the memo."

I laughed at him, but I didn't respond. I was too busy waiting on Mimi to say something slick, and boy was she right on time.

"Yeah, you's a fly motherfucker," Mimi said while drying her hands with a clean towel. "But'cha ugly ass still got a grill like a young Whoopi Goldberg."

"Excuse me?" D'Lovely shot back, placing his right hand over his heart as if Mimi had just stabbed him in it. "You wanna run that by me again?"

"You heard what I said. You're black, you're ugly, *you're nothing at all!*" Mimi exclaimed, imitating Mista from *The Color Purple*.

"Ugly?" D'Lovely frowned, looking Mimi up and down. "Well, sheeeiiiit, that ain't what'cha baby daddy said."

Me, Simone, and Diamond, the girl who was sitting in D'Lovely's chair, fell out laughing.

"See, now ya ass done went too goddamned far!" Mimi lashed out, looking at D'Lovely like she was ready to pop off. "Ya ass know good and the fuck well that I plays no games when it comes to my baby daddy. Now, you take that shit back!"

Damn, I wish I had me some popcorn. This ish was starting to get good. D'Lovely was known for putting a downlow nigga on blast. So, we all just sat there looking at him, wondering if he was gonna take back what he said about Mimi's baby daddy.

"I ain't playing wit'chu, D'Lovely," Mimi said as she rolled up her sleeves. "You take it the fuck back."

"Ooohhhhhh, so Miss D'Lovely hit a soft spot with that one, huh?" He placed his left hand on his hip and shifted his weight to the same side. "Well, hunnnnteeee, lemme tell you. That baby daddy of yours," he looked up at the ceiling and used his right hand to fan himself off, being extra dramatic, "that big ol' beef cake? Humph. He got a *fetish* for this peanut butter!"

My eyeballs damn near popped out of my head. I couldn't believe he said that. I was so shocked that I covered my mouth with both hands, hoping and praying the laughter inside of me didn't seep out into the airwaves.

"*Oh-no-the-fuck-you-didn't*!" Mimi shouted at the top of her lungs. She grabbed the curling iron that was plugged into her work station and bull rushed over towards D'Lovely.

I didn't want to laugh; I swear to God I didn't. But when D'Lovely screamed like a bitch and took off running with his hands raised in the air, I completely lost it.

"*Mimi, gurl, you better stop*!" D'Lovely screamed. He was running around the salon like a chicken with its head cut off, weaving through the rows of chairs where the customers sat.

"Stop, shit!" Mimi shouted back. She was hot on D'Lovely's ass, swinging the curling iron like a crowbar. "Ya flamin' ass done crossed the goddamned line! Outta all people, you know how crazy I be getting over Charles! Don't nobody come for my goddamned baby daddy, except *me*!"

Mimi's big ol' self got tired fast. She was huffing and puffing, and hunched forward with both hands resting on her chubby kneecaps. Looking up at D'Lovely, she said, "Nigga, I'ma bust ya fucking head. Talking 'bout my man got a fetish for some god-damned peanut butter!"

"Alright, Mimi, *alright*! I take it back," D'Lovely stated sincerely. "Bitch, you know you my gurl."

D'Lovely approached Mimi slow, and she didn't resist when he wrapped his arms around her.

"And just for the record, bitch, you started it. A bitch be knowing she look like Wesley Snipes with a twist of Forest Whitaker. But that don't mean ya ass gotta be reminding me."

"Boy, shut up." Mimi chuckled as she waved the curling iron in front of his face. "You lucky I didn't pop ya flamin' ass. Talking 'bout my man got a fetish for some dag-gone peanut butter." She cracked up laughing, and we laughed along with her.

Just as things were beginning to simmer down, my mommy and her boyfriend, Giovanni, walked through the front door.

Giovanni reminded me of the R&B singer Ginuwine. He was the light skinned, pretty boy type, with a blown-out S-curl, and a tight lil' body. He and Mommy have been together for five years now. He was cool at first, but

lately he's been getting on my freakin' nerves, always saying some stupid ish out of his mouth.

Now, my mommy, she was drop dead gorgeous. I looked just like her, just a younger and more petite version. We had the same cocoa brown skin with a light twist of vanilla. Our almond shaped eyes, long eyelashes, and thick juicy lips came courtesy of my grandmother, Francine. But our hazel-green eyes and our pointy lil' noses, were features that we inherited from my grandfather, Felix, who like my mommy and grandmother, was born and raised in the D.R. That's the Dominican Republic for those of you who don't know.

My mommy first came to the States in the late nineties to attend Drexel University. As the story goes, it was during that time when she met my daddy. He was dating one of her roommates, but all of that changed the second he laid eyes on her. Mommy's roommate was some Madonna looking, Italian chick who couldn't hold a match to my mommy's beauty. In no time at all, she had my daddy eating out the palm of her hand. My daddy was touching crazy fetty back then. Unfortunately, when I was five years old, the cops raided our house and my daddy went to prison for selling drugs.

It was the night before my first day of Kindergarten. We were chilling in my parent's bedroom watching the movie *White Chicks*. Daddy and me had just finished picking out my outfit for the first day of school. Daddy was sitting at the top of the bed counting a big ol' pile of money, and Mommy was sitting at the foot braiding my hair into two long ponytails. I was sitting on floor, right in between her legs. I remember this like it was yesterday. I was munching on a bowl of Cheez Doodles and laughing at the Wayans brothers when I heard a loud *Boom*! Then another one, followed by a loud *Crack*!

Daddy jumped off the bed and his money went flying through the air. He ran over to the window and said something to Mommy about a drug raid. At the time I didn't know what a drug raid was, but man was I about to find out. From the hallway, I heard a bunch of footsteps running up the stairs, and I remember thinking it was the Boogey Man coming to kill us. My five-year-old brain was too young to process what was happening. But yet and still, I was so afraid that warm pee soiled the pit of my panties and trickled down the insides of my legs. I broke down crying and quickly crawled underneath the bed.

Daddy was yelling at Mommy, telling her to grab the shit from the closet so he could flush it down the toilet. I peeked my head out from underneath the sheet that was dangling off the side of the bed, and looked up at Mommy as she ran towards the closet. She snatched open the door, reached inside and pulled out a black book bag. She tossed the book bag to Daddy, and the second he caught it, the bedroom door flew open wide. A masked man dressed in all black was standing on the other side shouting at Daddy. He had a big ol' gun pointed in Daddy's face.

"*Police! Don't you fucking move!*"

"*Don't shoot!*" Daddy said as he dropped the book bag and threw his hands in the air. "*Just calm down and take it easy. My girl and my daughter is in here!*"

The masked man and two of his partners tackled Daddy to the floor, and then placed him in handcuffs. A total of ten years went by before the next time I saw Daddy again, and that was last year on my fifteenth birthday. Mommy was the main reason I didn't see him; she wouldn't even allow me to speak to him over the phone. It was some bunked up ish Mommy did, try'na take me away from Daddy. But it's just like Daddy said on the first day he came home and we reconnected, it's the shadows of the game.

CHAPTER THIRTEEN

DOMINIQUE

After greeting everybody inside the salon, Mommy peeled out of her rabbit and fox fur coat and hung it on the coat rack beside the door.

"Hey, Boss Lady," Mimi greeted her back with a smile.

Simone and Diamond waved at her and smiled, but D'Lovely, being his overdramatic, animated self, just *had* to go above and beyond. He waved at Mommy with both hands, and smiled as though he hadn't seen her in a million years.

"Umm mmm *mmm!*" D'Lovely snapped his fingers, looking over Mommy from head to toe. "Gurrrrrrrl! You are looking *fee-yah-ierce!*"

"Well, thank you." Mommy blushed.

"No thanks needed, gurl." D'Lovely waved her off. "You know you a showstopper. So, just where in the tri-state is Giovanni taking you? Because dressed like that, it better not be no neighborhood bar."

Mommy was looking like a bag of money with big-face Benji's spilling out the top. Her new haircut was long on one side, but cut short and neatly trimmed on the other. Her ears, neck and wrist were blinged out from her diamond studded jewelry, and her sheer black cat suit was topped with her cherry-red, knee high Gucci boots and a red leather belt. Her thongs and bra were cherry-red too. I could see them through the sheer black fabric.

"He's taking me to Laff House to see Kevin Hart, you know his lil' funny ass is back in the city. Then after that, we'll probably just hit up a few clubs," Mommy replied. She looked at me and smiled, then walked over and gave me a big hug. "Hey, baby. How was school today?"

"The usual." I shrugged my shoulders, then popped the stick of gum in my mouth that I just removed from my purse. "We had a pop quiz in Geometry, a test in English, and another test in Biology. History class was exciting. Two of my classmates got into a fight, and my teacher, Mr. Powell, got punched in his face when he tried to break it up. But other than that, it was pretty much a typical day."

I looked at Giovanni, who was sitting in the first row of chairs, and caught him sneaking a peek at D'Lovely. He must have felt me watching, because he looked in my direction with a guilty smirk on his face.

"What's up, Nique-Nique? You good?"

I chucked up my deuces and pulled out my iPhone. It was Friday, so Twitter and the Gram just had to be lit. I went to my camera app and asked Mommy to take a selfie with me. She wrapped her arm around my neck and pressed her pretty face against mines. Mommy was way more conceited than me. So, the second I finished snapping a few pictures, she snatched the phone from my hand and selected the picture she felt represented her best.

"Ahn-ahn, Mommy, now you know you doin' the most." I laughed at her. I had just turned sixteen and still amazed me how much we looked like sisters, rather than mother and daughter.

"Nique-Nique, show me how to upload this picture and share it on my Facebook," Mommy said. She was holding my phone with both hands and looking at my Instagram app like it was Chinese arithmetic.

"Here, Mommy, give it to me." I reached for the phone, and she gave it back to me. In no time at all, I did exactly what she asked me. "What do you want me to write on the post?"

She thought about it for a brief second, then blurted out, "Bad Bitches R Us."

I smiled at her mischievously.

"Are you *sure* you want me to write that? Because Daddy's gonna have a fit when he sees it. He hates it when I use profanity in my posts. He says it's unbefitting of a young Queen."

Mommy placed her hands on her hips and gave me a look that said, *"Girl, you better do as I told you!"*

"Alright." I nodded my head. "But when Daddy sees this and he gets mad, this is all on you, not me."

"Girl, ain't nobody worried about Zion and all that back to Africa shit. I'm the one who raised you. His jailbird ass ain't do nothing but donate a little bit of sperm. So, I wish the fuck he would call his'self-checking me. I'll read that motherfucker faster than his black ass can blink."

"And I know that's right," Mimi said, sticking her nosey self in me and Mommy's conversation.

"Mimi, if you don't mind your own damned business," Mommy checked her. "Always getting in the middle of somebody's conversation."

"Now, you *know* I heard that!" D'Lovely chuckled and snapped his fingers three times, making the letter 'Z'.

Mimi scowled at him, and Simone burst out laughing.

I hate it that Mommy's was always bashing my daddy, calling him a jailbird and whatnot. I wanted so bad to check her, but doing so would have jeopardized me spending the weekend with Daddy.

I looked at Giovanni, and once again caught him lusting on D'Lovely.

You dirty dick, on the downlow motherfucker, I was thinking, but knew better than to say it out loud. My mommy loved Giovanni, and it seemed like whenever him and me bumped heads, she would always take his side. I'm really starting to hate Giovanni's ass.

"What's the matter, Nique-Nique?" Giovanni asked me, staring back with that goofy-ass expression on his face. "You a'ight?"

"*I fucking hate you.*" I mouthed the words after looking around to make sure nobody was watching me. "*You fucking creep.*"

Giovanni didn't reply. Instead, he just stood to his feet and headed towards the door. By then, Mommy and Simone had dipped off into Mommy's office. D'Lovely was putting the finishing touches on Diamond's hair, and Mimi's big ol' self was tearing up a platter of hot wings.

"D'Lovely," Giovanni said as he opened the door and stepped one foot outside. "Tell Felicia that I'm waiting for her outside in the car."

I shook my head and returned my attention to Instagram. Holding up my iPhone for everyone to see, I said, "Look, y'all! Me and Mommy got a hundred and thirty-four likes!"

Askari

CHAPTER FOURTEEN

ZION

It was 5:58 p.m. when I parked my Range Rover across the street from Felicia's hair salon; the same one she bought with the money she stole from me. As I sat there looking at the sign hanging above the picturesque glass front window, my mind traveled back to a dark place. Specifically, to a time when I wanted to kill Felicia for crossing me. Every night laid awake on my bunk staring up at the ceiling and thinking of all the ways to kill her. The only thing that changed my mind was Seekumbuzu and his words of wisdom.

When I explained the situation to Seekumbuzu, he broke it down so clear that I was mad at myself for not reaching the same conclusion. Seekumbuzu said to me, *"Zion, if you never taught your son how to fight, and he came home from school one day with a busted lip and a black eye, would you be mad at him? No, right? Because you never took the time out to teach him how to hold and throw his hands. So, if you never took the time out to teach that sista how to conduct herself in your absence, then how can you be mad at her for not acting accordingly?"*

Seekumbuzu's words struck a nerve, and I began to realize how wrong I was for seeing Felicia the way I saw her. In light of all the circumstances, I came to realize that Felicia was doing right by me, by doing right for our daughter. Dominique's a beautiful young Queen—smart and ambitious, an honor roll student, and a standout Lacrosse player. So, if for no other reason, I had to give Felicia her props for the excellent job she did with Dominique while I was locked away in prison.

Stepping out of my truck, I looked up at the sky and smiled. The color of the sunset was the perfect fusion of red, burgundy, and tan; the same color as a fresh, ripe peach. It reminded me of the final scene in *The Color Purple*, where Miss Ceily and her children were standing beneath the horizon of a descending sun.

Damnit, it feels so good to be free!

The rush hour traffic had died down, and Broad Street, from Susquehanna to Dauphin, was relatively empty. A white Maserati was parked outside of Felicia's salon, and her boyfriend, Giovanni, was leaned against the driver's side door. He was talking on his cell phone and smoking a cigarette. There was something about this dude that I didn't like, but I couldn't put my finger on it. Maybe it was the way he tried too hard trying to make himself appear to be good peoples, or maybe deep down inside I was a tad bit jealous, still holding onto the past feelings I had for Felicia. Either way, in the back of my mind, I made a mental note to keep tabs on this weirdo. Especially since he's living I the same house as my sixteen-year-old daughter.

"Brother Zion," Giovanni said when he saw me walking towards him. "Peace, black man. How you feeling?"

Giovanni extended his right hand, and I accepted the gesture with a firm squeeze. I wasn't down for the small talk, so I didn't engage. Instead, I just cut to the chase and asked him if Dominique and Felicia were inside.

"Yeah." Giovanni nodded his head while taking another drag on his Newport. "Nique-Nique's in there playing on her cell phone, you know how these kids are nowadays. And Felicia's back in her office."

See what I mean? I thought to myself. The only thing I did was ask this cat a simple question, but instead of giving me a straight answer, he had to go the extra mile being all Joe Familiar. So instead of replying, I just nodded my head and stepped inside the salon.

"*Daddy!*" Dominique beamed the second she looked up and saw me. She jumped out of her seat, then she ran over and wrapped her arms around my waist. "It's about time." She removed her arms from my waist and then glanced at her Movado watch. "It's 6:01 p.m., and *you, sir,* are one minute late."

It amazed me how Dominique loved me so much. After ten years of being apart, I assumed that when I came home our relationship, at best, would be somewhat strained. But, man, was I wrong. It was almost like the ten years we spent apart had never even happened. I was still Dominique's superman, and she was still my Cheez Doodle eating, sugar boop!

"Nique-Nique," I said after kissing her forehead and draping my arm across her shoulder, "where's your mom? I need to talk to her about something."

"She's in the back," Dominique said as she grabbed me by the hand and led me towards her mother's office.

Mimi, Felicia's road dawg, gave me a fake-ass smile, and the half-a-man that I refused to call *D'Lovely* looked at me and rolled his eyes. Now don't get me wrong, this *is* America and to each his own. But come on black man...*really*?

I started to check his punk ass for disrespecting me in front of my daughter, but one of the lessons that I learned in prison was to never argue or bump heads with a half-a-man. I reasoned that if he didn't care what he stuck in his mouth, then he damn sure didn't care what he let come out of it.

"Hey, Zion," Mimi said, as Dominique and me walked past her, "somebody called and left you a message."

I stopped walking and looked at her skeptically.

"Somebody called here and left me a message? Who?"

"The *Nineties*!" Mimi smiled like a demon. "They said give 'em they Range Rover back!"

The half-a-man burst out laughing, but simmered down quick when I shot his ass the look of death. I looked at Mimi and flexed my jaw muscles. I wanted to grind her fat, rolly polly, Miss-Piggy-looking-ass to bacon bits, but disrespecting women wasn't a part of my forte. So, to calm the beast that was welling up inside of me, I sucked in a deep breath and counted backwards from ten to zero.

Ten—Nine—Eight—

Dominique must have felt my energy, because she squeezed the palm of my hand and continued leading the way to her mother's office.

When we reached the door, Felicia was bent forward, picking through the paperwork in the bottom drawer of her file cabinet. Her back was to the door and her big ol' booty was tooted up in the air. I didn't want to look, but my eyes had a mind of their own. Her juicy, phat ass had me licking my lips, while the thickness of her thighs and her three inched gap had me rolling down memory lane.

Damn, she makes a brotha wanna tap that!

"Mommy?" Dominique said, as she stuck her head inside of the office. "Daddy's here."

"Did that sorry-ass nigga bring me my money?" Felicia replied. She was still digging through the file cabinet drawer and had no idea that I was standing right behind her.

I always knew that Felicia had been throwing dirt on my name. But to actually hear this woman talk bad about me to our daughter was enough to remind me how much I despised her.

"Have I ever missed a payment?" my smooth, deep voice caught her by surprise.

Felicia stood up straight and then turned around to face me. I released Dominique's hand, and then reached inside of my jacket to grab the envelope full of money that I'd brought along with me. The agreement between Felicia and me, was that aside from the $800 I gave her for child support every month, I still had to give her another $300 every Friday just to spend the weekend with Dominique. I hadn't missed a payment in the fifteen months that I'd been home.

"Here," I sat the envelope down on Felicia's desk, "since this is all you seem to care about."

Like a true vulture, Felicia scooped up the envelope. After peeling back the lid, she licked the tip of her thumb and flipped through the bills. I didn't even stick around to watch her count it.

"Come on, Nique-Nique, we out."

And with that, me and my baby got ghost.

CHAPTER FIFTEEN

DOMINIQUE

7:09 pm

From the look on Daddy's face to his overall demeanor, I could see that Mommy's actions had burned a spot on his brain. We were leaving the Golden Corral on Street Road in Bensalem, Pa., and Daddy wasn't being his usual fun-loving self. On the contrary, he seemed to be a little drained and caught up in his thoughts of Mommy.

"Daddy, I'm sorry for the way Mommy's been treating you."

"Nah, baby girl, you don't have to apologize," Daddy said, as we stopped at a red light on Roosevelt Boulevard. He flexed his jaw muscles, then he turned his head to face me. "I respect you too much to ever speak ill of the woman who birthed you. But what I will say is that some people just are who they are. That's just something I came to realize dealing with your mom. It's not even her fault. She just is who she is."

Daddy reached for his radio and turned on his Lauryn Hill CD. The sounds of my favorite song, *To Zion,* eased through the speakers, and I couldn't stop smiling. I was thinking of all the many nights I used to lay in bed, listening to this song and yearning for the day that me and my daddy, my Beautiful Zion, would be together again.

"Daddy? When they took you away, did you spend a lot of time thinking about me?" I spoke over the soulful music, staring at Daddy and waiting for his answer. Of course, I knew he thought about me, but I still needed to hear it. I guess it's just a daddy—daughter thing.

Daddy looked at me and smiled, then he reached over the console and caressed the side of my face. After that, he traced his finger down the bridge of my nose and then tickled the tip; the same way he used to do when I was little girl.

"Every day, baby girl. I thought about you every day," Daddy replied softly.

"Well, what did you think about?" I asked him with a bashful smile.

"I would think about your beautiful smile, the sound of your voice, your squeaky little laugh, and the cute way your bottom lip would poke out whenever you didn't get your way. I thought about the bond we shared, even before the first I had ever saw you. Every night when your mommy was pregnant with you, I would rest my head against her stomach and talk to you. I did it so much, that the second you were born, I told you how much I loved you, and you smiled at me, recognizing the sound of my voice. I thought about the times you would awaken in the middle of the night crying for a warm bottle and a fresh diaper. I would climb out of bed, change your little diaper, feed you a warm bottle, and then bring you back to bed with me and your mommy. So, yeah," Daddy nodded his head, "I thought about you a lot."

I continued smiling, cherishing the fact I had such a loving father. My daddy was the best. Not only was he the perfect example of what a man should be, my daddy was my motivation. He was the reason why I studied so hard, and why I always tried to carry myself like the beautiful black queen that I was born to be. I wanted to make Daddy proud of me, always.

"Daddy?" I called him once again when we stopped at another red light. "Did you ever dream about me?"

"Absolutely," Daddy quickly confirmed, looking at me as though I should have known better than to be asking such questions. "But the crazy part is that every time I dreamed about you, you were always five years old. I'm assuming that's because you were only five the last time I saw you, and that's how I remembered you the most. So back then, and even now, you're still my little baby. It doesn't matter how old you get; you could be married with children. But to me, no matter the time nor circumstance, you'll always be my baby."

My visage became blurred, as warm tears trickled down the sides of my face. The thought of Daddy being locked behind bars, trapped in a cell, all alone, away from me and Mommy, hit me like a ton of bricks. I was thinking of all the prison movies that I'd seen over the years. Specifically, the movie *Hurricane*, where Denzel Washington played the role of Rubin *Hurricane* Carter. I thought about a place in the prison they called *The Hole*, and I wondered if Daddy had ever spent time there. I imagined him all alone, trapped in darkness with the roaches and rats.

"Baby girl, don't do that," Daddy tried to console me. "Stop crying. You're gonna mess around and have me crying right along with you."

"But—But I missed you, Daddy. I missed you so much when they took you away from us. I wanted to come visit you, but—but Mommy wouldn't bring me. She—She turned her back on you, but—but I never did and I never will. I'll never stop loving you, Daddy. Never!"

I broke down completely, and Daddy pulled over on the side of the road. He wrapped me in his loving arms, and together we cried. We cried for all the special moments we missed, and for the lost memories we would never find. We cried for all of our lonely nights and the ten years we spent separated, heartbroken and yearning for one another's love and affection. Me and my daddy, my Beautiful Zion, we cried.

Askari

CHAPTER SIXTEEN

ZION

7:39 pm

After me and Dominique expressed our frustrations and released our pain, it was time to get back to business. It was a little past 7:30 and I was scheduled to meet my best friend, Atiba Muhammad, at our BTS rec center. Every Friday we held a group discussion with the youth in the city who attended the rec center.

When me and Dominique pulled up in front of the building, we noticed that a crew of young brothas were huddled at the corner having a rap cipher. We hopped out of my Range Rover, walked over and listened. Tone Boy, a neighborhood kid who was known for rocking the mic, was dishing out bars for days.

"My mama told me listen here, lil' nigga, better keep that pistol./ If you think the streets love you, when you're gone will they miss you?/ Them niggas you rydin' wit', they ain't official./ The same nigga that'll catch a body wit'chu, be the same one the district attorney use to come and get'chu./ Believe that shit./ This cocaine game you playing, boy leave that shit./ And I know this ain't the life she wanted for her first born, but I gotta take care of my first born./ So fuck working at Shop-n-Bag, I'ma cop, chop and bag./ Either that, or run around wit' a Glock and a mask./ I'm in a bad predicament, no high school diploma./ Can't get a good job, so I'm on the corna./ And I'm feeling like Hitler, crack houses like gas chambaz./ Filled wit' fiends, killing they lungs wit' glass bangaz./ My block a concentration camp, smokahs skinny as fuck./ Give the last pennies up for a hit of that stuff./ They'll sell they babies if they have to, to get a capsule, of the shit that look like cashews./ But what the fuck, cash rules."

I nodded my head and smiled, not for the content of Tone Boy's lyrics, but because of the way he chose to express himself. I mean, that cat even went as far as to compare the average drug dealer to the likes of Hitler. Why? Because he understood that selling drugs to his own people was the purest form of genocide. And I *knew* Tone Boy, I knew him *personally*. He was a good kid who came from a good family, and the closest he'd ever come to selling cocaine was Johnson & Johnson's baby powder. But through his lyrics, he was connecting with the misguided brothas who *did* sell drugs, showing them the ills of their current mind state. And sadly, a lot of these young brothas out here could relate to everything that Tone Boy was saying. Specifically, that raw, numb feeling of hopelessness, knowing the deck had been stacked against them long before they were even born. And in many cases, these young, misguided brothas come from a broken home—daddy dead or in prison, mommy on drugs, and at the age of twelve or thirteen they were forced to be the man of the house. They had three or four siblings to feed, but were too young to work. So, the only route they saw fit was running the streets; whether selling drugs or robbing people.

I'm not making any excuses, I'm just giving you the real. I'm exposing you to the shadows of the game; the story behind the scenes that most of us never see or read about. I'm explaining the unwritten mentality of the average corner boy. You know this little brotha, you see him every day standing on the corner trapping. He's got a face full of tattoos, a stolen gun on his waist, and no plans for the future because he doesn't have that ability to see that far. He was never taught to *think* that far. And worst of all, in his adolescent mind, his life expectancy is day to day.

Now, back to Tone Boy and his crew. They stopped rapping, then turned around to greet me and Dominique.

"What's going on, lil' brothas," I greeted them back, shaking their hands one at a time.

Dominique did the same, bringing smiles to all of their faces. Tone Bone, in particular, was smiling at Dominique harder than the rest. Supposedly, the two of them were *friends*. I knew better, but honestly, I didn't mind. My daughter was responsible, and Tone Boy was respectful.

I led the kids inside of the rec center, and as always, whenever I stepped inside of the building, I was proud of myself for making such an investment in the future of my people. In my drug dealing days, I'd done so much to destroy my community, so this time around I was determined to make a change for the better.

The rec center was an abandoned church that I purchased from the city. After paying to have it renovated from the inside out, I had it equipped with two classrooms, a computer lab, a kitchen, a weight room, and a full, indoor basketball court that occupied the second floor. The BTS center was a great escape for the youth who needed it. It was by far my greatest accomplishment.

"As salaam alaikum," I greeted Atiba, who was seated at the front desk taking attendance. I wasn't a Muslim, but Atiba was; he was a registered Muslim in the Nation of Islam. I didn't agree with his religious beliefs that Allah came in the person of Master Fard Muhammad and that Elijah Muhammad was his messenger. But what I *did* respect was that Elijah Muhammad did his best to raise our people up from a downtrodden state, and blessed us with such leaders as Malcolm X and Minister Farrakhan. Aside from that, Atiba was my brother and I respected his faith.

"Wa alaikum salaam," Atiba returned my greetings of peace. He stood to his feet and embraced me with a brotherly hug. Looking at Dominique, he smiled at her and gave a slight bow. "As salaam alaikum, little sister."

"Wa alaikum salaam." Dominique smiled back at him.

Atiba gave the same greeting to Tone Boy and his crew, and they each greeted him back. None of us were Muslims, but Atiba had that affect. He was a true brotha in every sense of the word, and you couldn't help but to respect him.

After speaking with me and Atiba for a few more minutes, the kids dipped off towards the classroom where our weekly discussion was being held.

Atiba settled his gaze on me. My brotha was 6'3" and a 195 pounds of rock-solid muscle. He had a medium brown complexion, a clean shaved face, and a neatly trimmed haircut. Like I previously stated, Atiba and me met a few years back while serving time in prison. He was one of the brothas that I met through Seekumbuzu, and together we established the BTS program at SCI Coal Township. The main objective of the program was to talk some sense into the younger brothas who were just coming through the system. Our work in the prison carried over to the streets, and I couldn't have been more honored to have such a strong, positive black man to call my comrade and friend.

"So, what's up, Zee? Are you ready for tonight's discussion?" Atiba asked me.

"Absolutely," I replied. "And assuming the kids read the book, I'm looking forward to an interesting discussion."

When we stepped inside of the classroom, we were surprised to see the kids had already began the discussion. They were going back and forth, breaking down the must-read text, *The Making of a Slave: The Willie Lynch Letter.*

"Yo, that's crazy how them white folks did our ancestors," said Tameeka, a seventeen-year-old, light-skinned sista with pinned back micro-braids. "Did y'all read the part where it talked about tying a black man to a wild horse and breaking him in, using the same exact methods that were used to break in the horse?"

"Yeah, I read it," said Michael, an eighteen-year-old, brown-skinned brotha with burgundy dreads. "But that wasn't the part that touched me the most," he continued while shaking his head. "The craziest part was how the slave-maker psychologically placed the woman ahead of the man, reversing the roles of the natural family structure.

"The slave-maker would take the man, his pregnant wife, and another man who wasn't related to the family and bring them all together. After that, he would tie the limbs of the father to four horses, and then set the man on fire. The blazing fire would cause the horses to take off running until they ripped the father completely apart. The slave-maker would then tar and feather the unrelated man and beat him within an inch of his life. All of this was done in front of the pregnant, black woman. The objective was to instill in the black woman so much fear, that it would seep into the soul of her unborn fetus. And when the child was born, if the child was a male, she would raise him to be totally submissive to the slave-master, fearing that if he wasn't, he would one day meet the same fate of his father or the unrelated male.

"So, in essence, the slave-maker placed the woman at the head of the family unit, using her to raise up generations of submissive, black men, who were subconsciously and psychologically afraid to death of the white man. How else could you justify a black man standing idly by, listening to the horrors of his wife, mother, or daughter being raped by the slave-master? He'd been conditioned that way."

"Yo, that's some deep-ass shit," said Shyheem, a young brotha from Brickyard.

"I don't know if y'all covered this already," Dominique interjected, "but what struck me the most was how the slave-master went to great lengths to turn our ancestors against one another. They turned the man against the woman, the old against the young, the light against the dark, and the house-slave against the field-slave. The book further stated that if properly implemented, this psychological slavery would last for over three hundred years. This was in the beginning of the eighteenth century, in 1712. So, I wonder if this is the reason, that we, in 2015, approximately three hundred years later, tend to think and act the way we do, whether consciously or subconsciously. You know what I'm saying? Like how we never have any unity among us, and how we tend to see one another as niggas and bitches, rather than brothers and sisters?"

Instead of butting in, Atiba and me remained silent. We smiled at one another and nodded our heads in approval. The message that we sought to convey was clearly making a mark with the youth in our community.

Man, these kids are smart!

A few seconds later, Atiba's wife, Hydia, entered the classroom and greeted me with a smile. Her long dreads were tucked beneath her soft-pink kimar, and the matching garb she wore covered her body from the neck down. Her cinnamon face was smooth without blemish, and everything about her said, *"Respect me, for I am Queen!"* I loved my sista. She was the epitome of a strong, black woman, and I admired her for the love and affection she showered upon our youth. She was the perfection reflection of Atiba.

"Okay." Hydia rubbed her hands together and slowly glanced around the classroom. "I'm listening to your views on this book. But did any of you sistas and brothas receive its true message?"

"Yeah, we got the message," Shyheem was the first one to answer, jumping out the jet with a parachute that didn't work. That boy knew dag-gone well how deep Hydia could get. And if he didn't, he was damn sure about to find out.

"Oh, yeah?" Hydia challenged his assertion. "Elaborate, please."

"Man, them crackers did us dirty," Shyheem replied, and I could see the hurt in his eyes when he said it.

"Those *crackers*?" Hydia asked him. Her head was slightly cocked to the side, and she was looking at him attentively. "What exactly do you mean when you say the words *cracker*?"

"You know." Shyheem shrugged his shoulders. "White people,crackers."

"That's racists," Dominique stated. She looked at me for reassurance, but I didn't give it. Instead, I directed her attention back to Hydia, knowing my sista was about to get busy.

"First and foremost," Hydia said, "the word *cracker* was a phrase that our ancestors used to describe the overseer, who by all means was the person cracking the whip, *literally*. However, in many cases, the overseer, himself, was a black man. So, the word *cracker* is synonymous with an oppressor, not a particular race. And secondly," she looked at Dominique, "this word *racist*, Nique-Nique, what exactly does it mean to be a racist?"

"That's when a person calls another person a nigger, or a spic, or a cracker," Dominique answered. "And to take it a step further, racism is when a person doesn't like another person based solely on the color of their skin."

"That is," Hydia paused for a few seconds, "absolutely incorrect."

"*Incorrect*?" Dominique frowned. "Incorrect, how?"

"Because the two scenarios just described amount to bigotry and prejudice, not racism."

"Sista Hydia, you're confusing me," Dominique said. "I don't understand."

"Me either," Shyheem, Tameeka, and Michael all stated in unison.

"I'm confused as hell right about now," said Raekwon another young brotha from Brickyard.

"Okay," Hydia replied, as she moved towards the center of the room. "I'm going to break it down to give you all a better understanding. Now, for a person to not like another person based solely on the color of their skin, this is what you would classify as *prejudice*. And for that person to call another person a nigger, a spic, or a *cracker*," she stated while making air quotes, "this is what you would classify as *bigotry*. But if that person has the *authority* to *treat* that other person like a nigger or a spic, *that*, my sister and brothas is what you would classify as racism. Racism only exists when bigotry and prejudice are accompanied with power.

"Now, back *to The Making of a Slave: The Willie Lynch Letter*. There were two main objectives to be learned from this text. The first objective was to shed light on the element of slavery that was written out of history, *the slave-maker*. We've heard stories and seen movies about the slave-trader and the slave-master, but never the slave-maker. Why? Because the omission of the slave-maker perpetuates the stigma that Africans naturally conformed themselves to being the white man's slave. This was not so. Our ancestors, in their natural state, were warriors, tribesmen, travelers, educators, cultivators, Kings and Queens. So, in order to break them out of their natural state and make them completely dependent and docile, it took a savagely, cruel, heartless individual; one who was intentionally written out of history.

"The second objective was to explain why Africans in America, and all though the diaspora, tend to treat one another the way we do. It explains why it is so hard for us to unite; why we often have distrust issues, a perpetual dislike, and a lack of concern for one another. It further explains why we tend to look down on, rather than uplift one another.

"Our psychological ills run so deep, that you can place an African-American, a Jamaican, a Haitian, a Dominican, a Puerto Rican, a Panamanian, a Cuban, and a Brazilian, all in the same room and they will swear up and down they are all a different people. When in all actuality, they each come from the same West African stock. The only difference is a matter of which European nation enslaved their ancestors; whether it was the English, the French, the Spanish, or the Portuguese. These differences are mostly reflected by the various languages we speak; all of which are European.

"It's really quite sad when you take it all in. But now that we've identified the poison," Hydia smiled, "it's time that we take in the antidote. And that beautiful information is contained in a text by one of our most renowned black scholars, Dr. Na'im Akbar. The title of his book is *Breaking the Chains of Psychological Slavery*."

Hydia looked across the room and settled her gaze on Atiba and me.

"Could you brothas go down to my office and grab those two boxes of books that I left on my desk?"

Happily, we did as she requested.

CHAPTER SEVENTEEN

ZION

"Tiba, you'll never guess what happened to me today," I said with a huge smile on my face. We were walking down the hallway headed towards Hydia's office at the rear of the building.

"I'm listening," Atiba shot back. "Go 'head and lay it on me."

"I met the most beautiful sista today. Her and her son came into the book this morning, and I'm telling you, bro ...this sista was bad. Like, Taraji P. Henson bad!"

"*Cookie?*" Atiba's eyes opened wide. "Cookie Lyons?"

"The spitting image, bro. The spitting image."

"Hey, now, hold on, Zee." Atiba stopped walking and folded his arms across his chest. "You're gonna have to do better than that, my brotha. I need the specifics."

"Alright. I'd say five-three, a hundred and thirty pounds, mid to late thirties. She has the prettiest honey-brown skin, no makeup needed, just a light touch of lip gloss. And her *body?*" I used my hands to demonstrate the figure of a Coke bottle. "That thang was like *plickity plow! Plickity plow!*"

We fell out laughing, the same way we used to do on the prison yard whenever we spoke about a phat butt and some thick thighs.

Plickity pow! Plickity plow!

Atiba closed his eyes and smiled. I'm assuming he was taking in the image of the master piece that I had just described.

"Alright, Zee." He opened his eyes and looked at me with a straight face. "I've got three questions for you."

"Go 'head and shoot."

"One, is she classy? Two, was she wearing a ring? And three, does the sista even know that you're interested in her?"

I answered his questions while rubbing my hands together.

"Is she classy? Bro, she was punishing her son by making him do a book report on *To Kill A Black Man.* As for questions two and three, she wasn't wearing a ring, and I'm pretty sure she knows that I'm interested."

"How can you be so sure?" Atiba asked me. "Did you tell her you were interested?"

"Absolutely," I quickly confirmed. "I told her through my eyes."

"You did *what*?" Atiba looked at me like I was crazy.

"I told her through my eyes, by the way I was looking at her."

Atiba cracked up laughing.

"Zee, come on, bro, you can't be serious! You mean to tell me this beautiful, classy, culturally grounded and single sista, *Cookie Lyons*,crossed your path, and you didn't even make a move?"

"Hold on, bro, you gotta remember, she had her son with her. I couldn't just make a move like that in front of her little man."

The look Atiba gave was a clear indicator that he didn't agree.

"Alright, Zee, if you say so. But what happens if you never see her again? Then, what?"

"That's not going to happen," I assured him.

"Oh, yeah? And how can you be so sure?"

"Because I gave her my business card."

CHAPTER EIGHTEEN

ERICA

7:58 pm

Well, goddamn, how much longer I gotta wait?

I was sitting in the lobby of the 26th District waiting for the po-po to bring out Reeko. I posted his bond over three hours ago, and they still haven't released him. Jabari and Tonya were with me when I paid it, but I told them to leave about an hour ago. Mainly because Jabari had a basketball game, and because Tonya's lil' fast ass was getting on my goddamned nerves. The entire time she was here, she was bitching and moaning about not cheating on Jabari with the nigga that he caught her creeping with. I done told him a million times about that girl, but the boy wouldn't listen. The bitch wasn't nothing but a thot-box with cum stains on it.

"Hey, you," I said to the police officer who was working the front desk. He was a skinny white boy who reminded me of a broke-ass Charlie Sheen. He had a military buzz cut, beady little eyes, and a crooked nose that was slightly cocked to the left.

"Yeah, *you*," I raised my voice when he looked around as though I couldn't have been talking to him. "How much longer is this shit gonna take? I paid my nephew's bail over three hours ago, and y'all still ain't released him. What the hell is the hold up?"

"You know, it's funny you asked me that," the officer replied with a smug expression. "I just received a fax from the courthouse saying he's being released on bond."

"Well, isn't that what the fuck I've been telling you?"

"Excuse me?" He squinted his eyes and stood to his feet.

"Excuse my ass when you kiss it. I paid y'all the fucking money, now release my nephew."

"Erica, calm down," a voice spoke up from behind me.

I spun around and saw the voice belonged to my lawyer, Mario Savino. He and Uzi were walking side by side, and Michelle, Savino's paralegal, was trailing behind texting on her cell phone.

Uzi's black ass was looking all stupid. He didn't want to come, but I made him. Because after all, he was the one responsible. I told his ass to stop giving that shit to my goddamned nephew.

"What's up wit' Reeko?" Uzi said as he stepped closer and wrapped his arms around me. "The young bul good?"

"Hell nawl, his ass ain't good. He's back there all alone, and it's all because of you!" I snapped at Uzi and pushed him away.

Yeah, I was dry snitching, but so-the-hell-what. Reeko's my nephew, and Uzi ain't have no busy giving him that goddamned dope. I told his ass about that shit.

Uzi backed away from me, then he cut his eye at the police officer standing at the desk. He started to check me for putting him on blast, but Savino gestured for him to keep quiet.

"I'm quite sure you already know who I am," Savino said, as he stepped forward and handed the police officer his business card. "Now, cut the shit and release my client."

The police officer scowled at him, then he mumbled under his breath before heading back to the holding cells to bring out Reeko.

CHAPTER NINETEEN

REEKO

"Yo, get the fuck away from my shit!"
That's what I shouted at the two mice who tried to jack me for my cheese sandwich. I was laying on the metal bunk in the small cell they had me in. My ribs were hurting, my right eye was completely swollen. My head was pounding like a sonofabitch. I wasn't not exactly sure, but I must had been back there for at least six hours. The municipal court set my bail at $30,000 with ten percent, so basically, I needed three racks to post bond. That was a few hours earlier, so I knew it had to be somewhere around eight o'clock.

I was hungrier than a mah'fucka. The only thing them pussies gave me to eat was a carton of juice and two funky-ass cheese sandwiches. I bodied the first sandwich, but held onto the second. It wasn't my first time being locked up in the district, so I already knew how dirty the cops be playing. They'll give a nigga two sandwiches and then hold him overnight, hungry as shit, without taking him to the county. So, for safe measures, I held onto the second sandwich to ward off any late-night hunger pangs. The bread on both sandwiches were stale as hell, and the one slice of cheese that was wedged in between was stiffer than candle wax. They ain't even have the decency to throw some meat on them mah'fuckas. At the very least, they coulda gave a nigga some bologna.

Nah mean?
Anyway, back to the two mice who tried to jack me for my shit. They were looking at me from a safe distance and making all these high-pitched noises, probably laughing at my dumb ass. They were hopping up and down and crawling through the bars at the front of the cell. And speaking of the cell, the shit was so small and cramped, that even though I was laying on the bunk, I could have reached out and touched the toilet if I wanted. The toilet was filled with another nigga's shit , and because it was broke, I couldn't flush the mah'fucka. The smell was horrible. Then, to make matters worse,

they had the air conditioner on full blast try'na freeze a nigga. The cell was so cold that I couldn't stop shivering.

"Hey, yo, Turnkey!" I shouted from the bunk. "Lemme get a blanket! It's colder than a mah'fucka in here!"

No response.

Frustrated, I looked around the graffiti covered walls. Some of the shit was written in pen, but most of it was scratched into the chipped, green paint. Nothing spectacular, just the everyday, typical jailhouse bullshit.

Death to All Rats!

Pussy, Stop Telling!

Fuck Da Police!

North Philly's Finest!

Jody Just Answered the Phone? Dat Nigga Fuckin' Yo Bitch!!!

"Hey, yo, Turnkey!" I continued shouting with my bottom lip quivering. "I need a mah'fuckin' blanket! It's fuckin' freezing in here!"

No response.

"Well, fuck y'all, then!"

I looked at my second sandwich and thought about eating it, but fuck that. They can kiss my ass, thinking they have me all hungry and depressed. I wasn't going for it.

I rolled off the bunk and slowly stood to my feet. A sharp pain shot up my left side and I grabbed my ribs immediately. My mouth was drier than the Sahara Desert, and I was beginning to feel dizzy; somewhat nauseous even.

Damn, them pussies fucked me up!

As I limped toward the front of the cell, the two mice took off running. I pressed my face against the cold, hard bars, but the only thing I saw was the holding cell directly across from mines. Inside of the cell, I saw two mah'fuckas stretched out sleeping. One of 'em was laying on the bunk, and the other one was passed out on the floor.

"*Hold the fuck up,*" I mumbled under my breath, recognizing the nigga who stretched out on the floor. "*That's Quiet Storm!*"

I was already mad that his stupid ass got me pinched. But to actually see him stretched out on the floor, sleeping like a baby without a care in the world, had me pissed off even more. So, I pulled my dick out of my pants, aimed it at Quiet Storm's face, and then opened up the floodgates. A couple of drops landed on the tier, but after that—*Sunshine*! Wet and warm and courtesy of my fuckin' balls! I was pissing so hard that some of the shit ricocheted off the bars and splashed against the front of my pants.

"What the—What the fuck?" Quiet Storm smacked his face when the first stream landed on his forehead. He popped up like a zombie, and I cracked up laughing.

"Reeko, you little bastard!" Quiet Storm shouted when he looked over and saw me pissing through the bars. "When we get to the county, I'ma stab you 'til my arm don't work!"

"That's only if I don't catch ya ass first!" I shouted back, shaking away the last few drops.

"I'm not playing wit'chu, Reeko! When I catch you, it's on!"

"Knock it the hell off!" the Turnkey bellowed as he slowly made his way toward us. I couldn't see him, but the sound of his jiggling keys was coming closer and closer. When he reached the front of my cell, he looked back and forth between me and Quiet Storm, and then looked down and saw the piss on the floor.

"You sonofabitches are no better than wild fucking animals," he scolded, still looking down at my fresh warm piss. "Johnson," he brought his eyes back to me, "get your shit. You're out of here."

"I made bail?" I asked him, automatically thinking about my Aunt Erica. Jabby must have told her what happened, and she came to get me.

"Yeah," the Turnkey snarled at me. "Now, get your shit and let's go."

He opened the cell, and I limped out slow. I was dizzy as hell, and my head was still pounding. I looked at Quiet Storm and gave him the finger.

"*Pussy, I'ma fuck you up when I catch you,*" I mouthed the words, so the cop wouldn't hear.

"Hey, yo, Reeko, man, put me up on the bail money." Quiet Storm looked at me like he wanted to cry. "I'ma pay you back, man, I swear on my mama."

"Nigga, I wish the fuck I would." I held my ribs and winced from the pain. "Fuck you think this is?"

"Come on, Reeko, man, *please*?"

"Nigga, smoke a dick and die."

CHAPTER TWENTY

ERICA

"Oh-hell-to-the-motherfucking-nawl!"

Those were the words that spilled out of my mouth when the police officer brought Reeko out into the lobby. He was hunched forward, holding his ribs and walking with a limp. I ran towards him and grabbed his face with both hands. His swollen right eye was completely shut and the front of his sweater was covered in blood.

"Why the fuck y'all had to do him like this for?" I shouted at the police officer, shooting daggers at his ugly white ass. "You motherfuckers ain't have to beat him like this. *Look at his fucking face!*"

"This is totally unacceptable," Savino scolded. "Just who and the hell do you people think you are?"

"They asses must be thinking they bullet proof!" I stepped towards the police officer, completely throwing caution to the wind. "It's about to be some consequences and repercussions for fucking wit' mines! You racist motherfuckers don't know who the fuck y'all dealing wit'!"

"Yo, Auntie E, chill," Reeko said in a shaky voice, as he reached out and pulled me back. "I'ma be a'ight, just chill."

"She better chill out," the police officer warned. He reached behind his back, but I couldn't tell if he was reaching for his gun or his handcuffs. Truth be told, I honestly didn't give a fuck.

"Everybody just calm down," Savino instructed. "Officer," he looked at the fake-ass Charlie Sheen, "give me your name and badge number."

"Listen, buddy, I just got here a few hours ago," the officer replied nonchalantly. "This is the work of the first shift, and the guys who brought him in won't be back until tomorrow. So, if you want, you can come back and talk to them in the morning. Because me, *personally*, I'm not giving you a goddamned thing."

"You know what?" Savino flashed him a threatening smile. "You bastards bit off more than you can chew, and I can show you better than I can tell you. You mark my words."

I was beyond pissed. Those motherfuckers ain't had no right beating on my nephew the way they did. Granted, Reeko's ass shouldn't have been out there selling drugs, but that still doesn't excuse the way did him.

"Reeko, you good, lil' homie?" Uzi asked him. That was the first thing he said since I put his ass on blast.

"Yeah, Uzi, I'm good," Reeko replied. "I'm just feeling a lil' dizzy."

"Don't you worry about a thing," Savino assured Reeko. "Not only are we going to beat this case, we're going to file a civil suit for police brutality."

"Yeah, that's right." I got up in the officer's grill. "Y'all asses is about to get sued."

"Whatever you say, ma'am," the officer replied with a smirk on his face. "That's the only thing you people know how to do."

"*You people*?" I screwed my face. "You racist ass, Ku Klux Klan, motherfucker!"

I balled my fist and attempted to swing, but Uzi grabbed me by the arm and pulled me close to him. I struggled to break free, but the hold he had on my arm was too damn strong. I twisted and turned, yanked and pulled, but he refused to let go.

"You better get her ass out of here!" the police officer shouted. He was reaching for his gun with one hand and pointing towards the front door with the other.

"Erica, just calm down!" Savino shouted, thrusting himself between me, Uzi, and the officer. "Just take it easy. We're going to get him, I promise."

"Don't make me say it again," the police officer threatened.

Uzi hoisted me over his shoulder, then he carried me outside. Reeko, Savino, and Michelle were right behind us. I was cussing Uzi out for causing this bullshit, but stopped when I looked back at Reeko. We were halfway down the ramp headed towards the parking lot when I noticed that Reeko had stopped walking. He stumbled backwards, then collapsed forward, going into a seizure the second he hit the pavement.

"Oh my God!" I cried out. "*Reeko!*"

I broke away from Uzi and knelt down beside my nephew. His convulsing body was stiff and hard, and thick, white phlegm was running out the side of his mouth. His left eye was rolled into the back of his head, and the only thing I could think about was keeping him from choking on his own tongue.

"Call an ambulance!" I shouted while turning Reeko over on his side. "Call an ambulance now! We gotta get him some help."

"There's no time for that," Savino said as he rolled up his sleeves. "Come on, Dawood, we need to get him over to the car. We'll only waste time waiting for an ambulance. We need to get him to a hospital as soon as possible."

Uzi's Audi coupe was too small to lay Reeko across the back seat, so they carried him over to Savino's Range Rover. Michelle and me were right behind them. I broke down crying and pressed my palms together. Looking up at the black, starless sky, I did the only thing that came to mind. I prayed to The Most High.

Please, Lord? Please don't let this baby die? Please?

Askari

CHAPTER TWENTY-ONE

KENYATTA

8:24 pm

"*I hate this stupid-ass house,*" I mumbled under my breath.

I slammed my bedroom door and then locked it, just in case Ma'Dukes tried to come in there trippin'. We were supposed to had been at Jabby's first game, but at the last minute she called me downstairs and told me we weren't going. It was times like this, that I wish my daddy were still alive. I know *he* would have taken me to see Jabby play. He died in a car accident when I was two years old, so I really didn't know him like that. But what I *did* know was that he loved basketball and that he loved his sons even more. So, clearly, if my daddy were still alive, he would have been there to see his son play ball. Especially, a son like Jabby. My big bro was a monster on the basketball court, and if I had to compare him to anybody in the NBA, it would have to be Kevin Durant. Because just like KD, my brother had a mean crossover and a super wet jump shot.

It's killing me just thinking about it!

I should have been front and center, watching the game from the half court line. But instead, I was sitting in my room stuck in the house with crazy lady.

"This the shit I *don't* like!"

"Say what, now?" Ma'Dukes shouted from the other side of my bedroom door. I'm assuming she must have been walking down the hallway when I said it.

"Nothing, Ma!" I quickly replied, thinking of something that rhymed. "I was umm—I was playing my X Box, and my joystick—it don't work right."

"Umm-hmm, you go 'head and keep it up, and one of my belts gon' show you some shit that you *don't* like!"

"Man, whatever," I shot back, barely above a whisper.

"What?"

"Nothing, Ma. Dang."

"Yeah, alright," she called herself punking me. My bedroom door was locked any ol' way, so it wasn't like she could have come in there and done something. Always try'na punk somebody with her bow-legged ass.

I hate this stupid-ass house!

Still mad about missing Jabby's first game, I plopped down at the foot of my bed and grabbed the remote control to my television. I turned it on and the first thing that popped up was Joseline Hernandez from *Love & Hip Hop Atlanta.* She was exercising in front of a full body mirror. Her skintight pants and cutoff T-shirt was sexy as hell, and I could feel myself getting excited. Her golden-brown skin was glistening with sweat, and her juicy butt and big ol' bottles were bouncing up and down every time she did a body squat.

Dang, shorty thick!

After watching Jocelyn for a few more seconds, I began thinking about Shameeka, envisioning the way she was running down the hallway butt ass naked. I promised myself that I wouldn't do it anymore, but I couldn't help it. I was bored as hell, and the images of Shameeka had me thinking about my favorite porn star, Pinky. So, from there on out, I was going to plead the fifth. All I'ma say is that a young nigga did what he had to.

Sheesh!

CHAPTER TWENTY-TWO

EBONY

Big Mama always taught us that when times get hard to call on the Lord, and that His love, grace and mercy would guide us through. So, there I was, down on bended knees, hands locked together with my head humbly bowed.

"Dear Heavenly Father, I come before You with a heavy heart. As a single mother struggling to raise two black men, I often want to give up and call it quits. But this is something that I simply cannot do. You designed me to be a strong black woman, so everyday I'm working hard and striving to be the woman You created me to be. I love my children more than I love myself, but it seems like the older they get, they less they respect me. I'm not trying to complain because I know and understand that others have it worse than me. Nor do I want to sound ungrateful, because I'm not. I appreciate every blessing that You've bestowed upon me and my family. So, basically, what I'm asking for is respite, Good Lord. Respite in the form of a devoted husband. One who's willing to love and respect me...treat me like a Queen and love my boys as if they were his very own. A Godfearing man. A man with ambition and a sense of humility. A strong black man. One who's capable of doing the one thing that I cannot, and that's showing my boys how to grow up to be just like him. Please hear my prayers, Lord. In the precious name of Your dear son, Jesus. Amen."

After reaching out to the One who created my mind, body and spirit, I immediately found a sense of comfort. God is good, and Big Mama was right, sometimes you just have to let go and let *Him*.

Wiping the tears from my eyes, I stood to my feet and got ready to take a much-needed shower. Kenyatta was in his bedroom acting out, mad at me for not taking him to Jabari's basketball game. But why should I reward either one for the stunts they pulled? And to be totally honest, missing Jabari's game was harder for me than it was for them. I mean, hell, it was the first time I missed one of

Jabari's game since the boy was in kindergarten. But it's just like Big Mama used to always say, *"This too shall pass."*

As I peeled out of my clothes and prepared myself for a much-needed shower, I couldn't help but to think about the handsome brotha that I'd met at the book store. His chocolate skin was rich and dark like Columbian coffee, and his pearly white smile reminded me of a bright full moon, proudly shining in the midst of a beautiful black sky. I wondered if Zion was the man that I'd been praying for. My long-lost soul mate. A love from a lifetime forgotten, centuries passed. A lifetime ago when Africa was the land, that we still called home. A past life when Zion was the King, and I was his Queen.   Does his heart still remember? Does his soul still remember? Does *he* remember—me?

I reached inside of my closet and removed his business card from my Chanel clutch.

"Zion Tumojawa," I read his name aloud, loving the way it rolled off the tip of my tongue. I glanced at the phone number listed and debated on whether or not I should give him a call. My heart was telling me to go for it, but my mind was telling me not to. So, to arbitrate my mixed feelings, I clutched the card with both hands, placed it against my chest and called on the Lord.

"Dear Heavenly Father, if this is him. If he's the one You designed specifically for me. Please, Lord, just give me a sign?"

My eyes were closed, and my stomach fluttered with butterflies. The room was completely silent, then all of a sudden, I heard my cell phone ringing.

"Umm mmm mmm! Yasss, Lord! Yasss! You may not come when we call, but you're always on time."

A small piece of my soul was hoping that Zion was the caller, but I knew he wasn't because I never gave him my number. Nevertheless, I still considered the ringing of my cell phone to be a sign from The Most High.

I grabbed the phone from my nightstand and saw the caller was my sister, Erica. I assumed she was calling on behalf of Jabari, sticking up for him the way she always does. But when I answered the call and placed the phone against my ear, I knew that wasn't the case. Erica was crying so hard, that I could barely understand what she was saying. And Erica never cried, and on the rare occasions she did—*Oh my God! No!*

"Erica, what's wrong? What's the matter?"

I was holding the phone with one hand and caressing my chest with the other. I was petrified to hear whatever it was that Erica had to tell me.

"Erica, I can't understand what you. You gotta calm down, so I can hear you."

"Ja—Jabari," Erica stuttered.

"*Jabari?*" My heart damn near leapt out of my chest. "What about Jabari? Is he hurt? Erica, did something happen to my baby?"

"Uhn-uhn," Erica sobbed. "It's—It's not Jabari, it's Reeko. The cops, they beat him up."

"*They beat him up?*" My octave escalated. "Well, is he okay?"

"No!" Erica shouted, then broke down crying even harder.

"Erica, I need you to calm down and tell me exactly what happened."

"Jabari called me and told me the cops beat up Reeko," she spoke slowly after taking a few seconds to calm herself down. "They caught him out there selling dope, but instead of just locking him up, they felt the need to beat on him."

"Well, what about Jabari? Did they beat him up, too?"

"Uhn-uhn." Erica sniffled. "Jabari was there when it happened, though. The cops only beat up Reeko. They left Jabari alone."

"Well, did they—did they beat him up bad?"

"Umm-hmm." She broke down crying all over again. "I think they mighta killed him. They beat that baby to death!"

My hands were shaking, and I could barely keep a grip on the phone. I was relieved to know that Jabari was safe, but it pained my heart to know that Reeko was beaten so bad, that Erica assumed he was dead.

"Erica, where are you? Which hospital did they take him to?"

"We took him to Temple."

"Did you contact Tony? Does he know what's going on?"

"I just got off the phone with him," Erica said. "He should be here any minute now."

"And what about Elisha?" I asked, referring to our older sister and Reeko's mother. "Did you do anything to track her down, so you could let her know what's going on?"

"*Elisha?*" Erica hissed at me. "To hell with Elisha. That sister of yours don't give a damn about Reeko. That bitch don't care about nothing but a crackpipe."

"Alright, Erica, just calm down. I'm on my way, but first I'm gonna try to find Elisha. She needs to know what's going on with her son."

"Whatever," Erica spat. "Just hurry up and get here."

CHAPTER TWENTY-THREE

SHAMEEKA

8:39 pm

The gymnasium was lit! Our varsity basketball team was going head up with our arch rivals Lower Merion High, and the building was jam packed. The bleachers and stands were filled with students and parents, and everybody was rooting for their respective high school. On both sides of the basketball court, the cheerleaders were doing their little one-two steps, flipping around and shaking their pom-poms, and the local media were crowded at both ends of the basket-ball court; all of them fixated on my boo, Jabari.

It was easy to follow the game and keep track because I grew up a Sixer's fan and used to frequent the games with my daddy. I hate to say it, but Jabari wasn't playing too well. He was missing most of his shots, and for the better part of the second half he was arguing back and forth with his coach and teammates.

The game clock was winding down to ten seconds and our head coach, Coach Morris, who also happened to be my history teacher, was running up and down the sideline ranting and raving like Tupac in *Above the Rim*. Our team was ahead by one point, but after a late in the game turnover, Lower Merion was setting up a game-winning shot. Their best player, #18 Kanye Lindsay, was dribbling the ball up court. He had already scorched us for 26 points, 11 assists, and 7 rebounds. So, obviously, he was the last person we wanted to see handling the ball.

"Robby, that's your man!" Coach Morris shouted at the boy who was guarding Kanye Lindsay. "Get outta zone, we're switching to man! Did you hear me? I said we're switching to man!"

As Coach Morris was shouting at Robby to switch his defense, Kanye Lindsay hit him with a devastating crossover. He stutter-stepped, dribbled to his right, and then hopped back quick, causing Robby to trip and fall.

"*Ooooohhhhhhhhhhhhhh!*"

The gymnasium went wild, as Robby lowered his head in embarrassment.

"What are you standing there looking stupid for?" Coach Morris continued shouting at Robby. "Shake it off and get back on defense."

The game clock was down to eight seconds and Kanye Lindsay was on a mission to score. He dribbled past Robby, cradled the ball, and then drove hard towards the basket. Jabari was guarding Lower Marion's star center, Keith Butler. He switched off of Keith and ran over to Kanye, who was already soaring through the air. Jabari jumped as high as he could, attempting to block his shot from behind. Unfortunately, Kanye's game was way too smooth. Still flying through the air, he switched the ball from his right hand to his left, and then lob it up to Keith, who was running up behind Jabari. Keith snatched the ball with both hands, cocked it back and then jammed in Jabari's face.

The gymnasium went buck!

"*Ooooohhhhhhhhhhhh! Agggghhhhhhhhhhhhhhh!*"

"*Time out!*" Coach Morris shouted over the celebration. He was looking at the referee and making the *time out* signal with both of his hands. "Goddangit! I want a time out!"

The referee blew his whistle and the game clocked stopped on six seconds.

"Time out. Ghosts."

CHAPTER TWENTY-FOUR

JABARI

I was leaned forward, hands on my knees and slowly shaking my head. My jumper wasn't falling, my legs felt heavy, and for some reason I couldn't finish at the cup. The ball kept going in and out.

What the hell is wrong wit' me? I thought to myself. *The game's almost over, and I only got eleven points and six rebounds? Yo, what the fuck!*

"Jabari?" Coach Morris signaled me out, sounding like he was born and raised in West Virginia. He was a skinny white dude who reminded me of Pete Carroll, the head coach for the Seattle Sea-hawks. He was frantically chewing on a piece of gum and looking at me like he wanted to snap me in half.

"Son, if you don't get your head outta your ass and get it in the goddang game!" he snapped at me. "Did I or did I not give you the keys to this goddang car?"

"You gave me the keys, Coach." I stood back straight and nod-ded my head.

"Well, goddangit, get out there and drive the sonofabitch!"

Instead of replying, I just wiped the sweat from my face with the front of my jersey.

"Alright, now everybody bring it in," Coach said as he dropped down to one knee. He pulled out his clipboard and magic marker, as we all crowded around him.

"We've only got one chance to finish this game, fellas. One. So, this is what we're gonna do. Robby," he looked up at Robby, then he scribbled a play on his clipboard, "you're gonna inbound the ball to Michael. Michael," he fixed his gazed on our sophomore for-ward, "you're gonna catch the ball at the top of the key, then give a touch-pass down inside the paint to Jabari. And Jabari," he swung his gaze to me, "you get this sonofabitch over and done with."

Coach stuck out his hand, and we held our hands over his.

"Perfection on there, fellas. One. Two. Three."

"*Perfection!*"

The game clock was down to six, and Lower Merion was ahead by one. The energy in the gymnasium was pure pandemonium. I looked around the stands for Ma'Dukes and Kenyatta, but I didn't see 'em. I saw Shameeka, though. She was holding up a cutout picture of my face and mouthing the words, "Come on, Bae, you can do it." I smiled at Shameeka, then I looked up on the top bleacher and saw Tonya. Her arms were folded across her chest, and I could tell that she had an attitude; probably because I was having a bad game. I doubt she noticed that I was smiling at Shameeka.

The referee blew his whistle, and both teams assumed their positions. My team was lined up in a single row, and the players from Lower Merion were crowded all around us. Robby was inbounding the ball from the half court line. Kanye Lindsay was standing right in front of him. He was waving his hands and jumping and down trying to block Robby's view. The referee was standing to Robby's left. He handed Robby the ball, and then blew his whistle, signaling the game was back on.

Blurt!

Me and my teammates broke out of line and ran to our designated spots. Robby inbounded the ball to Michael, and Michael touch-passed the ball to me. I was just beyond the baseline when I caught it. I looked up and saw the game clock was down to four. Keith Butler was giving me body, so I backed him down once. I hit his ass with a shoulder shimmy, spun around quick and got a clean look at the basket. I hopped off my back foot and put up a floater, praying my last shot would make up for such a lousy performance.

The gymnasium went quiet, as every eye in the building was studying the rotation of the ball. The game clock was down to three, and I could feel my heart thumping. I came down on both feet, watching the ball as it descended in slow motion.

Bump!

It bounced off the back of the rim.

Bump!

It bounced off the front of the rim.

Bump! Bump!

It rolled around twice and then came back out.

126

Shadows of the Game

Brrrrrrrrrrrnnnnnnnnnnnnnn!
The game clock stopped on zero.
Everybody from Lower Merion bum rushed the court.
I lowered my head in defeat.
The game was over.
We lost.

Askari

CHAPTER TWENTY-FIVE

JABARI

9:47 pm

Yo, I can't even front, it fucked me up that Ma'Dukes didn't come to my game. I knew she was mad at a nigga, but damn. Like, she really ain't come to my game, though? Ever since opening tipoff, I was searching the bleachers for her and Yatta, but they were nowhere to be found. Maybe that's the reason I played so bad. Well, one of the reasons, anyway. I was also thinking about Reeko, and the whole situation with Tonya and homeboy in the Benz was fucking with my mental. I couldn't escape the thought that Tonya was fucking this nigga, and if she was, then who was her baby's father? Him or me? And speaking of Tonya, she was out front waiting for me in the student's lobby. Ever since I caught her creeping with main-man, she'd been kicking this shit about not leaving my side until I forgave her.

Yeah, right.

I looked at my watch and saw the time was 9:47 p.m. My teammates were long gone, and I was the only one left inside of the locker room. I was seated on the wooden bench in front of my locker, leaned forward and tying the strings on my new Lebron's.

The click-clacking of footsteps caused me to look up. It was Coach Morris. He was walking toward me with his left hand stuffed down inside of his front pants pocket. His right hand was gripping the handle on his coffee mug, and the look he gave me was full of concern.

"What's going on, son? Is everything okay?" Coach Morris asked me.

"Yeah, Coach, everything's straight." I sat up and rested my back against the locker.

"Are you sure? You seemed a little distracted," Coach said while taking a sip from his coffee mug. He sat on the bench across from me and leaned forward slightly. "You know that you can talk to me about anything, right?"

"Yeah, Coach, I know."

"Well, gawn and release the bees from the comb," he quickly replied in his backwoods, hill billy vernacular. "Because clearly there's something bothering you. My superstar center gives me eleven points and then misses a wide open, game-winning shot? There's gotta be something going on. So, talk to me, son. What is it? What's bothering you?"

I took a deep breath and sighed.

"Today was a crazy day, Coach. Me and moms is beefing. My cousin got beat up by the cops, and I've been having some issues with my girl. I think she's cheating on me, Coach. I caught her steppin' out with another dude, and when I tried to confront her, the dude pulled a gun on me."

"Jabari?" Coach shook his head slowly. "Son, do you realize how special you are? How gifted you are, and the responsibility that comes along with having such a gift? And I'm not just talking about basketball, I'm talking about you as a person. You've got a younger brother who worships the ground you walk on. You've got a loving mother who's willing to lay her life down for you, and a sure shot chance at making it to the pros. Do you realize the position you're in?"

"Absolutely, Coach, why wouldn't I?"

"Because it seems to me that you're worried about everything except the right thing. Can't you see that you've got a good thing going here? I'm telling you, son, if you don't get it together, and fast, you're going to blow it."

"I'ma blow it?" I looked at him skeptically, assuming he was talking about the car and the house that my family was living in. "What the hell is that supposed to mean? Blow it, how?"

"Listen, Jabari, I've been coaching basketball for over thirty years now. And during that time, you can bet your last dingle berry that I've come across kids who would've done just about anything to be in your position. I've also come across a handful of guys who were fortunate enough to be in your position. But for some reason

130

or another, they somehow managed to blow it. You don't wanna be that guy, son, I'm telling ya. The worst thing you'd could ever do is turn out to be a wasted talent."

"A wasted talent? Nah, Coach, never that." I was beginning to feel agitated.

"Don't you tell me that!" he raised his voice, challenging me with his eyes. "I want you to *show* me, and not just to me. I want you to show it to your mother. I want you to show it your brother and the generation of guys coming up behind you. But most of all, son, I want you to a show it to yourself."

I stood to my feet and slung my gym bag over my right shoulder. Coach was burning me the fuck out, and I was mad at myself for even thinking that I could talk to this dude about my problems. I should have known his ass wouldn't understand me. And at the end of the day, the last thing I needed was a muhfucka preaching to me.

"Thanks for the talk, Coach, but I gotta bounce. I'll see you at practice on Monday."

"Jabari?" Coached called out, as I began walking away.

"Yeah, Coach, what's up?" I turned my head, but continued walking towards the door.

"Discipline, son, *discipline*. In order for you to achieve your goals, you've gotta have discipline. And it isn't hard. It's only a matter of making the right choice; the choice between what you want *now* and what you want the *most*. So, make the right choice, son. Make the right choice."

Instead of replying, I just nodded my head and kept it pushing.

When stepped outside into the student lobby, I looked over and saw Tonya. She was seated on the bench beside the vending machines, knocked out sleep. I started to creep past and leave her there, but I didn't. "Tonya?" I called her name and nudged her on the shoulder. "Come on, so I can take you home."

Tonya got up from the bench and followed me outside. Neither one of us said a word as the chilly, November wind smacked us in the face. Tonya leaned into me and nestled her face against my side. I started to push her away but at that point, my only concern was

Shameeka's BMW. The cranberry coupe was parked in the spot directly beside my Camaro. I could see Shameeka through the windshield. She was shaking her head in disappointment and scowling at me and Tonya. Tonya noticed her, too.

"And who the fuck is this bitch?" Tonya asked me, as she pointed at Shameeka's beamer. "She better not be out here waiting on you."

"Yo, slow ya roll," I told Tonya, giving her a stern look to calm that ass down. Unfortunately, my words fell on deaf ears. Because instead of Tonya doing what I told her, she was already acting ratchet—snatching off her earrings and mumbling something about beating a bitch's ass.

"Just tell me the truth, Jabari," Tonya looked up at me with tears in her eyes. "Is you is, or is you ain't fucking this bitch?"

I refused to answer.

"So, you *is* fucking this bitch!" She scowled at me. "Motherfucker gon' throw me shade 'cause a nigga gave me a ride home, but all the while he's out here freaking off with the next bitch. This nigga got me twisted."

By then, we were a couple of feet away from my car, and I could tell by Shameeka's face that she'd heard everything that Tonya said. Her lips were pouted and her wet, glossy eyes had me feeling like shit.

Fuck was I thinking bringing Tonya, knowing Shameeka would be here?

I started to tell Shameeka to go home and that I'd hit her up later. But before the words could leave my mouth, Tonya had already gone crazy. She ran up on the beamer, pulled open the driver's side door and snatched Shameeka out the car.

"Oww!" Shameeka screamed, as Tonya yanked her by the hair and gave her uppercuts nonstop. "Jabari, get her! Oww!"

"Ahn-ahn, bitch! You wanna be fucking the next bitch's man?" Tonya hissed at her, yanking and punching. "You gon' take this ass whuppin'!"

"Jabari, get her off of me!" Shameeka cried out, frantically trying to ward off the ass whupping. Her left hand was struggling to keep Tonya from pulling her hair, and her right hand was moving all around desperately trying to stop the wild punches from connecting with her face. "*Jabari, get her!*"

"Yo, shorty, what the fuck is wrong wit'chu?" I spazzed on Tonya. I pulled her off Shameeka and placed her little ass in a bear hug. "Didn't I tell ya ass to chill?"

"Boy, you better let me go!" Tonya bucked, tangled and twisted. "Don't be grabbing me, motherfucker! Grab her!"

"What?" I looked over just in time to see Shameeka swinging a wild punch. She caught Tonya dead-smack on the forehead, and then ran around to the driver's side of her beamer. She hopped back inside of the car and quickly locked the doors.

"Jabari, get off me!" Tonya continued shouting, flailing her arms and kicking her legs out like a crazy woman. "*Eeewwwwww, I'ma kill this bitch!*"

I released my hold on Tonya, knowing that Shameeka was safe inside of her car. But that didn't stop Tonya from running over and banging on Shameeka's driver's side window.

"Get'cha punk ass outta the car!" Tonya tugged on the door handle. "Don't get scared now, bitch! Get'cha ass outta the car and throw them thangs!"

"*Jabari?*" Shameeka shouted at me. "Who is this girl, and why is she acting like this?"

"Yeah, Jabari." Tonya looked at me and folded her arms. "Tell this bitch who the fuck I'm is."

Once again, I chose to remain silent. My ass wasn't saying shit.

"Oh, so now ya ass ain't got nothing to say?" Tonya fumed at me. She rolled her eyes, and then looked back at Shameeka. "I'm the wifey, boo-boo! The soon-to-be baby mama, Miss Numero the Fuck Uno!"

"*Baby mama?*" Shameeka mouthed the words. Her light-skinned face became beet-red, and I could clearly see the hurt in her eyes, as she looked to me for an explanation.

"You know what, Jabari? Fuck you!" Shameeka screamed at me. She threw the car in gear, then mashed out with her tires screeching.

Scurrrrrrr!

"Now, why the fuck you had to do that?" I looked down at To-nya.

"Why the fuck you did what'chu did?" Tonya fired back, snapping her neck and rolling her eyes.

"Jabari?" I heard Coach Morris calling my name. I looked back and saw him jogging towards me with a cell phone clutched in his hand.

"Yeah, Coach, what's up?"

"Here." He handed me the phone. "It's your mother."

CHAPTER TWENTY-SIX

EBONY

"Jabari?" I spoke into my Bluetooth, uncertain as to whether or not Coach Morris was able to reach him before he left. "Baby, is that you?"

"Yeah, Ma, it's me. What's going on?" Jabari's voice came through my earpiece. "How come you're calling Coach instead of me?"

"I've been trying to call you for the last half an hour, but your phone kept sending me to voicemail."

"Alright, so what's going on? Is everything okay?"

"No, baby, it's not," I spoke slowly, choosing my words carefully. I knew how close Jabari and Reeko were, so I didn't want to come right out and tell him what happened to his cousin.

"Well, what is it?" Jabari asked when I hesitated. "You're not saying anything."

"Jabari, it's Reeko."

"You're running late, Ma, I already know," Jabari spoke fast. "Auntie Erica already went down there to bail him out."

"But it's more to the story than just that. When they released Reeko from the district, he fell out and they had to rush him to the hospital."

"Aww, man," Jabari replied, and I could hear the pain in his voice. "But he's gonna be okay, though? Right?"

"I'm praying he is, but I can't say for sure. Kenyatta and me are headed to the hospital, so I won't know the full extent until I get there. The last time I spoke to Erica, she told me the doctors were still working on him."

"Which hospital did they take him to?"

"They took him to Temple."

"Alright, Ma, I'm on my way."

Click!

Instead of going straight to the hospital, I decided to make a detour. I was trying to find my sister, Elisha. I knew the odds of finding a crackhead on a Friday night were slim to none, but I had an idea as to where she'd might have been.

"Hey, yo, Ma? Where you going?" Kenyatta asked me from the passenger's seat. "We just drove past the hospital."

"I can clearly see that, Kenyatta. But first I wanna see if I can track down your Auntie Elisha. Hopefully, I can get her to come to the hospital with us."

"Good Luck with that one," Kenyatta replied sarcastically.

I shot him a look that was colder than icicles, then continued driving down Germantown Avenue. I was looking from left to right, hoping to see Elisha among the night time stragglers. I eased off the gas and coasted slow, but I didn't see her, so I kept on driving.

My sister's addiction was one of the darker spots in my life. She began smoking crack about sixteen years ago, when Jabari and Reeko were still in diapers. And ever since then, she's been a hot damn mess. A *"functioning addict"* was what she claimed to be, but all I was is a crack monster, one who doesn't care about anything, nor anyone else, except her and her precious little crack pipe.

I veered off of Germantown Avenue and cruised down 10th Street, only to be stopped at a red light on Cumberland. A crowd of guys were standing in front of the Chinese store on the corner, and one of them I recognized from the old neighborhood. His name was Kyle, and just like me, he was born and raised down Richard Allen.

"Kyle?" I called his name after rolling down the passenger's side window. I clicked on the dome light and leaned forward so he could see my face. "Kyle, let me talk to you right quick. It's Sweety Raw."

"*Sweety Raw*?" Kenyatta chuckled and looked at me like I was crazy. But little did he know, the educated sista that he and his brother called "Ma" was a project chick through and through, and was known for doing her thing back in the day.

"Hey, umm, who you said you was?" Kyle replied cautiously. He stepped back slow and reached behind his back.

"Boy, you better stop playing with me," I raised my voice and leaned in closer. "It's Sweety Raw from 10th and Poplar, Big Mama Johnson's granddaughter."

"Oooohhhhh, shit! Yo, Sweety Raw, what's happening, girl? How you?" Kyle smiled at me, then came over to the truck. "Damn, girl, you riding cleaner than a Muslim. What's this? The new Navigator?"

"Yeah." I nodded my head. "But listen, I'm looking for my sister, Elisha. Have you seen her?"

"Yeah, I seen her. I just left her crazy ass. She's around the corner at Treesha's house. You remember Treesha's, don't you? She was down with the crew back in the day."

"No." I shook my head. "I don't think so."

"Come on, now, you remember ol' crazy ass Treesha? *Miss Mae-Mae's granddaughter*? She grew up down the projects, too."

"You know what, I *do* remember Treesha. That's Tootie's and 'em lil' sister."

"Yeah, that's her," Kyle said with a smile. "She's still on that shit, too. Damn, lil' man, my fault." He turned his head to look at Kenyatta. "Had I known you was sitting here, I wouldn't have to be doin' all that mu'fuckin' cussin'. Hey, yo, Sweety Raw," he returned his gaze to me, "this Big Jabby's son, ain't it? The one was wit' him when them boys—"

"*Yes!*" I quickly replied, cutting him off mid-sentence. Kenyatta didn't know it, but he witnessed the murder of his father. He was too young to remember, and I planned on keeping it that way.

"Now, back to my sister," I digressed. "You said she's over at Treesha's house?"

"Yeah, she lives right over there on Delhi Street." He pointed at the vacant lot between Delhi Street and 10th "Come on, I'ma show you."

Kyle took off walking across Cumberland Street, and I parked my Navigator between Delhi and 10th. Looking at Kenyatta, I said, "Lock the doors and don't open them for nobody. I'll be back in a few minutes."

"Alright, Ma," Kenyatta's voice was dejected. I could tell from looking at him, he was thinking about his father.

That goddamned Kyle and his big-ass mouth!

I climbed out of my Navigator and followed behind Kyle. He led me to the next block over, but the street was so dark that I stopped in my tracks. The street lights were busted out, and there were no signs of human life. The ten or so houses on both sides of the street were essentially deserted, and from what I could see, the only car parked on the block was a broke down station-wagon. The back window had a bullet hole embedded in the center, and it's spray painted frame was sitting on cinder blocks.

This boy must'a lost his damn mind. I wish the hell I would take my ass down this dark-behind block.

"What's wrong?" Kyle asked when he turned around and noticed that I stopped walking.

"Are you sure somebody lives on this block?" I looked around and then took a step backwards. "Because it sure as hell doesn't seem like it."

"Aye, yo, Sweety Raw? Yo, I *know* you ain't got it in your mind that I would do something to hurt you? Girl, you damn near family? I would never..."

"I'm not saying that, Kyle. It's just that I'm not ...I'm not comfortable with walking down some dark-ass, deserted looking street."

"You ain't gotta explain ya'self." Kyle shook his head and frowned at me like I'd broken his heart. "Just wait here while I go and get Elisha for you."

Kyle continued walking, and I kept my ass there.

After stopping at the fifth house from the corner, Kyle ran up the steps and knocked on the door. A few seconds later, a skinny, brown-skinned woman emerged from the house, she said something to Kyle, then looked up the street towards me when Kyle pointed at me. The woman was Elisha. She waved her hands in the air and shouted, "Hey, sista girl? Come on down, so I can see you!"

"Ahn-ahn!" I shouted back. "You come up here! I need to tell you something!"

Elisha nodded her head, then she dipped one of her shoulders and bopped up the street. She was dressed in a green army jacket, a pair of jeans, and a scuffed-up pair of Timbs that were way too big for her feet.

138

"Ebony, girl, what'chu doing back in the hood?" Elisha spoke louder than what was necessary. She was holding a can of Natural Ice beer and had a Newport 100 dangling from the side of her mouth. "Girl, I heard you done gon' off and went Hollywood."

"Reeko's in the hospital," I gave it to her straight. "I came to get you, so I could take you down there to see him."

"Oh, yeah?" Elisha sucked in a puff of smoke. "Well, what happened to him? He done went and got himself shot?"

"No," I quickly replied, already seeing she was stuck on her same ol' selfish bullshit. "The cops beat him up and arrested him for selling dope. Erica bailed him out, but when she went to go pick him up, he passed out and slipped into a seizure."

Elisha puffed on her Newport and inhaled deeply. "The cops," she exhaled the smoke, "did they beat him up bad?"

"Erica didn't say. All I know is that she rushed him to the hospital. She never told me the full extent of his injuries, but I'm assuming he's hurt pretty bad. So, you need to come with me and see what's going on with your son."

"Uhn-uhn." Elisha shook her head *no*. "I'm fine right here."

"Excuse me?" I scoffed at the bitch.

"You heard what the hell I said. Ain't nobody tell that boy to be selling no goddamned dope. So, if the cops whipped his ass, then gooooood for him. Hopefully, they knocked some sense into his stupid ass."

The nerve of this bitch!

I wanted so bad to knock some sense into her ass, but I knew better than to waste any more of my time. It's bad enough that I bypassed the hospital just to go looking for her.

"You know what, Elisha, I hope your trifling-ass get everything that you fucking deserve."

"Umm-hmm." She smiled at me and then downed the rest of her beer. "I hope so, too."

Completely disgusted, I turned around and headed back to my Navigator.

"Hold on, Ebony, wait!" Elisha called out behind me.

"So, you're coming to the hospital?" I spun around and asked her, hoping she had enough love inside of her to be there for her only when he needed her the most.

"Uhn-uhn." She shook her head *no*, while reaching up to scratch her head. "I was wondering if you could loan me twenty dollars."

Refusing to entertain Elisha's bullshit, I hopped inside of my truck and slammed the door. I pressed down on the push start and threw the transmission in *drive*.

"Ma, what's wrong with Auntie Elisha?" Kenyatta asked, as he pointed at Elisha through the windshield. She was standing in the middle of the street throwing a temper tantrum.

"*Fuck you, Ebony! Fuck you, bitch!*" She grabbed her crotch with both hands, then stood on her tippy toes and thrust her womanhood at me. "*You stupid ol' stingy-ass bitch!*"

I started to hop out and put my foot in her ass, but what good would that have done? Besides, it was important that I went to the hospital so I could check on Reeko. If his own mother wasn't woman enough to be there to for him when he needed her the most, then it was up to Erica and me to carry the weight. It didn't bother me, though, because family was all we had. That's the way Big Mama raised us.

CHAPTER TWENTY-SEVEN

EBONY

10:11 pm

When Kenyatta and me walked through the sliding glass doors that led to the Emergency Room, I was surprised to see how uncongested it was. Friday nights in the ER were usually hectic, but strangely the ER's lobby was pretty much empty. Erica and Uzi were seated in the front row of chairs on the left side of the lobby, and across from them was a Puerto Rican girl who was doing her best to console a crying infant. The only other person was an older black woman who resembled Oprah Winfrey. She was slowly rocking back and forth, and had a King James Bible pressed against her bosom. Her chocolate brown face was covered in tears, and the distant look in her eyes told the story of a mother scorned. Unfortunately, it was the same story that black mothers throughout America knew all too well. The two of us locked eyes, but I turned away quick. The premonition I felt was that one day my own eyes would tell the same story.

"Ebony?" I heard Erica's voice calling my name. I was so caught up in my natural fear as a black mother with two black sons, that I momentarily forgot Erica was sitting there. She walked over and wrapped her arms around me. I hugged my sister back.

"Reeko's gonna be okay," Erica said, as she broke our embrace and stared into my eyes. She then looked at Kenyatta, and gave him the same embrace that she'd given me. "What's up, lil' man? You okay?"

"Sup, Auntie E? Yeah, I'm alright," Kenyatta said as he hugged her back.

I looked at Uzi, but for some reason he deliberately avoided my gaze. I couldn't prove it, but the feeling in my soul was that Uzi had given Reeko the drugs he was selling. Looking back at Erica, I said, "So, what are the doctors saying about Reeko?"

"They diagnosed him with Type-Two diabetes," Erica replied while resting her face on Kenyatta's shoulder.

"Type-Two diabetes? Well, goddamn."

"I know, right? And that's the reason he fell out and had a seizure. His blood sugar levels were so low, that he suffered a diabetic shock. That still doesn't justify the police putting their hands on him. They cracked his ribs and fractured his eye socket. My lawyer, Mario Savino, is filing a lawsuit on Reeko's behalf. He said he's suing the city for police brutality and for violation Reeko's civil rights."

I was elated to know that our nephew wasn't dead, but it still concerned me he'd been diagnosed with diabetes. Diabetes was one of the silent killers in the black community, and I was afraid that Reeko wasn't mature enough, nor responsible enough to manage such a disease. Clearly, this was something our entire family would have to keep tabs on.

"So, where's Tony? Did he ever make it down her?"

"Umm-hmm, he's here." Erica nodded her head. "He's in the back with Reeko. The doctor said only one of us could back there to see him."

"Praise the Lord," I expressed my gratitude. "Praise His Holy Name."

Now, don't get me wrong, I'm far from a *"Holy Roller"*. But what I *do* know is that God is The Most Merciful. He's known for moving in mysterious ways, and once again He was doing His thing, turning tragedy into triumph. Reeko was dead wrong for selling drugs, and the police who beat him were just as bad. But if none of that would have never happened, then how else would we know that Reeko was a diabetic. So, at the end of the day, our Lord and Savior was handling His business.

As Erica and me stood there talking, Jabari stepped inside of the lobby with Tonya right behind him. She wrapped her arms around Jabari's waist, and he nudged her away. The two of them must have been arguing before they came.

"So, whats up, Ma? What's the situation with Reeko?" Jabari asked when he approached us. "How is he? Is he doing okay?"

142

"Yes, Jabari, Reeko's fine," I told him. I was still mad at him, but at that point most of my anger had already subsided.

"How you doin', Miss Ebony?" Tonya greeted me. She was chewing on a piece of bubble gum and looking around the lobby when she said it. I flat out could not stand her. But on the strength of Jabari, I did my best to tolerate her. Erica was different; she rolled her eyes at the girl, and then walked back over to Uzi.

"I'm fine, Tonya. And you?"

"Oh, I'm a'ight," Tonya replied. She blew out a huge bubble, sucked it back in and continued chewing.

Ratchet! Just plain ol' ratchet, I thought to myself as I stood there shaking my head.

"Sup, baby bro? You good?" Jabari said to Kenyatta.

"Yeah, Jabby, I'm good." Kenyatta nodded his head. "But Reeko's not. The cops beat him up and gave him diabetes."

"*They gave him diabetes?*" Jabari asked with a confused expression on his face.

"Yup. That's what Auntie Erica told Ma."

Jabari looked to me for an explanation.

"First of all," I shot daggers at Kenyatta, "she wasn't even talking to you, she was talking to me. And secondly, that's not even what she said. Matter of fact, go sit'cha ass down. Get out of my face, Kenyatta."

Kenyatta lowered his head and walked away mumbling.

"And you?" I pointed at Tonya, "You take yourself over there with him. I need to speak to Jabari in private."

Tonya sucked her teeth and rolled her eyes, but I gave her a look that said, "*Girl, you better gawn and get somewhere!*"

As she walked away with an attitude that I couldn't have cared less about, I looked up at Jabari. He started to speak, but I spoke first.

"So, how was your game?"

"Not so good." He stuffed his hands down inside of his pockets. "We lost by one."

"Well, what about you? Did *you* have a good game?"

"Nah, Ma, I didn't. There was so much going on, that I couldn't focus. I only had eleven points and six rebounds. Then on top of that, I missed the game-winning shot."

I felt somewhat guilty for not being there to support him, but so the hell what. His ass shouldn't have done what he did.

"Now, I'm pretty sure you know the reason I didn't come to your game."

"Yeah, Ma, I know, and I apologize for having Shameeka in your room. I just need you to know that I wasn't trying to blatantly disrespect you. I didn't know you were getting off of work early, and I thought I had enough time to get Shameeka out of the house before you got home."

"This isn't about what you did, Jabari. It's more about what you *didn't* do. I'm a single mother with two black sons, and you're the oldest. So, not only am I expecting you to help me with your little brother, I'm expecting you to set a positive example. You need to be a better decision maker, Jabari. There's a repercussion for every action, and I need you to do better. So, more than anything else, I'm disappointed. I expect so much more from you, Jabari. So much more."

Tears began to well at the rims of Jabari's eyes, as he pulled me in close. He kissed the top of my head.

"I'm sorry, Ma. I didn't mean to disappoint you."

"I accept your apology, but my challenge for you to do better is still on the table. You're the man of the house and Kenyatta and me are depending on you to do the right thing. Our entire family for that matter; because if you make it, we all make it. You seriously need to keep that in mind."

"I'ma try, Ma. I promise."

"*Try?*" I pulled away from him, then looked into his eyes giving him the same look that Big Mama used to give me. "You know what I told you about the word *try*? To try is to fail. You either do something, or you don't."

"I *will*." Jabari gave me a bright white smile. "And I promise not to let y'all down."

"A'ight, now, I'ma hold you to that."

144

"I'ma hold myself to it. My word is my bond, and my bond is my life."

Askari

CHAPTER TWENTY-EIGHT

REEKO

When I opened my eyes, the first thing I noticed was Pops. He was taking a nap in the rocking chair a few feet away from my hospital bed. His meaty fingers were locked together, and his chubby hands were rising up and down on his beer belly. His salt-and-pepper locks were dangling out the bottom of his trucker hat, and his smoke-gray, *Members Only* jacket was zipped up to the collar.

I glanced around looking for any signs of my moms, but I didn't see her. It didn't surprise me, though; it didn't surprise me one bit. For as long as I could remember she'd been addicted to crack, and I shoulda known better than to think she would have been there for me during my time of need. That wasn't her style, and it probably never would be. At her very best, my moms was either hit or miss. There were times in my life where she did things to make it seem as though she actually gave a fuck, but mostly her crackpipe was King.

My pops loved her, though. I mean he had to, because he never completely turned his back on her. She would do something foul like steal a television or a microwave from the house, then her and Pops would argue and fight. Their fights would lead to Moms crying and making empty promises to stop smoking crack. After that, she would do a little stint in a rehab, come home and fly straight for a couple of weeks, then go right back to smoking chumpies.

That was the story of my upbringing, for the most part, anyway. But the last time she hit rock bottom, she did something that, as a man, I would have never been able to forgive. My Pops caught her sucking dick for a rock. It was a little over a year ago.

Pops came home from work early, and when he walked through the front door, he caught her trickin' off wit' the young bul, Twany, from the the Fairhill Projects. Pops kicked the shit outta Twany, then he kicked Moms outta the house. It's crazy now that I think about it, because a few months later Twany got smoked by the cops. They shot his ass about nineteen times, right in his own kitchen. Now, as far as my moms? Shit, she hadn't brought her ass back to the house ever since that day. She knew Pops woulda taken her back had she wanted to come home. So, I'm guessing that was her way of walking out on me and Pops for good.

Fuck it.

My throat was drier than a muh'fucka, and my left arm was itching like shit. I lifted my head from the pillow and looked down at my arm, try'na figure out what it was that had a nigga itching.

Ah-ha!

A butterfly I.V. was sticking out the crook of my arm. I closed my eyes, and for some reason a vision of Buckwheat from *The Little Rascals* popped up in the back of my mind. He said, *"I's sho' is hungry!"* My stomach growled and I coughed like a TB patient.

Completely drained, I laid my head back on the pillow and then looked over at Pops. He opened his eyes and smiled at me.

"What's up, Champ? How you feeling?"

"Tired and hungry," I told him in a dry, cracked voice. I was thinking about Buckwheat's crusty-looking ass when I said it.

"I's sho' is hungry!"

Pops reached out and grabbed the paper cup that was chilling in the cupholder attached to the bed frame.

"Here." He placed the cup against my lips. "Take a sip of this."

I curled my lips around the straw and slurped up the icy cool water. I slurped a few more sips and then turned my face away from the straw.

"Yo, Pops, can you run out and grab me a couple of Big Macs? I'm hungrier than a mah'fucka."

Pops reached out and softly caressed the top of my head.

"I'm not so sure about that, Champ. First we need to talk to the doctor and find out exactly what you can and can't eat."

"What I can and can't eat?" I looked at him like he was crazy. "Since when does an ass whuppin' dictate what a person can and can't eat?" I moved my jaw bone from side to side, checking to see if my jaw was broken. It wasn't. I then pressed my teeth against my choppas, confirming that all of my teeth were still intact. So, what the hell was Pops talking about.

"You got me confused Pops. What's going on?"

148

"Listen, Champ, I'ma give it to you straight wit' no chaser. The doctors ran a few tests, and they diagnosed you with Type-Two diabetes."

"*Diabetes?*" I frowned my face. "But I'm only eighteen, so how the fuck I got diabetes? That's an old person's disease."

I thought about Big Mama, knowing she was diagnosed with the same thing. Her diabetes had gotten so bad, the doctors had to chop off one of her feet.

"What the fuck?" I popped up and leaned forward, looking down to see if they chopped my shit off, too. They hadn't. Both of my shit-kickaz was still intact. I wiggled my toes one at a time to make sure.

"Pops, how the fuck I got diabetes?" My vision became blurred. "Is this shit gonna kill me the same as it did Big Mama?"

"No, Champ, *Hell, no.* You're gonna be just fine," Pops told me in a soothing voice. "I promise you that."

Pops wrapped me in his arms and squeezed me tight. I'm ashamed to say it, but I was crying like a bitch. I thought about Big Mama and cried even harder.

"Just calm down, Champ. Just calm down. Everything's gonna be okay."

Yeah, Pops, I hear you, I thought to myself. *But for some reason I don't believe you.*

Askari

CHAPTER TWENTY-NINE

SHAMEEKA

By the time I pulled into my driveway and parked my BMW beside Daddy's Jaguar, I was all cried out. I couldn't understand how something that made me feel so good, could be the same thing that hurt me so bad. For the past couple of months, Jabari had become my everything—my best friend, my lover, my sunshine in the rain, and my shoulder to cry on. But at that point, it seemed as though our time together was nothing but a lie; just a big, fat, motherfucking lie. At the very least, he should have told me that he had a girlfriend. I would have respected him more for being honest, and for giving me the opportunity to decide whether or not I wanted to deal with him, knowing that he already had a situation. I mean, hell, my goddamned feelings were involved, even though it was never my intention to fall in love. My mind and my heart were indirect conflict.

My brain was telling me to shake it off and go about my business, but my heart was telling me, "*Girl, you better fight for your man!*" Besides, I never told Jabari, nor anyone else for that matter, but just like Miss Thang, I was also carrying his unborn child.

As I killed the engine and climbed out of my car, I noticed the living room lights were still on. *That's odd,* I thought to myself while glancing at the time on my Gucci watch. It was a quarter after ten, way past my parents bed time. So, what were they doing still awake?

I leaned the answer the second I stepped inside of the house and found the two of them waiting for me in the foyer. My daddy was standing directly behind my mother, and each one was giving me an accusatory look.

"What's going on?" I asked them, as I peeled out of my jacket. "Why are you guys just standing there looking at me like that? This is so weird."

"Charlene," my daddy spoke first, giving my mother the green light to address me.

Askari

"Where were you today?" my mother asked me. The look she gave was daring me to tell her a lie.

"I was at school," I calmly replied while hanging my jacket inside of the closet.

"Well, I find that to be somewhat strange. Because earlier today, I received a text message from your principal. According to her, you haven't attended school for three days straight. So, again," she folded her arms across her chest, "where in the world were you?"

"I already told you." I looked back and forth between her and Daddy. "I was at school. So, clearly, Principal Jenkins must have made a mistake."

"You're lying!" she shouted at me.

"No, I'm not!" I shouted right back.

"Yes, you are!"

"Whatever."

"William, you better get this child before I smack her into next week." She placed her hands on her hips, and then gave Daddy a look that told him she meant business.

Looking at my father, I said, "Daddy, I didn't do anything. They're lying."

Now because I was a true-to-life *"Daddy's Girl"*, I was expecting him to have my back, the same as he always did. But boy ol' boy, he sure as hell shocked the shit out of me. He took a step forward and positioned himself right beside my mother. His pale, white face had a burgundy tint, and he was looking at me as though he could see straight through me.

"So, what do you have to say for yourself, young lady?"

The words he spoke carried so much venom, that I couldn't believe they came out of his mouth. He had never before spoken to me in such a manner.

"What do I have to say about what?" I whined like a baby. "I didn't do anything."

"You know what, Shameeka? You're really beginning to piss me off!" he snapped at me. "How in the world can you stand here

152

and lie to your mother and me with such guile? We didn't raise you this way."

"But, Daddy I'm telling you the truth." I began to cry, hoping that would force him to soften his stance. Unfortunately, my mother stepped in before it could work.

"You zip it up, Shameeka! You zip it up this very second!" my mother shouted at me. "You've been acting very peculiar these past couple of weeks, and I wanted to know why. So earlier today I searched your bedroom."

"*You did what?*"

"You heard me. I searched your bedroom."

"But, that's my personal space! You had no right going through my things!"

"I sure as hell did," she quickly replied. "And guess what I just so happen to find?"

She dug down inside of her pocket and pulled out the results from my home pregnancy test. I can't explain why, but my first reaction was to look at Daddy. He was shaking his head and looking at me like I ripped his heart out.

"But, Daddy?" I whined.

"Don't you but Daddy me." His voice was harsh and cold. "You've got a lot of explaining to do, young lady, beginning with the name of the sonofabitch who deflowered you."

Deflowered. The word bounced around my brain and then pierced my heart like a dagger. It was almost as though he didn't even see me as his daughter anymore, just a common street walker.

"Girl, you better say something," my mother demanded. She was giving me so much attitude, that her proper-acting-self reminded me she was originally from the Tasked Projects South Philly.

"Right now, Shameeka. We want answers," my daddy chimed in.

My breathing became heavy, and I couldn't stop the tears that were pouring out of my eyes. I simply didn't know what to say, especially to Daddy. So instead of replying, I shot right past them and ran up the stairs to my bedroom. The tears of my broken heart continued to fall, as thoughts of Jabari penetrated the depths of my soul. For the life of me, I just could not get it. I couldn't understand.

How can something that makes me feel so good, be the same thing that hurts me so bad?

CHAPTER THIRTY

ZION

10:24 pm

The mini library in my home office was one of my most prized possessions. I absolutely loved to read, and for the past year or so, I'd been piecing together an extensive catalogue of some of our most renowned black scholars—Dr. Wesley Muhammad, John Hendrick Clark, Na'im Akbar, Yosef Ben Jochannan, Chancellor Williams, Molefi Kete Asante, and Maulana Karenga to name a few. In addition, I was also able to track down a variety of books that were dedicated to the *true* history of my ancestors; my favorites being, *They Came Before Columbus, African Presence in Early Asia,* and *African Presence in World Cultures.* All of which were written by Ivan Van Sertima.

Tonight, however, my hour-long study session was dedicated to *Black Men: Obsolete, Single, Dangerous? The Afrikan-American Family in Transition.* This particular text was written by Haki R. Madhubuti. This brotha went to great lengths to breakdown and expose the psychological, physical, and social ills that plague our community, while at the same time providing a comprehensive guideline on how we should and must tackle those obstacles head on. This brotha goes in! He touched on everything from the HIV virus to the crack epidemic; from the resurrection of the black family unit to the true definition of black manhood; from the benefits of properly educating our children to the stigmas of mass incarceration; and most important, he highlights the necessity of living a healthy lifestyle. *That book is a hands-down must read for the black community.*

As I continued my study session, going back and forth between reading, highlighting, and jotting down notes, my cell phone vibrating on the desktop.

Vrrrrrm! Vrrrrrm! Vrrrrrm!

I sat the book down and picked up the phone. Looking at the screen, I saw the caller was Atiba. I accepted his incoming call, then placed the phone against my ear.

"Peace, Black Man. Talk to me."

"Hey, Zee, are you watching the Republican debate on CNN?"

"Not exactly," I replied, as I looked up at my television and saw Donald Trump. He was speaking at one of his rallies, with his toupee blowing in the wind. The volume was down, so I couldn't hear what he was saying.

"I'm tuned in," I told Atiba, "but the volume's down and I really wasn't watching. I wasn't planning on watching until after I finished studying."

"Well, turn up the volume real quick and check out Donald *Dump*. This turkey burger done lost his mind."

I did as my brotha suggested, and listened closely. Trump was ranting and raving about Muslims. Specifically, he was calling for a band on all Muslims entering into the country.

"Do you hear this crap?" Atiba asked me, clearly agitated and upset. Like I previously stated, my brotha and his family were devout Muslims in the Nation of Islam.

"Just who and the hell is this devil referring to?" Atiba continued. "Is he talking about the Nation? The Sunnis? Or is he talking about the Shia's and Sufis? Does he even realize that black people make up thirty percent of the Muslims in this country? Whatever happened to the land of religious freedom? This is ridiculous. The Messenger was right, that devil ain't nothing but a dag-gone liar."

To make it plain, none of this was surprising to me. I'd been keeping a close eye on Donald Trump ever since he championed the phrase, *Make America Great Again*. What exactly was that cat try'na say? He was a capitalist in every sense of the word, so was he speaking in terms of economics? Because if that were the case, then economically speaking, America was at her *greatest* when *my* people were enslaved by *his* people, and the American society, as a whole, benefitted tremendously from the free labor that *my* people were forced to provide. So, yeah, you can bet your bottom dollar that I'd been keeping tabs on this toupee-wearing weirdo.

"And what about the Muslims overseas who are serving in the U.S. military? Is he referring to them as well?" Atiba continued to point out.

"I'm really not sure, my brotha. But what I *can* say is that Donald Trump is the last person America needs in the oval office, even though the largest demographic, the poor white Americans, are giving him their undying support. And obviously, we both know why."

"You can say that again. See, that's the reason us black people need to come together and do for ourselves like The Messenger taught us. We need to build our own nation and stop begging the white man for a piece of his, then get mad when we're treated like second class citizens. It doesn't make any sense."

After talking to my brotha for the next twenty minutes, I disconnected the call and then went upstairs to check on Dominique. Her bedroom door was closed, so I gave it a light knock.

Knock! Knock!

"Nique-Nique, you okay in there?"

"Yeah, Daddy," I heard her voice from the other side of the door. "You can come in, it's open."

I turned the knob and gently pushed the door open. Dominique was stretched out across the foot of her bed. She was laying on her stomach, propped on her elbows with her feet dangling off the side. Her Apple iPad was laying on the bed flipped open in front of her, and Tone Boy's face was on the screen. They were talking on Tango.

"What's up, Brotha Zee?" Tone Boy greeted me with a smile.

"What's going on, Lil' Brotha," I returned his greeting, but couldn't bring myself to return his smile. It was kind of weird seeing a teenaged boy in my daughter's bedroom, even though he wasn't physically there.

"So, what are you guys getting into?" I asked them.

"Studying," Dominique said, then she held up one of my favorite books, *No Disrespect* by Sista Souljah. Tone Boy did the same.

It was clear to me that Dominique and Tone Boy were really into one another. I guess that was a good thing, because I'd much rather see my sixteen-year-old daughter interested in one boy, rather than the plural.

"Nique-Nique," I leaned forward and kissed the crown of her head, "don't be up too late. And Tone Boy," I looked down at the iPad screen, "I wanna see you at the rec center on Monday. I need to talk to you about something."

I needed to make sure that Tone Boy and me were on the same page when it came to the love of my life. I also made a mental note to have a similar conversation with Dominique. My baby was still young and had a lot to learn about boys. So, as her father, I had every intention on schooling my baby to the game.

"A'ight," Tone Boy replied. "I'm cool with that."

"And Nique-Nique," I looked at her with a cautionary, raised brow, "I'm not playing. It's getting late, so I'm gonna need you to warp this up within the next half an hour."

"Okay, Daddy." She looked up at me and smiled.

My baby was so beautiful, and for reasons I couldn't explain, my mind traveled back to the day she was born. My princess was becoming a queen right before my very eyes, and I couldn't lie, it was really starting to trip me out.

The birth of a daughter, my gift and my curse.

CHAPTER THIRTY-ONE

JABARI

11:34 pm

"Come on, boo, why you can't forgive me?" Tonya pouted and stuck out her bottom lip. We were parked in front of her house, and I hadn't said a word to her since the situation between her and Shameeka.

"The only thing he did was give me a ride home," she insisted. "If anything, I'm the one that's supposed to be mad. You were straight up sharing my dick with another bitch, but yet and still I'm willing to forgive you. So, why come you won't forgive me?"

"Listen, Tonya, I'm tired as shit, and I still gotta drive all the way back to Willow Grove. Can't you just take ya ass in the house and let a nigga bounce?"

"Nope." She shook her head defiantly. "Not until you forgive me."

After a few minutes of not speaking to one another, Tonya got up on her knees and leaned over the center console. I knew what she was about to do, but I played stupid.

"Yo, Tonya, what'chu doin'?"

"I'm making my boo remember why he loves me so much," she replied with a devilish smile, seductively biting down on her bottom lip. She nibbled on my earlobe, then reached down and caressed my dick through the fabric of my jeans. I rocked up quick and wasted no time unbuckling my pants. I mean, what else was I supposed to do? Keep acting like I was mad? Yeah, right. A good ol' fashion chewy was exactly what I needed.

Tonya spat in the palm of her hand, and then stroked me nice and slow. I swear that shit felt like magic.

"You like that, Daddy?"

"Ummmm! Hell, yeah."

She stroked faster and tongued me down at the same time. I broke away from her kiss and gently grabbed the back of her neck.

"Yo, stop playing and step to ya business."

"Gladly," she said with a smile, then she lowered her head and spat on my dick. "Umm! Thick and juicy, just the way I like it."

She gripped my soldier with both hands, Kim Kardashian style, and then twirled her tongue around the helmet. After that, she slowly brought me to the depths of her tonsils.

"Slurp! Slurp! Ummmm! Slurp!"

The car was so small, that neither one of us could barely move. So, to give us a little more room, I pushed back the seat and lifted up the steering wheel. Tonya got loose and started going ham— sucking and moaning, slurping and stroking. I gripped the back of her head and pushed it down, causing her to gag and cough.

"Ahn-ahn, Jabari, why you do that for?" She popped her head up and looked at me like I was crazy.

"Yo, what'chu talking 'bout?" I laughed at her. "I ain't even do shit."

"Yah-huhn, yes you did!"

"A'ight, shorty, whatever you say." I continued laughing.

"I'm not playing wit'chu, Jabari. Don't be pushing down on my fucking head."

"Yeah, yeah, yeah." I pushed her head back down. "I was only playing wit'chu. Now stop talking, and lemme get this nut."

Tonya sucked me off for another five minutes, and I came hard inside of her mouth. I told her how much I loved her, and how good she made me feel. She wiped her mouth with the back of her hand, and then smiled like a little girl on Christmas morning.

"So, is you staying over or what?" Tonya asked me, still wiping her mouth. "My mama ain't home, and we can do it all night if you want."

"Nizzaw. Maybe next time," I told her. "But I love you, though."

"Aww, baby, I love you, too."

She attempted to kiss me, but I turned my head.

"Shorty, you trippin'. You better go 'head wit' them cum-stained lips."

"Well, fuck you, then." She laughed at me, then cracked open the door and climbed out the car. "Call me when you get home."

"I got'chu."

Tonya sped-walked towards her house, and I pulled off the second she stepped inside.

Askari

CHAPTER THIRTY-TWO

TONYA

After locking the front door behind me, I ran into the kitchen and grabbed a turkey baster from the drawer. I stuck the tube inside of my mouth and then pressed down on the dropper until it slurped up every bit of Jabari's cum. My pussy was still wet, so when I pulled my pants down and pushed my thongs to the side, it didn't take much to slip the turkey baster way up inside of me. Luckily for me, I was ovulating. So when I pressed down on the dropper and coated my womb with his million dollar seeds, I was praying them mutha-fuckas came with a checkbook.

Now, I know what y'all are prob'bly thinking: *Tonya's a grimy ass bitch*! Oh well, kiss my ass, so what. Jabari was my muthafuck-ing meal ticket, so fuck y'all. I mean, hell, I done already lied to the nigga when I told him he got me prego. So, if my black ass didn't show and prove, the joke would have fucked around and been on me.

Fuck that!

Whatever it takes to be the wife of an NBA baller, then that's what the fuck I was willing to do, turkey baster and all. So, like I said before, y'all can pucker up and kiss my ass.

Muthafuckas always wanna be judging some-damn-body.

Askari

CHAPTER THIRTY-THREE

JABARI

Monday, November 23rd, 2015

10:15 am

It was a brand-new week and I was back to being focused. We had a team meeting a few hours ago, right before the start of first period, and Coach Morris gave us a much-needed pep talk. He told us that the season was still young, so if we tightened up and won the rest our games, we could earn a rematch against Lower Merion in the state championship. I was sure to bring the flame in that one. This shit was personal. Keith Butler got his card punched when he dunked on me and made me a part of his highlight reel. It wasn't even three days ago, and he already had a million views on You Tube. It was cool, though, because the next time we meet I was going to show him why they call me Big Jabby.

Believe dat!

The bell rung, signaling the start of fourth period. I had lunch and study hall for the next two periods, so the plan was to post up in the student lobby and kick game to some of the honeys. I was dipped in a fresh pair of PRP jeans, topped off with a cream Moncler sweater jacket with sycamore buttons. My grid belt and cinnamon-brown boots were courtesy of Balenciaga, and my bookbag was a tan and white Gucci Python. My fresh cut was lined up to perfection, and my waves were spinning like a puddle of water with a pebble dropped in the center. The Rollie on my wrist was one of the watches that my pops left me, and the fragrance of my body oil was Somali Redwood.

As I made my way towards the student lobby, this lil' brown skinned, slim goody named Rickina tried to holla at me as she walked past in the opposite direction. Shorty was old news, so I chucked up my deuces and kept it pushing. I wasn't in the habit of chasing old pussy, so I didn't. Rickina *did* have a helluva shot, though. Her dick sucking skills were aaahhhhh, but her ride game was on a beanski. Shorty used to be popping that thing like Ciara, and be loving it when a nigga get to sucking on them titties.

Damn, I thought to myself as Rickina walked away switching her lil' bubble butt. *Maybe I should call her tonight. Nah mean? See what that ride game be about.*

I laughed it off and continued walking down the hallway. Up ahead, I spotted Shameeka. She was standing beside her locker fronting like she ain't see the kid coming.

Damn, shorty was beautiful, flawless, way prettier than Tonya. She kinda reminded me of the R&B singer Jordan Sparks, just a tad bit thicker. She had a buttery tan complexion, a pointy lil' nose, and the sexiest pink lips a nigga had ever seen. She was the type of beautiful that didn't require any makeup, just a light touch of lip gloss. Her dark, wavy hair was pulled back into a long ponytail, and I couldn't help but to feel some type of way about her. I had crazy love for shorty, but I knew I couldn't take it there.

Tonya was my number one, and Shameeka would never have that spot. So, to keep it one hunnid, I'm kinda glad things ended the way they did. Shameeka deserved to be somebody's number one, and since she would never be mines, I'd rather she go out find a dude who was willing to give her everything that she deserved.

"What's up, Meek?" I spoke in a casual voice. "You good?"

Shameeka shot me the ice-grill, scowled at a nigga from head to toe, and then looked away as though I wasn't even standing there. She was obviously still mad at me, and rightfully so. I was dead wrong for making our relationship appear to be one thing, when it was really something else, even though I never came right out and told Shameeka she was my girl. At the very least, I shoulda told her about Tonya and the baby.

"Damn, Meek, it's like that?" I asked her with a guilty smirk on my face. "You ain't got no holla for ya boy?"

I waited for a response, but Shameeka just sucked her teeth.

"Well, fuck it." I shrugged my shoulders and walked away.

"Jabari?" Shameeka called out behind me.

I turned back around and noticed she was crying. I hate it when females cried, especially the ones I cared about. My heart was beating for shorty, but I refused to let it show. The situation was bad enough, and if I told Shameeka how I truly felt it would only make things worse. So, instead of expressing my true feelings, I just focused on doing something that would make her stop crying.

"Damn, Meek you were looking like Ronda Rousey a couple of seconds ago. But now you're standing here crying. What type of bipolar shit is that?" I said with a smile, hoping Shameeka would smile, too, but she didn't. She sobbed even harder, and before I knew it, she was pressed against me, with her arms wrapped around my waist. Her warm tears were wetting up the front of my sweater.

"Yo, stop crying." I gently caressed her back. "Everything's gonna be okay."

"No, it's not." She shook her head and squeezed me tighter. "Jabari, I'm in trouble."

"Trouble? What kind of trouble?"

"*Big trouble,*" she quickly replied.

It was killing me to see her cry, so I used the back of my sleeve to wipe her tears away. People were walking up and down the hallway staring at us, but I didn't care. Especially since most of them already assumed that me and Shameeka were together.

"Well, you know you can still talk to me about anything, right?" I said, as I led her over to an empty bench. "So, tell me what's wrong. What's going on?"

Shameeka sat down on the bench, and then looked up at me with her eyes all puffy. She took a deep breath and shook her head slowly.

"Jabari, I'm pregnant."

"You wanna run that by me again?" I asked her, praying that my ears were playing tricks on me.

"I'm pregnant, I said."

"Pregnant?" I looked at her with a creased brow. "Are you sure?"

"Of course, I'm sure!" Shameeka snapped at me. "I was late this month, so I took a pregnancy test and the results were positive. I'm having a baby."

Completely deflated, I sat down beside her and cracked my knuckles one-by-one.

"And I'm guessing you're telling me this because the baby's mine?"

She nodded her head *yes*.

"But how is that even possible?" I asked. I was looking at her skeptically, wondering if this was her way of persuading me to leave Tonya. "Not once did I cum inside of you. I pulled out every single time, so how can I be the father?"

"That doesn't mean anything, Jabari. You *do* know what pre-cum is, right?" She wiped the front of her face, and then looked at me waiting for an answer.

I sat up straight and sucked in a deep breath.

"Listen, Shameeka, I ain't try'na come off the wrong way or nothing, but I really can't stand that right now. I'm only eighteen, and I already got a baby on the way wit' my girl, Tonya. My mom don't even know, 'cause I'm afraid to tell her. So, what am I supposed to do now, tell her I got *two* girls pregnant? I got love for you, Meek, I really do. But I'm going though enough as it is. I'm just not ready to be father of two kids. I'm not."

"Jabari, you sound so selfish," Shameeka pulled my card. "You're only thinking about yourself. What about me? What about the life that's growing inside of me? Doesn't that mean *anything* to you?"

"Shameeka, I *am* thinking about you," I sternly replied. "This time next year I'll be away at Duke University, then after that who knows. I could be drafted by any team in the NBA and be thousands of miles away from you and the baby. I'm sorry, Meek, but this is too much for me to deal with. I've got mad shit going on, and I just can't deal with this shit, too."

"*This shit?*" Shameeka hastily replied.

"Come on, dawg, you know what I'm try'na say."

168

For the next few minutes, we just sat there in silence. The both of us were sorting through our own thoughts and feelings. I can't say what Shameeka was thinking, but I sure as hell know what I was thinking—abortion.

"So, what about ya peoples?" I asked her. "Do they know?"

"Unfortunately, yes. I didn't tell them, though. My mother found the results of my pregnancy test when she was snooping around my bedroom."

"Well, do they know I'm the one who got you pregnant?"

Shameeka shook her head *no*.

"They asked me who the father was, but I refused to tell them. I thought it'd be better if you and me spoke first."

"Listen, Meek, I'ma give it you raw and uncut. You've got your whole life ahead of you, and the same goes for me. A baby will only get in our way and hinder our dreams. I think our best option is to get an abortion."

"*An abortion?*" Her eyeballs damn near popped out of her head. "My family's Catholic, we don't believe in abortions."

I stood to my feet and adjusted my book bag.

"Well, that's the best I can come up wit'. If you want, I'll even pay for it, and when it's time to get it done, I'll go down there with you."

Shameeka broke down crying and covered her face with both hands. It hurt like hell to see her going through it the way she was, but what could I do? I had already taken my stance. There was nothing else to say, so I walked away and linked up with some of my teammates in the cafeteria.

Damnit, Jabari!

Askari

CHAPTER THIRTY-FOUR

EBONY

11:15am

The time on my watch was a quarter after eleven, and with forty minutes left on my lunch break, I had about twenty minutes to go for mines. Then after that, head back to Center City where I worked as a social worker in the welfare office.

There was simply no way I could spend another night lying in bed thinking about this man, wondering if he was the one. My yearning heart was telling me, *Yass, girl, yass!* But my intellectual mind was telling me, *Girl, you better pump your brakes and take some time to get to know this brotha.*

My yearning heart was trumped by my intellectual mind, so there I was, parked outside of the Afrikan Arts book store, hoping to learn more about this beautiful brotha named Zion.

After throwing the transmission in *park* and killing the engine, I reached down inside of my purse and pulled out my MacBook. I flipped the lid and examined my reflection in the compact mirror. My eyeliner and lip gloss was on fleek, and my new hairstyle intensified my natural beauty. Satisfied, I clamped my MacBook back together, tossed it inside of my purse, and then climbed out of my Navigator. I was dressed in a cream, Prada business suit and a white blouse. My peep-toe Cavalli pumps were a shade lighter than my cinnamon-brown BCBG handbag, and my black, oversized Fendi shades were propped up on my forehead.

As I approached the store's entrance and reached for the door handle, my heart was thumping a million beats per second, and in the back of my mind, I couldn't resist the urge to play Twenty-One Questions. *What if he wasn't interested? What if he didn't find me attractive? What if he was married? Or even worse, what if he was gay?* I didn't think so, but then again you never know.

Stepping inside of the store was like déjà vu. Once again, my nasal was greeted with the sweet aroma of a burning Frankincense.

The melodic sounds of Neo-Soul were bumping through the sound system; only this time it was Lauryn Hill instead of Jill Scott. Looking around the store, I immediately spotted Zion, who was seated at a table in the back-right corner. He was reading a book and sipping on a cup of hot tea.

"Now the joyyyyy in my worrrrld lives in Zionnnnnn!"

"Damn, L-Boogie, you sho'nuff hit the mark with that one," I said to myself, loving the beautiful tone of her legendary voice.

Zion must have felt my energy. He laid the book on the table, then he looked in my direction and smiled. His manicured dreads had a razor-sharp outline, and his rich chocolate complexion had a natural glow. He stood to his feet, and I admired him from head to toe, shifting my stance when my pussy became moist. His cream Polo shirt and faded blue jeans fit him just right. He moved from around the table and slowly began walking towards me.

Umm mmm mmm! I thought to myself, as I looked down and sized up the bulge in his crotch. *Is that a shotgun, sir? Or are you just happy to see me?*

"Ebony, right?" Zion said with a chuckle, noticing the way I was staring at his junk.

Embarrassed that he'd caught me looking, I looked up at his handsome face and said, "Huh?"

"Your name? It's Ebony, right?" He extended his right hand to shake mines.

"Oh, so you remember my name?" I said with a smile, loving the feel of his soft palm pressed against mines.

"Of course, I remember. It's not every day that I'm blessed with the presence of a Queen so beautiful." He released my hand and then looked around the store. "Where's little man? Kenyatta. You didn't bring him?"

"No, not today," I answered his question, astonished that he not only remembered my name, but my son's name as well.

"Oh, okay." He nodded his head. "So, how can I help you? Are you looking for anything in particular?"

"Umm, not exactly," I nervously replied, and then bit down on my bottom lip.

172

I wanted to tell Zion how much he'd been on my mind, and how I couldn't go to sleep at night without fantasizing that his firm body was pressed against me. I wanted to tell him these things, but I didn't have the courage. I was afraid he didn't feel the same way.

"Listen, Ebony," Zion broke the awkward silence, "I'm a firm believer that a man should never have a problem expressing himself. So, with that being said, would you mind if I asked you a few questions?"

"No, not at all. I wouldn't mind. You can say whatever you feel the need to."

Zion sucked in a deep breath and exhaled slowly.

"Alright," he rubbed his goatee, "I'm kinda putting myself out there by saying this, but ever since Friday, I haven't been able to not think about you. And I was wondering, you know, whether you had a man or not. So, do you?"

I smiled at him like a teenaged girl who just experienced her first kiss, and for the first time my yearning heart and intellectual mind were finally on the same page. My mind, body and spirit were screaming, "*Yasss! Yasss! Yasss! Jesus, you da man!*"

"So, is that a no, a yes?" Zion asked, referring to my bright, wide smile.

"That's a no," I quickly confirmed. "It's just me and my two boys, Jabari and Kenyatta."

"Okay." Zion nodded his head and returned my smile. "So, I wouldn't be stepping on any toes by asking you to join me for dinner this weekend?"

"Nope, not at all," I told him. "No toes being stepped on over this way."

"Alright, so will you join me for dinner this weekend?"

"Absolutely." I nodded my head. "Just tell me when and where."

My heart was beating way faster than normal. *Was it love*? Maybe. *Lust*? Oh, you better believe it! I wanted to smack it up, flip it, rub it down, oh noooooooo!

"How about you chose the time and location," Zion said in a smooth voice, snapping me out of my thoughts. "Because after all, you're the one who's blessing me."

"Oh, yeah?" I gave him the side eye, then folded my arms across my chest. "And how am I blessing you exactly?" The octave of my voice was challenging, but the smile on my face didn't give gave it any credence.

"It's just like I told you," he licked his lips and stared into my eyes, "it's not every day that a brotha has the fortune of being in the presence of a woman so beautiful. And when I say beautiful, I'm referring to your energy, the way you carry yourself and how you interact with your son. So, objectively speaking, when it comes to a woman of your stature, *blessed* is the only word that seemingly comes to mind."

Good Lawd, this brotha's go me blushing right about now!

"You don't agree?" he asked with a prying smile.

"I mean, I'm a'ight." I brushed my shoulders off, making him laugh.

"Ohhhh, so you're beautiful *and* funny?"

"I try," I replied with a straight face, causing him to laugh even harder. "So, when and where? This is *your* idea, so it's all on you. You lead the way, and I'll follow."

"You know what?" He wagged his index finger. "I have a better idea. How about I cook for you?"

"You," I pointed at him, "cook for me?" I pointed back at myself.

"Yeah," he replied with a chuckle. "I'm known for throwing down a little bit."

"Oh, is that right?" I blew on my knuckles, then brushed them against my shoulder. "Well, Umm, I'm known for doing a little throwing down myself."

"Well, it seems to me we've got us a little competition in the making," Zion said as he slowly rubbed his hands together. "How about we do this, I'll cook for you on the first date, and you cook for me on the second date. Then after that, we decide who's the best when it comes to throwing down in the kitchen."

"Challenge accepted."

I extended my right hand to seal the deal, and Zion accepted the gesture with a soft handshake. He gently caressed the back of my hand with the front of his thumb, and my body temperature escalated.

"So, umm, just when and where is this competition taking place?" I asked, as I damn near creamed on myself. "And just so you know, I'm not the type of gal who goes to a guy's house on the first date. So, keep that in mind."

"Most definitely," Zion shot back. "I figured as much. I was actually thinking about my rec center. We have a kitchen on the first floor. You can meet me there at seven o'clock on Saturday, and I'll show you who's the *real* boss of the kitchen."

"Did you just say that you own a rec center?"

"Umm-hmm." He released my hand, and I found myself breathing again. "We've been running it for about a year now."

"*We?*" I asked, praying he wasn't referring to a wife or a girlfriend.

"Yeah. Me, my comrade, Atiba Muhammad, and his wife, Hydia. The three of us run the day-to-day operations."

"Wow. That sounds pretty interesting."

"It is," he replied. "We work with the youth in our community, helping them with their homework and teaching them to think outside of the box. It's a beautiful thing."

"Sounds like it." I glanced at my watch. "Okay, so Saturday at seven o'clock. But you still haven't given me the address."

"It's the old church on 17th and Hunting Park, you can't miss it."

"And trust me, I won't." I glanced at my watch once again, then returned my gaze to Zion. "Well, I better get going. My lunch break is almost over and I need to get back to work."

"Do you still have my information?" Zion asked, as he followed me to the door.

"I sure do. I have it right here." I patted the latch on my purse.

"That's what's up. Hopefully, you'll give me a call later."

"I most definitely will," I said, as he brushed past me and pushed open the door.

I stepped outside and strutted back to my Navigator, throwing a little umph in my hips because I knew he was watching. I climbed inside of my truck, started the engine, and then rolled down the window.

"And, Zion?" I called out. He was still standing in front of his store. "I couldn't stop either."

"You couldn't stop what?" He gave me a strange look.

"Thinking about you," I finally confessed, cracking a smile when I said it.

Zion smiled back and waved his hand as I pulled away slow.

I looked in my rearview mirror, and began shaking my head.

"Thank you, Lord. Thank you."

CHAPTER THIRTY-FIVE

KENYATTA

12:39pm

"Gucci, get'cha stupid-butt outta here!" I shouted at my Auntie Erica's miniature Yorkie. I was laying on the couch reading my book, and the stupid dog kept jumping on me.

"I'm not playing wit'chu," I warned her. "Get'cha stupid self outta here!"

"Yatta? I know you ain't down here yelling at my baby like that?" Auntie Erica said as she came into the living room. She was dressed in an olive-green Gucci jumper and fly pair of Gucci boots the same color as butterscotch Timbs. A red and green Gucci belt was wrapped around her waist and clamped together by a solid gold, double-G buckle. The jumper was zipped down at the top showing off her Gucci link necklace, and her iced-out double-G earrings were dangling from her lobes. Her silky, black hair was shiny and long, and her Chanel No. 5 reminded me of Ma'Dukes. They both wore the same fragrance.

"Boy, don't be talking to Gucci like that," Auntie Erica said as she squatted down. She looked at Gucci, who was nibbling on my shoe string, and motioned for the stupid dog to come to her. "Come to Mommy, baby. Come on, come to Mommy."

Gucci jumped off the couch and scampered over to Auntie Erica.

"That's my baby," Auntie Erica cooed, talking to the dog like she was actually a baby. She scooped Gucci up in her arms and continued cooing at her. The shit was kinda weird, but funny at the same time.

Auntie Erica's crazy as hell!

"Her love her Mommy, don't she?" Auntie Erica asked, while rubbing her nose against the side of Gucci's face. "Yes, her do love her Mommy. Her love her Mommy so much."

Gucci looked at me, and I swear to God the little fucker stuck her tongue out at me.

You little bastard! I chuckled to myself thinking about the movie *Honey I Shrunk The Kids* In the back of my mind I had a vision of Buck Bundy, the dog from *Married With Children* His ass got zapped by the shrink machine and turned into Gucci's little ass. The thought made me crack up laughing.

"Yatta, don't be laughing at me and my baby." Auntie Erica chuckled. She came over and sat down beside me, still rubbing her nose into the fur on Gucci's face. My Auntie Erica was drop dead gorgeous. She looked a lot like my mom, just a little taller and a few shades lighter.

I refused to use the term babysitting because I was not a baby, but Auntie Erica was watching me for the day. Ma'Dukes be bugging, always try'na treat me like a baby, even though I was a teenager now. According to her, I was not responsible enough to be in the house by myself. So, a few hours earlier she dropped me off at Auntie Erica's, which was ten minutes away from her job. She's a social worker at the welfare office downtown. I was cool with it, because aside from Auntie Erica being my favorite aunt, her house was the shizney, straight up lit! Especially, the kitchen. She had every single cupcake, ice cream flavor, cereal and pop tart known to man. And that was just the tip of the iceberg.

Her boyfriend, Uzi, had a footlocker that was filled to the rim with nothing but video games. Dude wasn't around much, but whenever I stayed the night and he *did* happen to come home, we would stay up into the wee hours of the night playing X-BOX. I would sucker him out of his money, too? I mean, what in the world would make a grown man think that he could beat a teenager in a video game? The last time he tried, he ended up buying me a new pair of Jays.

Damn, I hope he comes home before it's time to leave.

"Yatta," Auntie Erica said while pointing at the book in my hand, "what'chu over there reading?"

"To Kill A Black Man," I answered, then held up the book to give her a better look at the cover.

"Well, does it have any pictures?" she asked me after taking the book from my hand and flipping through the pages.

I laughed at her and shook my head *no*.

"Eew." She playfully scowled at me, rolling her eyes. "What'chu got a problem wit' me asking about the book having pictures? Because the way I see it, the pictures would've told the whole story, and I wouldn't have had to waste time reading the damn thing."

"Yo, Auntie E, lemme find out."

"Find out what?" She snapped her neck and got up in my grill. "Spit it out, young bul. What'chu try'na say?"

"Nothing." I laughed at her, then leaned back so she couldn't go upstairs on me.

"Alright, Yatta, I gotta make a quick run," she said as she sat Gucci down and stood to her feet. "If Uzi comes home, just tell him that I stepped out for a minute. And if your mom calls, tell her that I'm upstairs taking a nap. That girl would lose her mind if she found out I left you here all alone."

"Okay," I said. "But on your way back, can you stop at Tony Luke's and grab me a cheese steak?"

"Chicken or beef?" she asked, as she took off walking towards the door.

"Chicken," I told her, "with triple cheese, mushrooms and onions."

"Got'cha." She nodded her head while pushing open the door. "And Yatta," she turned back around to face me, "other than family, don't let nobody inside of this house. And do not...I repeat...*do not* go upstairs in my bedroom."

"I got'chu."

"Kenyatta, I'm not playing with you. Stay out of my bedroom."

"Didn't I just say I got'chu?"

"A'ight, now." She blew me a kiss. "I love you, behave yourself, and I'll be back in an hour."

The second she stepped outside and locked the door behind her, I hopped off the couch and ran over to the window. I peeked through the blinds and watched her as she climbed inside of her Porsche

Panamara. I waited until she pulled off, then slowly made my way up the stairs. My destination? Auntie Erica's bedroom. Had she never mentioned it, I probably would have never thought about it? But because she did, my curiosity got the best of me.

What the hell is so special about her bedroom?

CHAPTER THIRTY-SIX

KENYATTA

"Dang, it smells like weed in here?" I said to myself, as I stood in the middle of my Auntie Erica's bedroom. The large room was spotless, reminding me of one of them interior design magazines that Ma'Dukes be getting in the mail. Her King-size bed had four columns and a silk canopy that was draped across the top. I remembered seeing something similar in one of my Pinky pornos, and just like that, in the snap of a finger, I was thinking about watching a porn movie and getting my shit off .

My Auntie Erica's a freak, so I knew her and Uzi had some pornos in the stash, but where?

As I stood there looking around the room, I figured the nightstand was a good place to begin my search. But when I opened the top drawer and looked inside, I damn near jumped out of my skin.

"Agh!" I shouted, scared to death and taking a few steps backwards. "Auntie Erica done chopped Uzi's dick off!"

Urf! Urf! Ugggrrrr! Urf!

I looked back and saw Gucci. She was standing outside the door barking at me and growling, probably cussing me out in her doggy language telling me to stay out of her *Mommy's* bedroom.

Completely ignoring Gucci, I walked back over to the nightstand. I looked down at the brown skinned dick inside of the drawer, realizing what it was. I had never seen a dildo that looked so real. It was thick and long, and shiny like brown leather. It had a huge set of balls and thick veins going up and down the sides. The only reason I knew what it was, or what it had to be, is because of Jabby. He sat me down one day and told me all about sex. He showed me one of his girl-on-girl porn videos, and the two chicks in the movie were fucking each other with these cream-coated sticks. I asked Jabby what they were, and he told me they were dildos. But the dildos in the movie were pink and purple, nothing close to the one I was looking at.

"*Damn*," I mumbled under my breath, thinking about my own dick and how small it was compared to the dildo. "I wonder if my shit's gonna be that big when I grow up."

After closing the drawer, I had a vision of Auntie Erica sticking that thing inside of her coochie. The vision was so clear that my stomach became nauseous.

"Eeew!" I shook my head, desperately try'na shake away the image. "Auntie Erica's a freak-a-leak! Eeew!"

Urf! Urf! Urf!

"Gucci, shut ya bitch-ass up!" I snapped at her, cursing out loud because nobody was around to hear me say it. I turned around to see what Gucci was doing and noticed she was ransacking the bottom of Auntie Erica's walk-in closet. I walked over and looked down at the green duffle bag she was chewing on.

"Get'cha little ass outta here!" I nudged her away with the tip of my sneaker.

I knelt down and felt the top of the bag. It was big and bulky, and whatever that was stashed inside was hard like metal. I pulled back the back zipped and slowly opened the bag.

"Dizzamn!"

I couldn't believe my eyes. The entire duffle bag was full of guns. Some were black, some were silver, and some were bigger than the others. I reached down inside of the bag and pulled out one of the smaller ones. Being careful to keep my fingers away from the trigger, I held the gun to my face and looked down inside the barrel. The dark, little hole had a burnt smell that reminded me of charcoal. Inside of the cylinder, I noticed there were five hollow-tipped bullets. The six bullets, I assumed, was down at the bottom of the black barrel. I couldn't explain why, but I stuffed the gun in my back pocket. After that, I reached back down and zippered up the bag.

About an hour later, I was sitting on the couch playing Madden 16. The entire time I was thinking about the gun. It was stashed in my book bag, and my book bag was hanging on the coat rack beside the door. I was also thinking about Ma'Dukes and the ass whupping she would surely give me if she knew I had it, Jabby, too, for that matter. He would probably give me body shots for like an hour straight, or at least until I shit on myself.

Nah, man fuck that! I'm putting that muh'fucka back!

I dropped the joystick, and then went over to grab the gun from my book bag. I pulled back the zipper and reached inside, but before I could grab the gun, I heard keys jiggling from the other side of the door.

Oh, shit! It's Auntie Erica!

Completely shaken, I zipped up the bag and then hauled ass back to the couch. The front door opened no sooner than I picked up the joystick. Auntie Erica came in the house, closed the door behind her, then reached over and thumbed in the digits on her home security system.

"Sup, boo? You ready to eat?" She smiled at me, then held up the paper bag she was holding, our two cheese steaks were sticking out the top.

"Umm-hmm." I nodded my head, looking back and forth between her and my book bag.

"A'ight," she said as she took off walking towards the dining room. "Well, let's get it. 'Cause these cheese steaks are smelling hella good, and I'm hungrier than a hostage."

I turned the game off and followed her into the dining room.

Damn, man, Ma'Dukes is gonna fuckin' kill me!

Askari

CHAPTER THIRTY-SEVEN

EBONY

4:43pm

Yes! I'm finally off of work! I thought to myself, as I pulled out of the 12th Street parking garage. Mondays were the absolute worst. Because after a two-day weekend, kicked back and chilling, it was always hard going back to work and getting right back into the groove of doing things. So now that *Miserable Monday* was finally over, I had to pick up Yatta from Erica's house and then head back home. The plan was to take me a nice hot bubble bath, followed by a nice hot shower, and then sip on a glass of wine as I prepared dinner for me and the boys.

A red light on the corner of Broad and Federal brought my Navigator to a stop. The rush hour traffic was usually one of my pet peeves, but not today, nope, not at all. The weather was uncharacteristically warm for the month of November, about 73°. The sun was shining bright, and the sounds of Fantasia had your girl jamming behind the steering wheel.

"You're always on my minnnnnd. When you come around, I get shyyyyy. When I see youuuuu. When I see youuuuu. Never know when you might walk by, so I gotta be right on time. When I see youuuuu. When I see youuuuu.

A Chinese lady in the next lane over was looking at me like I was crazy, but I honestly didn't care. If only she knew what I knew, her little Chinese ass would have been jamming too. *Ms. Ebony Beatrice Johnson done went and found herself a man!* You heard me, Cheena? Good! Now, you run and tell somebody *that*!

Obviously, I was still thinking about Zion, yearning to know any and everything there was to know about him. I wanted to know where he grew up, where he lived, whether or not he had any chil'ens, and if so, how many? I wanted to know what made him happy, so that way I could always be the one who made him smile. I wanted to know what made him sad, so that way I could always refrain from doing it. I wanted to know the full extent of his wisdom, and spend late nights and early mornings picking his brain. I wanted to know the feeling of his intimate touch, the taste of his skin, the texture of his tongue and most definitely I wanted him to know mines.

In my thirty-eight years of living, only two men could honestly say they had experienced the passion of my body. My children's father, Big Jabby, and my ex-boyfriend, Terry. Both men added layers to my chocolate. One for the better, and the other for the worst.

Big Jabby was my first love. It sounds crazy but we fell in love way back in kindergarten, and *got married* in the second grade—Ring Pops and all. He loved me and the boys to no avail, and not a day went by where he didn't cross my mind. We grew up together down Richard Allen, and to be totally honest, I couldn't remember a time in my life when we didn't know one another. Our families were extremely close. His grandmother, Miss Val, and Big Mama were best friends, so our love for one another was natural...pure.

Just like Jabari Jr., Big Jabby was a high school basketball star. Well over six-foot-nine, he was the best baller to come out of North Philly since Hank Gathers and Rasheed Wallace. He had a full-ride scholarship to Duke University, and every other D-1 college for that. But the streets were vicious, and the game was cold. So, once they got a hold on Big Jabby, they never let go.

Big Jabby was always infatuated with making money, so when he started selling crack in the 11th grade he blew up in no time. Within his first year of hustling, he went from slinging caps to slinging weight, and by the time we graduated from Benjamin Franklin he was already sitting on a nice chunk of money. He had four corners in the Bad Lands and half of Richard Allen on lock. So, obviously, by the time his first semester of college rolled around, going to Duke was the furthest thing from Big Jabby's mind. I literally watched him go from a Ford Taurus to a Pathfinder, from a Pathfinder to a Lexus, and from a Lexus to a 600 Benz. He even purchased a house for me and the boys down in Bear, Delaware.

Everything was cool, at least I thought it was. I didn't know it at the time, but Big Jabby was stuck in the middle of a turf war.

There were a gang of drug dealers from South Philly who called themselves *The Grip Boys,* and they were pressing Big Jabby hard, solely for the sake of taking over his drug operation. They gave him an ultimatum: either get down with the program or die.

But Big Jabby, being who he was, he simply wasn't going for it. He flat out refused, and made it clear that he would much rather go to war. He was so defiant, that one night, while he and me were partying at the Transit nightclub, we were approached by this guy named *Mook,* who we both knew from the projects. He told Big Jabby that one of The Grip Boys, some guy named *Smack,* had placed a $20,000 ticket on his head. I'm wasn't sure if it was the liquor talking, or Big Jabby's pride, but he got up in Mook's chest.

"Well, since you wanna be this nigga's messenger boy," Big Jabby jabbed his finger into Mook's forehead, *"you tell that bitch-ass nigga, I got sixty on his and another thirty on his baby mu-hvah's!"*

After that, he cracked Mook upside the head with a champagne bottle and knocked him out cold. That was a big mistake. Because just like Big Jabby, Mook was also a major player in North Philly. He had a crew of young wolves from the Bad Lands who called themselves *The Block Boys,* so it didn't take long before the beef was on.

About a week later, Big Jabby was gunned down in cold blood. He was leaving the barbershop on Woodstock and Susquehanna, where he'd just finished taking Kenyatta to get his first haircut. He was standing beside his Benz and strapping Kenyatta down in his car seat, when three shooters dressed in all-black approached him from behind. They didn't even try to rob him, they just blew his brains out, right there on the spot and right there in front of my baby. According to the police officer report, Kenyatta was found scream-ing in his car seat. He was covered in his daddy's blood, and smack-ing his face trying to wake him back up. The top half of Big Jabby's body was still inside the car, hunched over Kenyatta. But from the waist down, they left him in the gutter. He died trying to protect our baby from the gunfire.

At the time of Big Jabby's murder, Kenyatta was only two years old and Jabari was seven. That was eleven years ago, 2004, the same year we lost Big Mama. My entire world came crashing down. I lost the house in Delaware, and me the boys had to move back to the same hood we left just a few months earlier. Loneliness and depression crept in fast, and before I knew it, I was searching for love in all the wrong places. That's how I met Terry.

It was New Year's Eve, 2005, and I was celebrating with a couple of my girlfriends from work. We were chilling at the 40/40 Club in Atlantic City, having a few drinks and getting our party on. That's when we were approached by this handsome, smooth talking brotha named Terry. He was clearly interested in me, even though he bought a couple of rounds for my girls, too. Terry and me exchanged numbers, and a few months later he was living in my two-bedroom apartment with me and my boys.

Our first year together was like a ghetto fairytale, but all of that changed on the night of our first anniversary. It was New Year's Eve, 2006. I wanted to go out and celebrate, but Terry insisted we stay home. That alone had me pissed the hell off. I was beginning to notice a trend with Terry, and I didn't like it. It seemed as though he wasn't happy unless I was cooped up in the house, cut off from the outside world. He was so persistent on making me stay in the house, that eventually I lost my job and had to get on welfare. Then, on the rare occasions where I *did* go out and have a good time, Terry would cop an attitude. That particular night, however, I couldn't have cared less about Terry and his funky little 'tude. If he didn't want to go out and celebrate, that was on him. No sweat off my back. I needed a babysitter any ol' damn way.

So, the plan was to hang out with the girls for a few hours, and then head back home to bring in the New Year with Terry and the boys. But when I walked through the door at 11:35 p.m., the boys were asleep, and Terry was sitting on the couch watching television. A half empty bottle of Hennessey was sitting on the coffee table, and from the look on Terry's face I could see he was drunk. He got up from the couch and staggered towards me looking crazy as hell— one side of his hair was neatly braided, but the other side was bushy and wild. A demonic look covered his face and his eyes were blood-shot red.

"Lemme smell ya panties, bitch."

I looked at him like he was stupid, then attempted to brush past him to go check on the boys. That's when he snatched me by the back of my hair and flung me backwards. I crashed into the front door and slid down to the carpet.

"Terry, what the hell is wrong with you?" I shouted at him, then I shook away the dizzy spell that flooded my brain.

"Take ya panties off and lemme smell 'em!" Terry demanded. *"I know ya lil' smutt ass was out there fuckin'!"*

I stood to my feet and straightened out my clothes.

"Take my panties off"? I scowled at him. *"I'm not taking off—"*

Wham!

He punched me square in the nose, giving me the lightbulb effect. I was dazed and shaken up pretty bad, but I didn't fall.

Wham!

Another punch landed across the left side of my face, and I went down hard. The only thing I could think to do, was to curl up in a ball.

Wham!

Terry kicked me in the ribs, and I yelped like a wounded dog.

"Got the nerve to tell Terry what she not gon' do?" he continued shouting, referring to the both of us in the third person. *"Bitch must'a lost her rabid-ass mind!"*

"Terry, I'm sorry!"

"Not at all, bitch! Ya stankin' ass ain't sorry. But'chu about to be!"

Terry snatched his belt off and flipped it into a loop.

Wham! Wham! Wham! Wham! Wham!

After whipping me with the belt, he returned to the couch and continued watching television, acting as though nothing had ever happened.

That was the first time I had ever been abused by a man. Thick globs of blood were dripping from my nose and mouth. My head was hurting so bad that it felt like King Kong was trapped inside. My pride was hurt, and my spirit was damn near crushed.

"Mommy?" I heard Jabari's voice.

I looked up and saw him standing in the hallway. He was dressed in his Spider Man pajamas and rubbing his eyes with the back of his hand.

"Is everything okay? What was that noise I heard?"

"It was nothing, baby. Just go back to bed."

I was so glad the living room lights were turned off, and that Jabari couldn't see my face.

"Are you sure?"

"Didn't she just tell you wasn't nothing goin' on?" Terry snapped at him. *"Now, take ya lil' bad ass back to bed."*

Jabari, sensing that something was wrong, looked at Terry. He then returned his eyes to me, and I could see he was crying.

"Everything's fine, baby, I promise. Now, go back to bed."

I was so afraid Terry might attack him, too. So, I prayed to God, asking that He send Jabari back to his room without asking any more questions. My prayer was answered.

As soon as Jabari went back in his room, I peeled myself off the floor and staggered into the bathroom. Once inside, I cut the lights on and examined my face in the mirror. I had two black eyes, my nose was swollen and bloody, and my bottom lip was split down the middle. I was so furious, that I wanted revenge. I wanted to do something to Terry's ass so bad, but he was too damn big.

At six-foot-three, two hundred and ten pounds, he was seventy pounds heavier and one foot taller than. So instead of doing something to physically harm him, I did the next best thing—I called the cops. It had taken them a half an hour to get there, and the entire time I was locked in the boys' room. I didn't come out until I heard Terry shouting.

"Who the fuck is that knocking on my goddamned door this late at night? The po-lice? Well, what the fuck y'all want? The bitch called y'all and said what? A'ight, man, slow ya roll. I'ma open the door."

The second I heard the locks click and the door being pulled open, I emerged from the bedroom and limped out into the living room. Two police officers were standing at the door talking to Terry.

"Jesus Christ!" the younger of the two police officers exclaimed. He was looking at me when he said it.

"Ma'am?" the older police officer addressed me, then he pointed his flashlight at Terry. *"Is this the guy who assaulted you?"*

"Umm-hmm, it was him." I nodded my head and broke down crying.

"Sir, I'm gonna need you to turn around and place your hands behind your back," the younger police officer stated to Terry.

"For what?" Terry slurred back. *"I ain't done shit, not a single goddamned thing."*

The older police officer grabbed Terry by the arm, and when he pulled away, both officers tackled him to the floor.

"You're under arrest, you woman-beating-son-of-a-bitch," the older police officer hissed at Terry, as he placed him in handcuffs.

"Under arrest? For what?" Terry questioned when they snatched him off the floor and stood him up straight.

"Domestic Battery," The older police officer growled back.

"Domestic Battery?" Terry slurred. *"Now, y'all wait one goddamned minute. I need somebody to tell me what time it is."*

The younger police officer glanced at his watch, then he looked back at Terry. *"It's a quarter after midnight."*

"Oh, helllll naw!" Terry stomped his feet. *"You muthafuckas can't arrest me! That's a Statute of Limitations!"*

"A Statute of Limitations?" The older police officer looked at him quizzically. *"What the hell does that have to do with anything?"*

"It's got everything to do with this shit!" Terry screamed in his face. *"This shit y'all talking 'bout? Man, that shit happened last year!"*

The older police officer scowled at Terry, then he motioned for his partner to take him away. *"Take his stupid ass outside to the car."*

"This some bullshit!" Terry shouted while being pulled out into the hallway. *"Statute of Limitations, goddamnit! Y'all locking me up for some old shit! This shit happened last year!"*

Unfortunately, that wasn't the last time Terry put his hands on me. My stupid ass forgave him and dropped the charges, and for the next four years I had to walk around wearing extra makeup and oversized sunglasses to cover up the bumps and bruises. Eventually, I left Terry's sorry ass, but not before I stabbed him in self-defense.

All of that is behind me now, and I had got a good feeling things would be better this time around. Because not only did God have my back, it was just like Big Mama used to always say, *The third times a charm!*

CHAPTER THIRTY-EIGHT

DOMINIQUE

5:18 pm

When I stepped inside of Mommy's hair salon, the usual suspects, D'Lovely and Mimi, were at it again. They were shouting and pointing at one another. Simone was wedged in the middle looking back and forth between them like she was watching a ping-pong match.

"Hey, y'all," I greeted everybody as I wiggled out of my book bag and hung it on the coat rack.

"Hey, Nique-Nique," they greeted me in unison, then took turns giving me a hug.

I looked at Simone and placed my hands on my hips.

"Girl, what are these black folks in here arguing about?"

"Kanye and Amber Rose," she replied with a devious smile. "It's starting to get good, too. You came just in time."

"Ahn-ahn, this shit ain't starting to get good, it's starting to get *ree-al*!" D'Lovely boasted, looking me square in the eyes. "This chick," he pointed at Mimi, "got the nerve to be calling me a liar, talking about Amber Rose ain't one of my homegirls from back in the day. Dat ass is from South Philly, right around the corner from my grand mammie's house. Me and this bitch been kicking it since the fifth grade. And to take it a step further, *I'm* the one who told the bitch to chop her hair off and dye the rest blonde. Mimi better ask somebody."

"Umm-hmm, that's what'cho mouth say," Mimi shot back, shaking her head in disbelief. "Just because you might'a knew the bitch back in the day, doesn't mean that you know the bitch now. And she for *damn sure* ain't tell you nothing about sticking her fingers in Kanyé's buns. Ya flamin' ass is always exaggerating sum'n."

"And how the hell would you know?" D'Lovely glared at her. "You don't know what my gurl told me when she kicked his undercover ass to the curb. So, don't even go there, Mimi. Do *not* the fuck do it."

"Yes, I do know," Mimi insisted. "Because the bitch is restricted from talking about the details of their sex life. I saw the shit on E! News. They were basically saying that Kanyé cut her a check to keep quiet."

"Umm-hmm." D'Lovely pursed his lips and rolled his eyes. "Black folks is always talking about some goddamned 'they'. *They* said this, and *they* said that. But never wanna tell you who the fuck is *they*. So, who the fuck is 'they', Mimi? Who the fuck is 'they'?"

"*E! News!*" Mimi shouted in his face. "Ain't that what the hell I just said?"

"Chil' please," D'Lovely said with a smile. "And assuming what you're saying is true, then why would a grown-ass man payoff his ex to keep quiet about their sex life? Riddle me that, Mimi. Riddle me that."

"I don't know," Mimi replied, shrugging her shoulders. "Maybe was packing a little peter or sum'n. How the hell should I know?"

"Umm-hmm." D'Lovely continued smiling, then he used his left hand to fan himself. "It just goes to prove my point. That nigga was hiding sum'n...*in his ass*! Hashtag-fingers in the booty!"

Me and Simone fell out laughing. D'Lovely was funny as hell, always saying something crazy.

"So, Miss Nique-Nique," D'Lovely said in a sing-song voice, "how was your day?"

"It was okay," I said.

"Did you meet any cute boys?" He gave me a wink.

"Did I meet any cute boys?" I looked at him sideways, releasing a nervous laugh. "D'Lovely, if you don't gawn and get somewhere."

"*Whaaaat?*" He placed his hands over his heart. "Miss D'Lovely was a lil' mama once. I know what time it is."

"Boy, bye." I laughed at him and playfully punched him on the shoulder. "So, where's Mommy? Is she back in her office?"

194

"Umm-hmm," D'Lovely said as he returned to his salon chair. "She's back there with Giovanni doing only *Gawd* knows what. Now, let the church say amen."

"Boy, shut up!" Mimi laughed at him and pushed the back of his head. "Giovanni ain't even back there. He left about fifteen minutes ago."

"Oh, hell to the nawl!" D'Lovely said, as he reached up and smoothed out the back of his finger waves. Scowling at Mimi, he said, "Heifer, I know good and the fuck well ... them lil' chocolate wedges you call fingers did *not*...just touch Miss D'Lovely's 'do. Gurl, get'cho life! Everybody and they mama know better than to be touching Miss D'Lovely's 'do. But nooooooo, ya lil' chunky ass just had to go against the grain."

Me and Simone burst out laughing, and Mimi shot us the look of death. Squinting her eyes at Simone, she said, "*Simone*, out of all people, I know ya stupid ass is not over there the fuck laughing. Ain't you the same one who got fired from the M&M factory for throwing away all the W's?"

"So, what." Simone pouted. "From the way I was looking at 'em, I really thought they was printed upside down. I didn't they were M's."

"Ahn-ahn, y'all, I can't!" I said, as I raised my hands in defeat. "I'ma get back with y'all later. I need to go in the back to check in with Mommy."

When I reached the back of the salon and peeked my head inside of Mommy's office, I noticed she was talking on her iPhone. I started to walk away to give her some privacy, but she gestured for me to come inside. I sat down across from her and looked at her face. I was thinking to myself, *how can a woman so beautiful, treat the father of her only child so ugly?*

I loved Mommy to death, but I hated the way she treated my daddy. I also resented the fact that she kept me away from him for so long. Like ten whole years, though? Really?

"So, what's up, diva? How was your weekend?" Mommy asked me, after she disconnected her call.

"It was okay," I spoke somberly, thinking about Daddy when I said it. This was the first time Mommy and me spoke since last Friday, when Daddy came to pick me up.

"Just okay?" She looked at me with a raised brow. "Usually, you're full of energy and floating on Cloud Nine whenever you return home from one of your weekend visits. And now you're telling me it was just okay? Did Zion do something to piss you off? 'Cause if he did, you know I ain't got no problem cussing his ass out."

"Mommy, you can't keep doing that. That's not cool."

"Doing what?" she asked me. "And what's not cool?"

"Talking down on my daddy, and treating him like trash whenever he comes around. That's not cool, Mommy. That's not cool, at all."

"Well, excuse the fuck outta me!" Mommy snapped her neck and rolled her eyes. "You're acting like that motherfucker doesn't talk bad about me."

"He doesn't," I quickly defended Daddy. "Not around me, anyway. He respects me too much to speak bad about my mother."

"So, what are you saying, Dominique?" She raised her voice and leaned in across the desk. "Are you saying that *I*," she pointed at herself, "the one who took care of you while that jailbird was locked in a cell, doesn't respect you? Is that what you're telling me?"

"No, Mommy, that's not what I'm saying," I spoke calm, even though she had her finger pointed in my face. "All I'm saying is that my daddy's a good man, a *king*, and he doesn't deserve to be treated this way. I just think you need to lay off him a bit."

"You know what, Dominique?" She still had her finger pointed in my face. "Maybe what I need to do is put an end to you and Zion's little weekend getaways. Maybe that's what the fuck I need to do, since ya lil' grown ass got the nerve to be telling me what I *need* to do."

I took a deep breath and sighed.

"Listen, Mommy, I'm not a little girl anymore. I'm sixteen now. And to be totally honest, there's nothing you can do to keep me away from my daddy. It's not happening."

"Oh, is that right?"

"Yes, Mommy, it is. Because I'm not—"

Slap!

Her right hand landed across my face, and my cheek went numb. I couldn't believe she smacked me. I was so angry that my hands began trembling. I wanted to smack her ass back, but I didn't. I was thinking about Daddy, knowing he'd be upset if I raised my hands to my mother.

"Ahn-ahn, now what the fuck is you standing up for?" Mommy shouted, as I hopped up on my feet. "I know ya lil' ass ain't try'na get buck!"

I started to say something that would knock her off her high horse, but I kept it to myself. Because once again, I was thinking about Daddy.

"Where the fuck is you going, Dominique?"

I didn't reply, I just kept on walking. I couldn't take it anymore. I was going to go live with my daddy.

Askari

CHAPTER THIRTY-NINE

ZION

5:48 pm

I was sitting behind my desk at the rec center, listening to *Keep Ya Head Up* by Tupac. Listening to Pac was a coping mechanism I developed while spending my time in prison. His lyrics were so real, and I found them to be a great source of motivation, especially during the times I was stagnated and mentally exhausted. It still amazed me that Pac was only twenty-five when those cowards took him away. My brotha was a *KING*; a true warrior in every sense of the word. Sometimes I sit back and wonder how my beloved brotha would have addressed the issues of today's America. I could see him now...determined and proud, fist to the sky, shouting: "*Black Power*!" While at the same time, admiring the younger generation for their dedication and fearlessness; their palms in the air and shouting at the top of their lungs, "*Black Lives Matter*!"

Sadly, a lot of us don't even realize that with the death of Tupac Shakur, we were robbed of one of our most precious jewels, maybe even the Malcolm X or the MLK of my generation. I mean, look at it like this:

If Brotha Malcolm would have died at the age of twenty-five, he would have only been a hustler on the streets of Harlem. And if MLK would have died at the age of twenty-five, he would have only been a Baptist minister. So, you can only imagine what Pac would have become.

Even now, in 2015, almost twenty years after his demise, can you imagine the powerful voice he would have been for our people? Can you imagine the type of educator and motivational speaker he would have been? Trust me, we lost something very special. Just listen to what he said about honoring and uplifting the black woman, telling us brothas that because of *her*, we *are*:

"*And since we all came from a woman, got our name from a woman, and our game from a woman. I wonder why we take from our women, why we rape our women, do we hate our women? I think it's time we kill for our women, time we heal our women, be real to our women. 'Cause if we don't, we'll have a race of babies that will hate the ladies and make the babies. And since a man can't make one, he has no right to tell a woman when and where to create one. So, will the real men get up? I know you're fed up, ladies. But keep ya head up."*

As I sat behind my desk nodding my head to the music, I heard a knock at the door. I looked up and saw Tone Boy standing outside in the hallway. He was wearing a gray hoody, black jeans and a red Phillies fitted.

"Brotha Zee," he greeted me with a smile. "You told me to come holla at'chu, so what's up?"

I turned the music down and stood to my feet.

"Come in, lil' brotha. Have a seat."

Tone Boy stepped inside of my office, and we shook hands firmly.

"This is about Nique-Nique, isn't it?" Tone Boy asked, then he sat down in the chair beside my desk.

"Most definitely," I replied while returning to my seat. "The two of you have become quite close, and I was wondering what your intentions are."

"My intentions?" He bit down on his bottom lip and began cracking his knuckles. "I'm not exactly sure what'chu mean."

"I'ma put it like this, how do you see my daughter? Do you see her as just another girl, or do you see her as someone special?"

"I consider Dominique to be someone special," he replied without hesitation, not once breaking eye contact.

"Oh, yeah?" I leaned back in my chair and caressed my goatee. "Special in what way?"

"You know, she's different from the other girls." He flashed me a bashful smile.

"Different? Different, how? What makes Dominique so different?" I was pressing hard, loving the sight of Tone Boy squirming in his seat.

"Well, for starters, she's smarter than most of the girls I know. She's beautiful and funny. She has a good heart and she's always encouraging me to follow my dreams as a rapper. I can talk to Dominique about anything, and she can do the same with me. Basically, she's a good person. I really like her."

I was satisfied with Tone Boy's response, but still I dug deeper. Why? Because as black men, one of the many things we lost during slavery was taking charge of our woman. We've been conditioned, subconsciously, to allow any man, whether he's fit for the task or not, to enter his way into our bloodline through our women. This was something I refused to do. I needed a generation of kings, not peasants. Kings produce kings, and peasants produce peasants. My daughter deserved a king.

"So, lemme ask you something, and please don't take it the wrong way."

"I won't."

"Are you sexually active?" I got right to it. "With Dominique, or anyone else for that matter?"

"Yes, sir, I am." Tone Boy lowered his head. "But not with Dominique," he quickly added, returning his gaze to mines. "She's still a virgin, and that's one of the things I love about her. Most of the girls my age are different when it comes to that. I'm not looking down on them, or anything like that. It's just, you know, when I get married, I want my wife to know me and only me in that particular way."

I was born at night, but not *last night*. So, I knew that nine times out of ten, Tone Boy was lying through his teeth. I would love to think that my sixteen-year-old daughter was still a virgin, but chances are that simply wasn't the case.

"So, you're saying that one day, you could see yourself marrying Dominique?" I asked him with a cautionary raised brow.

"Absolutely." Tone Boy smiled. "When the time's right, and with your blessing, of course."

"But you and Dominique are only sixteen," I reminded him. "In the next couple of years, the two of you will be going off to college. You'll be meeting new people and experiencing new things. So, how can you be so sure that your feelings for Dominique won't change?"

"Well, this is something that me and Nique-Nique already talked about. We've decided that we're both going to Temple. So that way, we can still be close to home, and be close to one another at the same time."

I sat there quietly, carefully absorbing the words that were coming out of his mouth. I liked Tone Boy a lot, and I couldn't think of a better prince for my princess.

"I'll tell you what," I looked Tone Boy square in his eyes, "as long as you continue to respect Dominique and treat her like the beautiful black queen she is, I have no problems with the two of y'all being together. I trust you, and I trust Dominique. I also trust that both of y'all are responsible enough to nurture a healthy relationship. I just want y'all to slow down a bit, you know? And not rush things."

"That's what's up, Brotha Zee," Tone Boy said with a smile. "And I promise not to let you down."

As I reached across the desk to shake Tone Boy's hand, I was taken by surprise when a female voice began screaming my name.

"Brotha Zee! Brotha Atiba! Somebody help me, *please!*"

Tone Boy and me looked at one another, then we dashed out of my office. The first thing I noticed was Haneefah, one of the little sistas who attended the rec center. She was standing at the entrance screaming and crying. The front of her Hollister jacket was covered in blood.

"Haneefah, what's wrong? What happened to you?" I shouted back, as I ran down the hallway towards her. "Are you okay? Did somebody hurt you?"

"No!" she cried out, fervently shaking her head. "It's not me, it's Shyheem! He just got shot!"

I brushed past her and ran outside. I was looking around for Shyheem, but I didn't see him. "Haneefah, where is he?"

"He's around the corner, laid out in front of Gratz!" Haneefah replied, then she took off running. "Brotha Zee, come on! We gotta help him!"

"Zee, what's going on out here?" Atiba asked when he emerged from the building. "I was sitting in my office, and I heard someone screaming."

"It's Shyheem," I told him, as I took off running behind Haneefah. "He just got shot."

Askari

CHAPTER FORTY

ZION

A large crowd of spectators were gathered in front of the Simon Gratz high school. There were so many, it was virtually impossible for me to get a visual of Shyheem. Some of the spectators were crying, some whispering to one another and pointing, and some were just standing around recording with their cell phones.

"Please, everybody just back up and give us some room!" I shouted as Atiba and me made our way through the crowd. "Come on, y'all, back up!"

The large crowd parted down the middle, and I immediately spotted Michael, another kid who I knew from the rec center. He was crouched down beside Shyheem, squeezing his hand and coaching him to fight.

"Brotha Zee!" Michael shouted when he saw me running towards him. "We gotta hurry up and get him to the hospital! I'm not sure if he's gonna make it!"

"Michael, I need you to back up," I said, then I knelt down beside Shyheem.

The little brotha was doing bad. His gray, Nautica sweatshirt was soaked in his own blood, and burgundy air bubbles were sprouting out from the four or five bullet holes that peppered the front of his chest. He was laying on his back and looking at me with glossy, wet, horrified eyes.

"Broth—Brotha Zee," Shyheem panted. "Don't—Don't let me die."

He coughed up a thick wad of burgundy goop, and a deep guttural sound bellowed from the depths of his lungs.

"Stop talking, Shy. Just take it easy and stay calm," I consoled him. I could see he was struggling to breathe, so I rolled him on his side.

"Michael, did anybody call 911?"

"Yeah," Michael replied. He was shuffling from side to side and nervously biting down on his fingernails. "I called them about five minutes ago, right after it happened."

"Does anybody have a car?" I shouted at the crowd. "We need to get him to the hospital. *Now!*"

Nobody offered a response, so I dug down inside of my pocket and pulled out the keys to my Rover. "Here." I tossed the keys to Atiba. "Run back and grab my truck from the rec. We gotta get the little brotha some help."

I looked up at Michael, as Atiba took off running.

"What the hell happened? Who did this to him?"

"It was Reakwon," Michael blurted back. "Shyheem stepped on his Jays, and Raekwon shot him."

"*A pair of sneakers?*" I asked him with a creased brow. "Raekwon shot this brotha over some goddamned sneakers?" I looked down at Shyheem and saw the blood gushing from the four exit wounds on his back.

"Yeah." Michael nodded his head. "Raekwon's crazy as shit. He's always talking about clapping somebody, and he finally did it."

"But—But what happened?" I asked him, then I looked back down at Shyheem.

"We were on our way to the rec, me, Shyheem and Haneefah, and that's when we bumped into Raekwon. He was hanging out with some of his boys from Haines Street. Shyheem stepped on his Jordan's by mistake, and Raekwon went crazy. He pulled out a gun and demanded that Shyheem get down on his knees and lick away the scuff mark. Shyheem wouldn't do it, and that's when Raekwon started shooting."

I looked up and saw Atiba running towards us.

"Come on, Zee. Let's get him over to the truck."

I grabbed Shyheem under his shoulders, and Atiba grabbed by his ankles. We lifted his body, but then quickly put him down when a gut-wrenching, snarling-like sound escaped his lungs. A thick clump of gooey, dark blood sprang from his mouth and his head lollied to the side. I looked at Atiba, and shook my head slowly.

206

Shyheem was gone.

A deathly silence hung in the air, and then all of a sudden, I heard the bone-chilling wails of a woman screaming. It was Barbie, Shyheem's mother and a childhood friend of mines.

"*Ahn-ahn, no! Not my baby, no!*" Barbie screamed, as she ran up on us. "*Not my Shyheem! Lord, no!*" Barbie rushed me with a barrage of wild punches, and I covered my head with both hands. I didn't even try to stop her.

"*Get away from my baby, Zion! Get'cha ass away!*"

After pushing me out the way, Barbie dropped to her knees and then wrapped her arms around Shyheem. His lifeless eyes were locked wide open, and his bloody body was stiff and limp. His blank expression remained the same as Barbie pressed his face against her bosom.

"*Lord Jesus, please?*" Barbie yelped, as she looked up at the sky. "*Not my baby, Lord. Not my Shyheem! Give him back! Give him back to me, Lord! Please?*"

It felt like someone had stabbed me in the heart, so I could only imagine what Barbie must have been feeling. Struggling to hold my tears back, I reached out and wrapped her in my arms. There was nothing I could say or do to stop Barbie's pain, so I squeezed her tight and gently rocked her from side to side.

"This—This is all your fault," Barbie sobbed, then she pushed me away. "I trusted you, Zion. I trusted you to look after my son, and look what happened. My baby's gone, Zion. My Shyheem is gone."

A lump formed in the back of my throat, and a brisk chill ran down the length of my spine. The same way I approached Barbie when I first came home from prison, was the same way that I approached Raekwon's mother. I requested that both sistas allow me to be a mentor to their teenaged sons. These sistas trusted me. They gave me free reign to step in and be a father figure to their sons, as they came into their own as young, black men, but somewhere along the line I dropped the ball. Shyheem's blood was on my hands, *literally*, and Raekwon's impending jail sentence was something that I was all too familiar with. So, when Barbie called me out, accusing me of being responsible, I couldn't help but to wonder if the sista was right.

Was I responsible?

CHAPTER FORTY-ONE

JABARI

6:24 pm

When I stepped inside of the house, I could tell from the gun bust that Ma' Dukes was in a good mood. The aroma of my favorite meal smacked me dead in the face, and the sounds of Fantasia were bumping from the sound system in the living room. I slipped out of my Balenciaga's and sat 'em beside the front door. Ma' Dukes was just like Big Mama, she'd dig in ya ass about wearing shoes inside of the house. That was one of the effects from growing up in the projects. You never knew what type of filth you stepped in while walking down the hallway or riding the elevator. So, whenever you stepped in the crib, it was mandatory that all shoes be checked in at that door.

Damn, that grub smells good! I followed my nose to the kitchen.

"Sup, Ma what's good?" I asked while sliding up beside her. She was standing at the stove, bopping from side to side, and sipping on a glass of white wine. I wrapped my arms around her and kissed the top of her head.

"Oh, hey, baby!" She looked up at me and smiled. "I'm fixing you and Yatta's favorite: baked ziti and Big Mama's cheddar biscuits."

"I already know. I smelled 'em the second I stepped in the house. So, how was your day?"

"*My day?*" She smiled at me, and pointed at herself. "It was off the shiz-nah-eezy!"

"Off the *what*?" I cracked a smile and then grabbed one of the biscuits from the sheet pan laying on the stove.

"Well, isn't that the way y'all be saying it?" She nodded her head, then began moving her hands like a rapper spitting a verse. "Off the shiz-nah-eezy?"

"Aye, yo, cool out, though," I told her while shaking my head. "First of all, I'm way too old for my mom's to be talking like Lil' Scrappy. And secondly, what was so special about your day that made it *off the shiz-nah-eezy*?" I laughed at her, using my fingers to indicate quotation marks.

Clearly feeling herself, she gon' look me up and down.

"Humph, well wouldn't you like to know."

"Yeah, a'ight." I laughed at her. "Whatever that's supposed to mean. So, what's up wit' Yatta? Where is he?"

"He's out back feeding the dog."

"A'ight, I'ma go out there and check on him."

"Umm-hmm." She nodded her head, and then took another sip of wine. "And you tell him I said to get his butt back in here, so he can wash up and get ready for dinner. It's almost time to eat."

"Fa'sho."

After slipping on the old pair of Timbs that I kept beside the patio door, I stepped outside into the chilly November weather. Looking across the yard, I spotted Kenyatta. He was down on his knees, leaned forward and reaching into the dog house. Our pit bull, Red Man, was standing beside him wagging his tail.

Fuck is he reaching in the dog house for?

"Yatta, what'chu over there doing?" I asked him, as I stepped down from the patio. Kenyatta backed out of the dog house and spun around quickly. "Fuck is you in there doing?" I looked at him suspiciously.

"Who? Me? Oh...ah, ah, nothing."

Red Man ran up on me, but before he had the chance to jump up and put his dirty paws on my Moncler sweater, I cocked my fist back and he stopped in his tracks. His stupid ass knew better than to be jumping on people, especially me. The last time he tried, I knocked his ass out with a vicious right hook.

Returning my attention to Kenyatta, I said, "What'chu digging in the dog house for? You was hiding sum'n?"

"Nah-ahn." He shook his head *no*. "I thought I saw a rabbit."

I could tell his lil' ass was lying, so I called his bluff.

"Nigga, that's bullshit. Ya ass was in there hiding sum'n."

210

"Nah-ahn, Jabby. I wasn't hiding nothing."

"So, what'chu looking all suspect for?" I asked him with my eyelids squinted. "You better tell me what'chu was hiding. 'Cause if you don't, and I get myself dirty try'na find out what it is, I'ma *bust* ya lil' ass. Now, tell me what the fuck it was."

"But Jabby, I wasn't' hiding nothing. I thought I saw a rabbit, I swear. "

"Go, stand over there by the patio. And you better not move."

"But, Jabby."

"Don't make me say it again!"

Kenyatta began crying, so I knew for a fact that he was up to some bullshit. I moved over to the dog house, then I looked back at my brother. He was crying and biting his nails.

Yo, what the fuck he was doing in here?

I bent down in front of the dog house, but just as I stuck my hand inside, Ma' Dukes began shouting my name. Not my first name, but my *full name*. So, if you grew up in the hood with a black mom, then you know that could've only meant one thing…*trouble*!

"Jabari Maleek James, Junior! Boy, you better ya ass in this goddamned house!"

I looked down at Kenyatta, and he quickly looked away.

"Don't just stand there looking stupid." I pointed at the patio door. "Get'cha ass in the house. We gon' deal wit' this shit later."

Askari

CHAPTER FORTY-TWO

JABARI

"Ma, what's going on?" I called out, as me and Kenyatta entered the house through the patio door. I slipped out of my boots and looked around the kitchen, but I didn't see her. "Yo, Ma, where you at?"

"I'm in the living room!" she lashed out. "You get'cha ass in here! *Right now!*"

What the fuck is wrong wit' her? I asked myself, as I took off walking. *She was cooler than a fan just a few minutes ago. So, why is she so mad all of a sudden?*

My questions were answered the second I stepped into the living room. Ma' Dukes was standing there talking to Shameeka and her parents, so right away I knew what it was. I looked at Shameeka, but she lowered her head, refusing to meet my gaze. She reminded me of a scared, little girl who had just finished crying. Her moms was standing right beside her, and her pops was leaned against the door. His arms were folded across his chest, and his usual pale face had a flush red tint. He and his wife were both looking at me.

"So, what's this I'm hearing about you getting this girl pregnant?" Ma' Dukes asked, as she turned around to face me. "Is this true?"

I looked at Shameeka and caught her staring at me. Her beautiful eyes were begging me to forgive her for throwing me under the bus.

"Boy, you better answer me," Ma' Dukes demanded. She sat her wine glass on the coffee table, looking at me like she was ready to pop off.

"I 'on't know." I shrugged my shoulders. "I mean, I guess it's possible."

"You don't know?" Shameeka's moms asked me. "*You guess?* Well, what exactly are saying, young man? Are you calling my daughter a hoe?"

"No, ma'am. Not at all," I quickly replied.

"Well, then what *are* you saying?" Shameeka's pops interjected. "Because it sure as hell sounds like you're calling my daughter promiscuous."

"No, sir. What I'm trying to say is that I don't know. Me and Shameeka wasn't exclusive. She was free to do her thing, and I was free to do mines. So, for all I know, she could have been seeing somebody else."

"*Jabari*?" Shameeka whined. "How could you say something like that?"

"Because it's true, Shameeka. It's not like we were together. We were kicking it, and that's it."

"But, Jabari," Shameeka cried, "I was loyal to you. I loved you, and I still do. And you're really going to stand here and treat me like this?"

"Shorty, I ain't treating you like nothing. All I'm saying is that we weren't together like that."

"Oh my God, Jabari, this is wrong. This is so wrong!"

"Shameeka, you stop that crying," her moms scolded her. "You stop it, right this second."

"But, Mommy, I love him!"

"I don't care," her moms shot back. "This boy is beneath you. I've told you before about slumming it with these no good city boys."

"Wait. What?" Ma' Dukes got up in her grill. "I know good and goddamned well ya lil' bougie ass ain't just say that your daughter was better than my son?"

Shameeka's moms popped fly. "Well, if the shoe fits..."

"*Oh-hell-to-the-muthafucking-nizzaw!*" Ma' Dukes snapped out. She slipped out of her house shoes and pulled off her earrings. "Bitch, I'm from Richard Allen, born, bred and muthafuckin' raised! I will draaaag yo' ass!"

"Oh, yeah?" Shameeka's moms tried to get buck. "I'm the goddamned district attorney. So, you go ahead and do it. Your little ghetto ass will be locked up so goddamned fast, you won't even know what hit you! So, you go ahead and do it. You fucking touch me!"

Ma' Dukes cocked her hand back and attempted to swing, but I grabbed her by the arm. I was afraid that Shameeka's mom would make good on her promise, so I pulled Ma' Dukes back and held her close to me.

"Get off me, Jabari! Get the fuck off me!" Ma 'Dukes struggled against my strength. "I'ma stomp the bones out this bitch! Ol' bougie-ass bitch! Coming up in my house like she Michelle Obama or some-goddmaned-body! Talking shit! *Jabari, lemme go!*"

"Jabari, you better hold onto ya mammie," Shameeka's moms instigated with a smile. "She touches one hair on my goddamned head, *one* and she's fucking out of here. *Gone!* You'll be driving upstate to visit her at Muncy."

"Bitch, ya ass ain't all that!" Ma' Dukes shouted, still struggling to break free. "Wit'cha smutt-ass daughter that lil' bitch ain't nothing but a thot monster waiting to happen!" She kicked her foot at Shameeka's moms, and then wailed on me because I wouldn't release her. "Jabari—let me—*go!*"

"Yo, Shameeka, get'cha fuckin' peoples!" I shouted at her. "You see me try'na hold her back! Get'cha peoples and roll the fuck out!"

"Calm down, young man, there's no need to be bent out shape," Shameeka's moms said to me, still smiling. "And by the way, did you tell your mother that you're expecting ghetto twins?"

"*Ghetto twins?*" Ma' Dukes stopped struggling, then she looked up at me for an explanation. "What the fuck is this bitch talking about?"

"This *bitch*," Shameeka's moms popped her neck, "is referring to the second young lady your son impregnated like a stray dog roaming the streets. Umm-hmm, that's right," she continued smiling as she headed towards the door. "Mr. Basketball Star is about to have his hands full. So, if I were you, I'd be teaching him how to balance a checkbook."

"Yo, *Shameeka?*" I flipped out. "Get'cha drawin' ass moms, dawg! Fuck is you doing?"

Shameeka's pops rolled up his sleeves and began cracking his knuckles. "You're not getting away with this, you little punk."

215

"Aye, yo, ol' head, if you don't sit'cha lil' white ass down somewhere."

"Come on, Daddy, let's go," Shameeka said as she grabbed the back of his shirt. "He's not even worth it."

"I'll be seeing your ass again," he threatened while looking me in the eyes. He was stretching his arms and bopping around, fronting like he wanted some smoke. I assumed it was a pride thing, because he *had* to know he wasn't fucking with me. "This shit isn't over, pal. It isn't over by a long shot."

"Whatever, fam. Get the fuck outta my house."

When the door close behind them, I released my hold on Ma' Dukes and she wasted no time giving me the grind up.

"Goddamnit, Jabari? What the hell is wrong with you?" she asked me with tears in her eyes. "Whatever happened to wearing condoms? At the very least, you should have been smart enough to protect yourself."

"I do be wearing condoms. It's just that sometimes, I be finding myself caught in the moment. And even then, I still be pulling out."

"*Pulling out*?" She looked at me like I was stupid. "How the hell is that supposed to stop you from catching a disease?"

"Come on, Ma, it's not even like that."

"What is it like then, Jabari? Because I'm telling you now, that House In Virginia, that *HIV*, it's not a goddamned game!"

"Dang, Jabby. You got *two* girls pregnant?" Kenyatta asked me with a stupid-ass grin on his face. "Dang, bro. You was knocking 'em down, huh?"

"Yo, take ya lil' ass upstairs!" I snapped at him.

"For what?" Kenyatta shrugged his shoulders. "I already heard everything that y'all was talking about."

"Boy, you better take ya ass up them goddamned stairs!" Ma' Dukes spazzed on him. "*Now!*"

"Dang, man, always try'na treat somebody like a baby," Kenyatta complained as he ran up the stairs.

"You keep on running that mouth of yours, and I'ma *bust it*!" Ma' Dukes shouted from the bottom of the stairs. "Do you see what I'm talking about?" She returned her gaze to me. "The more you

216

don't listen, the more Kenyatta does the same. You're supposed to be setting a positive example around here."

"A'ight, Ma, I apologize." I raised my hands in defeat. "But I'm telling you the truth. Even though I wasn't wearing a condom, I was still pulling out. So, who's to say I'm the one who got 'em pregnant?"

"Boy, you just don't get it," she chuckled with a sarcastic disbelief. "You really don't get it."

"Get what? What is it that I don't get?"

"You know what, Jabari? Get the fuck outta my face. I can't even stand to look at you right now."

She stormed off towards the kitchen and left me standing there in silence. I started to follow her, but I didn't. I knew it was better to give her some time to cool off, so I slipped my shoes back on and headed out the door.

I was on my way to go kick it with Tonya.

Askari

CHAPTER FORTY-THREE

ZION

8:27 pm

After spending the past two hours with Barbie and her family, I decided to head home and call it a night. I was mentally exhausted, and emotionally at a stalemate.

When I came home from prison, my goal was to show the next generation a better way. I wanted to instill in them a sense of hope and a sense of pride, and encourage them to love themselves and to love one another. I wanted them to know, understand and appreciate their history, and give them the motivation to never allow that cruel history to repeat itself.

Unfortunately, what I didn't realize is that our younger generation had become so disconnected with themselves. The complexity of the hood was something that I no longer recognized. Even in my past life as a young hustla, wild and reckless, when it came to my hood, I still had a sense of responsibility. It was a misguided one, but a sense of responsibility, nonetheless.

The OG's who came before me emphasized the importance of looking after and taking care of the hood. They even put together an unwritten code of ethics for the hustlers of my generation to follow: *no selling drugs in school zones; no selling drugs in, or around playgrounds; no shootouts during the day time hours; the neighborhood had to be kept clean; the elderly had to be respected and taken care of; ten percent of all profits were set aside for free lunch and after-school programs; and by all means, little boys were restricted from playing grown men games.*

These unwritten rules from the 60's and 70's were no longer existent, and *"The Game"* as we once called it was essentially over. What we see today are only the remnants, something that I often referred to as the *Shadows of the Game*.

In the days of my father and the hustlers before him, it was essentially unheard of for a young brotha, like Raekwon, to be carrying a gun. Why? Because the older brothas would have checked him—*quick*. They would have taken the gun, kicked him in the ass, and then sent him home crying to his mother. So, despite the fact the OG's from the 60's and 70's were doing dirt themselves, they still understood and recognized their responsibility to educate and cultivate the next generation. But somewhere along the line— more than likely the crack era of the 80's—the brothas of my generation threw our younger brothas to the wolves.

There's a Shyheem and a Raekwon in every hood in America, and from the time they were old enough to walk and talk we've been telling them: *"Boy, you better stop crying and be a man,"* or *"Boy, you better man up"*. But what we never took the time to teach them what being a *man* actually meant. Consequently, our next generation of young black men were forced to figure it out on their own, mistakenly believing the accumulation of material items defined their manhood.

The concepts of being a good son, a good husband and a good father was replaced by a lust for fast cars and flashy jewelry. The protection and provision of the black woman and child was replaced by a fetish for sneakers and clothes. And the responsibility to educate and cultivate our young was replaced by a desire for money and power.

This was the case with Shyheem and Raekwon. When Shyheem stepped on Raekwon's Jordan's, he wasn't just stepping on a pair of sneakers, he was stepping on something that Raekwon considered to be an extension of his manhood. As a result, Raekwon, being misinformed, was willing to defend his *manhood* at any and all cost.

So, as black men, *original men*, how do we respond when tragedies such as these continue to plague our communities? Do we sit back, point our fingers and condemn? Or do we take responsibility for what *we*—grandfathers, fathers, uncles—*didn't do* to prevent a young brotha from looking in a mirror, pulling a gun and killing his own reflection? Do we realize that we're failing these young brothas by neglecting to teach them what it truly means to be a man? Or better yet, do we even know the definition ourselves?

CHAPTER FORTY-FOUR

ZION

When I turned off of Stenton Avenue and cruised down my block, I noticed that Felicia and Giovanni were standing on the step of my walkway, and a Philadelphia police officer was knocking on my front door. His blue and white squad car was parked in front of my neighbor's house, and Felicia's Maserati was parked across the street. I pulled over and climbed out of my Rover, nervous as hell. I was thinking the worst, and praying that Dominique was okay. I looked at Felicia, hoping to get an answer, but she was already screaming at me and pointing.

"There he go! That's him right there! Now, take his black ass to jail!" She began running towards me, but Giovanni grabbed her by the waist. "Giovanni, lemme go!" She was twisting and pulling. "That motherfucker stole my baby!"

"Felicia, calm down," Giovanni pleaded with her. "Just let the cops handle it."

"Motherfucker, I ain't calming down shit!" Felicia continued screaming and making a scene, acting like she was trying to get at me. "This motherfucker got the nerve to be poisoning my god-damned child? Try'na turn her against me! Fuck that shit! *Giovanni, lemme go!*"

"Are you Zion Tumojawa?" the police officer asked, as he walked over towards me. He was a skinny, white dude with pasty skin and straggly red hair.

"I am," I confirmed with a slight nod, looking back and forth between him and Felicia. "But what's the problem? Is there something wrong with my daughter? Where is she?"

None of this was making any sense, and I was beginning to feel worried. Why was Felicia acting so crazy? Did something happen to Dominique? Did she make it home from school?

The police officer attempted to answer my questions, but before he had the chance, he was rudely interrupted by Felicia's next outburst.

"Didn't I just tell you this motherfucker kidnapped my god-damned daughter?" she screamed in his face. "So, what the hell is you standing there talking for? You 'posed to be taking his black ass to jail!"

"Hold up, I did *what*?" I looked at Felicia like she stole something. "Woman are you crazy?"

"You know what'chu did, motherfucker! You kidnapped my baby, and I'm pressing charges!"

Staring at Felicia, I could see she was under the influence of some type of drug, presumably Perc 30's or Xanax. Her pupils were dilated, and she was moving and talking slower than usual.

"Ma'am, I'm going to need you to calm down," the police officer said to Felicia, giving her a stern look. She calmed down a bit, and he returned his gaze to me. "Alright, sir, now according to the information I've gathered thus far, I *know* you didn't kidnap your daughter." He cut his eye at Felicia when he said it. "Apparently, your daughter and her mother had an argument, and she ran away from home. We have reason to believe that she's here with you?"

"Yes, the fuck he did kidnap her!" Felicia accused. "His black ass ain't got custody of Dominique, *I* do! So, if Dominique's inside of his house without having my permission, I'm pressing charges!"

"Ma'am, I think it'd be best if you returned to your vehicle," the police officer suggested. He was grinding his teeth, and his freckled face was beginning to turn red. "You," he pointed at Giovanni, "I'm going to need you to escort your friend here back to the car. Her irate behavior is making the situation harder than it needs to be."

"Yes, sir." Giovanni nodded his understanding. He grabbed Felicia the arm, but she pushed him away.

"Not the fuck at all, I ain't gotta go nowhere!" Felicia refused. "My tax dollars pay this motherfucker's salary. So therefore, *I'm* the bitch that's calling the shots! That shit ain't the other way around!"

"*Ma'am*?" the police officer raised his voice, then he whipped out his handcuffs. "If I've gotta say it one more time..."

Felicia scowled at me, and then stomped off back to her car.

"Alright, now what's going on with my daughter? You said she ran away from home?"

"Well, that's according to what I've gathered so far. Your daughter and her mother had a disagreement of some sort, and she took off. We're assuming she's here with you."

"Well, all of this is news to me," I explained while looking the officer square in his eyes. "I'm just now coming home from work, and the last time I seen Dominique was when I dropped her off at school this morning. So, if for any reason she *is* inside of the house, then I'm just now knowing about it."

"I figured as much," the police officer replied while returning his handcuffs to the latch on his belt. "But at the same time, the lady does have a valid complaint. According to Miss Diaz," he nodded at Felicia, "she's been awarded full custody of your daughter. So technically, if your daughter's in there, this could present a major problem. I'm not try'na be a dick, I'm just being honest wit'cha."

"And I appreciate that. But it's just like I told you, I'm just now coming home from work, and I'm not even sure if Dominique's here. So, if you want, we can go inside and take a look around?"

"That would be great," the police officer said as he followed me to the front door. When we stepped inside of the house, the first thing we saw was Dominique. She was stretched out on my leather sofa, sound asleep.

Askari

CHAPTER FORTY-FIVE

DOMINIQUE

"Nique-Nique?"

I was knocked out on the sofa when I heard Daddy calling me. I could feel his hand caressing my back, and then gently nudging my shoulder.

"Come on, Nique-Nique, you gotta get up. Did you hear me, Princess? I said you gotta wake up."

When I opened my eyes and caught a glimpse of the police officer standing beside the door, I damn near lost my mind. I hopped up from the sofa and bear-hugged Daddy. I was having flashbacks of the night they took him away from me.

"No! You can't take him!" I shouted at the police officer. "Not again, I won't let you!"

Daddy wrapped me in his arms, and he held me tightly. I squeezed him tighter, and he squeezed me back. The police officer just stood there staring at us.

"Everything's okay, Princess. I'm not going anywhere," Daddy whispered in my ear.

"Daddy, you can't leave me," I begged him. I was crying hysterically and squeezing around his waist. "I can't lose you, Daddy. Not again, I can't."

"Princess, you can never lose me," Daddy cooed in my ear, then he kissed me on the forehead. "I'm not going anywhere, I promise."

"Well, then what is he here for?" I pointed at the police officer. "And why is he bothering us?"

"It's your mother," Daddy told me in a soft voice, then he kissed me once again. "She called the police and reported you missing. She said you ran away from home."

"I did, Daddy. I did run away from home," I admitted, while looking up into his soft brown eyes. "I wanted to stay with you, Daddy. I belong here with you. You're my everything."

Tears began welling at the rims of Daddy's eyes, as he bit down on his bottom lip. Taking a deep breath, he said, "And I belong with you, Princess. But unfortunately, that's not the case right now. You're still a minor, and your mother has full custody of you. I wish there was something that I could do, but for right now my hands are tied. I'm sorry."

"You're goddamned right, you're sorry!" Mommy bellowed from the doorway. She was ice-grilling Daddy, and Giovanni was holding her by the waist. I was completely shocked. I had no idea they were standing outside on the porch. Mommy looked at me and folded her arms across her chest.

"Get your shit, Dominique, and let's go."

I shook my head *no*, and then I looked up at Daddy.

"Do something," I begged him. "I don't want to go with her, I wanna stay here with you."

"Over my dead ass body!" Mommy shouted. "Now, for the last time, get your shit and let's go, Dominique! And just so the fuck you know," she looked back at Daddy, "all these lil' weekend getaways, that shit is the fuck over. Ya ass will not be seeing my daughter no goddamned more. And I mean that shit."

Daddy shook his head and sighed. "Whatever, Felicia. If you say so."

"*Motherfucker!*" She charged at Daddy, but Giovanni pulled her back.

"Ma'am!" the police officer shouted. He pulled out his stun gun and aimed the barrel at Mommy's chest. "You try that again, and I will put you down. Do you got that?"

"Anyway." Mommy dismissed him with the flick of her hand. Looking at me, she said, "Bring ya ass, Dominique. Let's get it."

As she spun around and headed out the door, I looked at Daddy and noticed the tears that were trickling down his chocolate face. I had never seen him cry before, and it hurt my soul to see him that way. Completely forgetting about myself and my personal plight, I reached up and wiped his tears away. The roles between us had been reversed. I had become the comforter, and Daddy was the one being comforted.

"Don't worry, Daddy, you'll see me again. Everything gonna be okay, I promise. Because even if she makes good on her threat, I'll be eighteen in two more years."

A new wave of tears were welling at the rims of Daddy's eyes, but I wiped them away before they had a chance to fall.

"Just two more years," I promised him. "Then after that, it'll just be you and me, Daddy. The King and the Princess. Okay?"

Daddy nodded his head and squeezed me tightly. His thick arms were trembling, and I could feel the heat from his body seeping onto mines. I held him for a few more seconds and then stood up on my tippy toes, kissing the tip of his nose. It was the same way I used to do as a little girl.

After telling Daddy how much I loved him and how much he meant to me, I grabbed my belongings from the living room closet. I hugged him once more, and then headed out the door with the police officer right behind me.

When I climbed in the back seat of Mommy's car, I placed my hands to my face and cried like a baby. And when Mommy pulled away, I got up on my knees and looked at Daddy through the back window. He was standing in the middle of the street watching us drive away. His brown eyes locked on mines, and he mouthed the words, *"I love you, Princess. Don't ever forget that."*

I smiled at him and wiped my tears away.

"I won't, Daddy. I won't. Just two more years."

Askari

CHAPTER FORTY-SIX

EBONY

9:16 pm

Thoughts of Jabari ran through my mind as I turned off the shower spigot. I stood there silently, hoping and wishing that my frustrations and disappointments could drip away like the beads of water trailing down my soft, brown skin, from my head to my toes, and then quietly down the drain to a faraway place never to be seen again.

I was so upset with my first born. His decision-making skills were beginning to scare me, and it seemed as though there was nothing I could do to steer him in the right direction.

As a small child, whenever Jabari would act out, all I had to do was give him the *look*. Then later, as a preteen, a couple of whacks from a wooden brush was enough to set him straight. But now that he's eighteen, 6'11 and 258 pounds, what was I supposed to do? *Beat him?*

Mentally exhausted, I stepped out of the shower and grabbed a warm towel from the towel rack beside the door. After wiping myself dry and removing my shower cap, I threw on my bathrobe and headed down the hallway. I needed to sit down and talk to Kenyatta. The father-like influence that Jabari had over my baby was something that I couldn't deny. So, I needed to talk to him and let him know that Jabari's actions were nothing he should mimic or admire.

"Yatta?" I called his name while gently tapping on his bedroom door. I turned the knob, but before I pushed it open, I said, "Baby, you dressed?"

The reason I asked is because the last time I barged inside of his room, I caught him doing what little boys do at the age of thirteen. *I damn near went blind.*

"Yatta?" I called him once again, and then pushed the door open when he didn't respond. Surprisingly, the room was empty. I assumed he was downstairs watching a movie on the big screen, so I walked down the hallway and descended the stairs.

"Kenyatta, I know you're not down here watching TV," I admonished, as I reached the bottom of the stairs. "You know you gotta get up at six in the morning, and it's a quarter after nine. So, if I were you, I'd be taking it down for the night."

When I stepped down into the living room, the TV was showing a rerun of Martin, but Kenyatta was nowhere to be found.

"Kenyatta Lateef James?" I raised my vice to let him know I wasn't fooling around. "Boy, you better get up them stairs and get'cha lil' butt in the bed!"

After checking the dining room, I headed towards the kitchen assuming he was fixing himself a late-night snack. But when I reached the kitchen, it was empty.

Now, where the hell this boy done went to? I asked myself, while standing there scratching my head. *Maybe he's in the garage lifting weights.*

I was just about to check the garage, but then turned my head when I heard Red Man barking. I looked out the sliding glass door that led to the patio, and spotted Kenyatta. The motion detector lights were shining bright, allowing me to get a clear view. He was crouched down in front of the dog house, and Red Man was standing right beside him.

This boy must'a bumped his damn head, out here playing with the dog this late at night.

I tightened the belt on my bathrobe and opened the patio door. The weather had changed dramatically. A blanket of frost covered the back lawn, and the barren branches on the willow trees that surrounded the back yard were swaying to the rhythm of a cool gust. The warm November sun had been replaced by a white, crescent moon, and the calm blue sky had transcended into a purple abyss, sporadically sprinkled with the flickering of bone white stars.

"Kenyatta?" I called his name after sticking my head through the crack in the door. "Just what in the world do you think you're doing?"

Caught off guard, Kenyatta spun around quickly. He was standing about thirty feet away from the house, and had a shiny object clutched in his right hand. He looked at me, and then looked down at the object. Bringing his gaze back to me, he said, "Huh?"

"Boy, don't *huh* me. You heard what I said. You're supposed to be getting ready for bed. And what's that?" I pointed at the shiny object.

He looked back at the dog house, and then looked down at the shiny object. Shrugging his shoulders, he said, "Nothing, Ma. It's nothing."

"Oh, yeah?" I opened the glass door a little bit wider. "Well, bring nothing here, so I can see what it is." Kenyatta took a deep breath, and then began walking towards me. The closer he came, I could see he was holding a piece of aluminum foil. "See, Ma?" He held it up in the light. "I told you it was nothing, just some left over biscuits from dinner. I was feeding 'em to Red Man."

"So, why were you standing over there at the dog house?"

"I just told you. I was feeding Red Man the biscuits."

"But Red Man's greedy as hell." I looked at him skeptically. "Usually, whenever we come outside to feed him, he's already waiting at the door with his tail wagging and his mouth drooling. So, why would you go over to the dog house? That doesn't make any sense."

"Well, that's because—umm—umm. Oh, yeah, that's right. I was checking to see if the heater was still working. It's starting to get cold, and I was making sure that Red Man was nice and warm."

I looked Kenyatta square in his eyes, and the second he looked away I knew something was wrong. My motherly intuition was on full blast, telling me to look inside of the dog house, which is exactly what I did. I slipped on the flats that I kept beside the door and began marching towards it.

"Hold up, Ma, wait. What'chu doing?" Kenyatta asked, as I shot right past him. "What'chu going over to the dog house for? There's nothing in there," he continued in a shaky voice.

I ignored his ass, and kept right on walking. Red Man was a few steps ahead of me, tail wagging and looking over his shoulder as if he were leading me to something. When we reached the entrance to his wooden shack, he laid down on the frost-covered dirt and began barking. Kenyatta was looking at Red Man like he wanted to kill him, and the look I gave Kenyatta was the same.

"If there's something in here that's not supposed to be, then I'd suggest you tell me."

"I already told you, there's nothing in there," Kenyatta stuck to his story. "Now, can we please go back in the house?"

His shaky voice and watery eyes only furthered my suspicions. So, after rolling my sleeves back and hiking up my bathrobe, I squatted down at the entrance. The harsh aroma of dog food and wet Pit bull smacked me in the face. It stank something terrible, but not enough to keep me from reaching inside.

"Ma, wait!" Kenyatta blurted out.

I pulled my hand back and looked over my shoulder. Kenyatta was crying. His bottom lip quivered, and his skinny frame was shivering from the weather.

"Kenyatta, what the hell is in here?" I asked him in a serious tone.

"If I—If I tell you, will you promise not to beat me?"

Looking at my baby's face, I could feel my heart splicing down the middle. For Kenyatta to even ask such a question, was enough proof that I was in for a rude awakening. What was he hiding that was so bad, he assumed that I would give him a spanking? And this was coming from a child who never received a *real* spanking a day in his life.

"Yatta," I took a deep breath and released it, "what the hell is inside of this dog house?"

"First, you gotta promise me," he cried. "You gotta promise not to beat me."

"Baby, I promise that I'm not going to beat you. But you seriously need to tell Mommy what's going on. What the hell are you hiding in there?"

My heart was beating out of my chest, and despite the cold weather I was beginning to have hot flashes. My brain was moving at a thousand miles per second, sifting through the possibilities of what he'd might say.

"Is it cigarettes?" I asked him. "Have you been smoking?"

Still crying, Kenyatta shook his head *no*.

"*Well, what the fuck is it?*" I screamed at him, way past the point of having patience. "Is it drugs? Are you using drugs?"

Again, Kenyatta shook his head *no*.

"Baby, whatever it is, we can talk about it," my voice cracked. "You know that you can talk to Mommy about anything. So please, baby, just tell Mommy what it is."

"It's a—it's a gun," Kenyatta mumbled, then he shamefully lowered his head.

"A *what?*" I shouted at the top of my lungs, causing him to take a few steps back.

I was boiling with rage, and could literally feel my body trembling. Any and everything that was destined to go wrong with a thirteen-year-old boy carrying a gun ran through my mind, as I began to feel nauseous.

"Mommy, calm down," Kenyatta pleaded. "Don't be mad at me, please? I won't do it again I swear!"

Completely ignoring him, I plopped down on all fours and frantically dug inside of the dog house. I didn't even flinch when my fingers came in contact with the slimy texture of a chewed-up milk bone. It was too dark to clearly see inside, but I was able to make out a dingy old blanket and the driver's seat cushion that Red Man slept on. I flipped over the cushion, and that's when I found it.

Lord Jesus, please? This can't be happening!

I felt the length of the barrel, and then traced my fingers along the grooves of the cylinder. It was sure enough a pistol—the God-forsaken tool that changed the course of my life many times over. My chest grew tight and it was hard to breath.

Is this really happening?

Is my mind playing tricks on me?

Was my thirteen-year-old son really hiding a gun?

I must have been having an out-of-body experience. The back yard was spinning. Red Man was barking and Kenyatta was crying, still begging me not to give him a spanking.

"Where—the fuck—...did you get this?" I snarled at him with my teeth clinched. I was back on my feet with the gun in my hand, slowly closing the distance between us.

"I—I found it," Kenyatta stuttered.

"You found it?" I continued walking him down. "You found it, where?"

He shrugged his shoulder and nervously chewed on his thumb knuckle.

"I don't know. I just—I just found it."

Wham!

I smacked his little ass so hard, that he stumbled backwards and fell to the ground.

"Come on, Mommy, please? You promised you wouldn't beat me!"

"Motherfucker, I lied!" I shouted back, and then snatched him off the ground by his shirt collar. "Now, get'cha ass in the house and take off them goddamned clothes!"

"But Mommy, you promised!"

"*I don't give a goddamn!*" I screamed in his face. "Ya lil' ass wanna be big and bad, and playing with guns and shit? Boy, I'ma *break* you the fuck up!"

CHAPTER FORTY-SEVEN

ZION

9:27pm

After hitting the weights and running a few miles on the treadmill in my basement, I was ready to call it a night. My heart was heavy, and I was outright depressed. I'd been working so hard to make a difference in the lives of our young people—my daughter's included—and then just like that, in the snap of a finger, all of my hard work was beginning to unravel. I thought about Seekumbuzu and the promise I made to dedicate my life to the struggle. But at the same time, I was thinking about Uzi and the shit he was kicking in front of my bookstore the other day.

"I'm just giving you the real, bro. The Christians only care about the Bible. The Muslims only care about the Qur'an. The hustlas and stickup boys? If it ain't about the bag, them niggas don't give a fuck. And these bitches? These stanking-ass skally wagz? These bitches don't want nothing but a dick to suck, and a muh'fucking welfare check. And half of 'em don't even spend that shit on they fucking kids. So, how the fuck is you supposed to fix some shit like that?"

Maybe Uzi was right, maybe I did bite off more than I could chew. Life was so much easier when I was slinging them thangs and stacking that fetty. But with knowledge comes responsibility, and now that I knew what I knew, and could clearly see the plight of my people's struggle, how could I call myself a man and just sit back without doing anything to change it for the better?

Still frustrated, I slipped out of my sweaty clothes and headed towards the bathroom. I was halfway down the hall when I heard my cell phone ringing; it was downstairs on the dining room table. I started to disregard it, but then I thought about Ebony, remembering she was supposed to be giving me a call. I couldn't even front, I hauled ass down the stairs praying it was her. But when I picked up the phone and looked at the screen, I realized that it wasn't. It was, however, the next best thing; it was Sista Hydia. She wasn't at the rec center earlier, but I was more than certain Atiba had told her everything that happened.

"Peace, Black Man," Hydia's voice eased through the phone. "I was talking to my King, and he told me what happened. He also said that you were taking it hard and coming down on yourself. So, I was calling to check on you, to see if you were feeling okay."

"Thanks for calling, sis. I'm alright."

"Black Man, you and my King are the strongest brothas I know. But between the two of you, it's hard for me to tell which one is the most stubborn. You claim to be okay, but the sound of your voice is telling me otherwise. I'm not going to pry, because I overstand that you're dealing with this tragedy in your own, unique way. I just need you to know that your community loves you, and that we appreciate all of your hard work and dedication. You're doing a phenomenal job, and don't ever forget that."

I took a deep breath and sighed.

"Thanks, sis. I appreciate that, I really do."

"I'm only speaking the truth," she quickly replied. "And Black Man, you have to remember only a coward can stand on the sidelines and have an opinion about an ongoing war. It takes a hero, or better yet a *warrior* to strap his boots on and willingly place himself on the front line, and that's exactly what you're doing. You could have easily come home from prison and hopped right back in the game, but you didn't. You sacrificed your personal gains for the betterment of your community, for the betterment of our youth, which is essentially the betterment of our future. So, for that, Black Man, you have every reason to hold your head up high."

"Hold my head up high?" I questioned. "How can I do such a thing when two of our brothas lost their lives today? Shyheem's stretched out in the morgue, and Raekwon's facing a Life Sentence. Sista, I failed those brothas. I took on the responsibility to show them a better way, and I failed. Can't you see that?"

"I most certainly don't," Hydia spoke with conviction. "And I'd appreciate you for never saying that again. Zion, you're a gem. And for every Raekwon and Shyheem, there are dozens of young black men who benefit tremendously from your time and effort. Now, make no mistakes about it, what happened today was nothing short of a senseless tragedy. But what's a war without casualties? My prayers go out to both families, but we can't get caught up and be down on ourselves about what happened. We shall and must continue to push forward. Black Man, we still have work to do."

Listening to my sista's logic brought a reassuring smile to my face. Her spoken words were the truth, and without a doubt they had given me the strength I needed to keep moving forward.

"Hey, umm, sis, would you mind if I switched gears for a minute? I need a woman's perspective on something."

"By all means, Black Man, proceed."

"After everything that happened at the rec, when I returned home Felicia was waiting outside with the police. She was try'na get me locked up, talking about I kidnapped Dominique."

"No, the hell she didn't!" Sista Hydia exclaimed. "Zion, are you serious?"

"Sista, I'm dead serious. She was really out there try'na get me locked up."

"For allegedly kidnapping your own daughter?"

"My own daughter," I quickly confirmed, still sick to my stomach from the thought.

"So, what happened?"

"Apparently, Dominique ran away from home and was coming to stay with me. So, when I pulled up in front of the house, Felicia, her fruity-ass boyfriend, Giovanni, and a police officer were standing out front waiting on me. The police officer was knocking on the door, and Felicia was hooting and hollering, talking about pressing charges on me."

"And what did the cop say?"

"He was basically saying that Felicia's accusations didn't make any sense. She admitted that Dominique had stayed over for the weekend. But because it was Monday and Dominique was still there, she was accusing me of kidnapping her. I didn't even know Dominique was there. The last I saw her was earlier this morning when I dropped her off at school."

"Umm mmm mmm, now this chick *know* she needs an ass whipping."

"And this is the crazy part, because Felicia has full custody of Dominique, she's saying that I can't see her again until she turns eighteen."

"Well, if you need me, Black Man, you know I got'cha back. 'Cause I got no problems coming up outta this hijab. I'll throw on some sneakers, Vaseline my face, and then go out and handle my business. You know The Nation don't raise no punks. There's a whole lot more on the menu than just bean pies and bow ties, we serve up butt whippings too. That dizzy chick better ask somebody."

"Chill out, Lailah Ali. It's not even that deep." I laughed at my sista, knowing she was speaking the truth.

"But it *is* that deep," she vehemently stated. "Doesn't she realize that little sista needs her father? There are so many little sistas out here just yearning for the love and affection of a father, and praise be to Allah, Dominique has one. A *strong* one, at that, and this chick is try'na block her blessing? Ahn-ahn, Black Man, this heifer just don't know!" she raised her voice. "The problem is that you're a man, so you can't put your hands on a woman. But *me*? Oh, I'll drag that ass up and down Broad Street, from South Philly to Uptown."

I cracked up laughing, thinking about Sista Hydia getting down and dirty, and throwing them hands. She was usually so classy and refined, that I almost forget she was born and raised in the Wilson Park projects. But even then, no matter how good it would feel to see Felicia getting her just due, I could never bring that type of drama to the mother of my child.

"Stop laughing, Black Man, because it's really not funny," Sista Hydia stated with a chuckle. "Because I really am serious. I'll break my foot off in that girl's ass. She sho'nuff got the right one."

"I know you would, and that's the reason I'm laughing," I told her, still laughing at the thought of Felicia catching them hands. "But seriously, though, from a woman's perspective, why do you think Felicia's hates me so much? Granted, I went to prison for ten years and left her all alone to raise Dominique. But now that I'm home and doing everything I possibly can to be a good father, why is she giving me such a hard time?"

"Well, that's an easy one," Sista Hydia shot right back. "She's kicking herself in the butt for not being there for you when you needed her the most. And now that you're back home, looking and doing good, but refusing to have any dealings with her outside of y'all's daughter, she's making you feel the burn. And because Dominique is the only power she has over you, she's using that baby against you."

"Damn, Sis, that's foul," I replied, while shaking my head. "Does a woman really have to go that hard just to get back at a man for not wanting her?"

"Correction," Sista Hydia checked me, "a *real* woman doesn't act that way. Those are the characteristics of a grown little girl. And speaking of a woman, just when in the world do you plan on getting one? Because me and my King are tired of you playing the third wheel whenever we go out. It started off as cute, but now it's just sad. You seriously need a woman, Black Man."

"I'm working on it, Sis. I'm working on it."

"Oh, I know," she giggled. "My King told me about Cookie."

"Well, damn, does Atiba tell you *everything*?"

"Humph, he better, if he knows what's good for him. Now, back to Miss Taraji P. When am I going to meet her?"

"Whooooaaaa. Put the horse back in the stable. Can I at least get the chance to know the sista first? Sheesh!"

"Alright." Sista Hydia sighed. "If you say so. But just in case she isn't the one, I know some beautiful sistas down at the Temple. But you know you have to be a Muslim first."

"Yeah, yeah, yeah."

"What? I'm just saying. You know the Fruit don't be playing no games when it comes to us sistas."

"With that being said, I'm gone, Sis. Tell my brotha I send my love, and I'll see y'all tomorrow at the rec."

"Insha Allah. And we love you, too, Black Man. Peace."

"Peace."

Askari

CHAPTER FORTY-EIGHT

EBONY

9:54 pm

Thinking about Big Mama, I decided to borrow a chapter from her infamous book of discipline, *The Questions Asked After Kicking A Kids Ass.*

Whenever Sadie-Mae would give us a spanking, she would come back a little while later with a bowl of ice cream and a slice of cake. Being the wise woman she was, it was done to let us know that she loved us, and that she wasn't kicking ass just for the sake of kicking ass. But most importantly, she knew it would make us more receptive to the questions she wanted answers to. So, after giving Kenyatta a thorough ass whipping, I took another shower and then headed downstairs into the kitchen to fix him a bowl of ice cream. Not only did I need my baby to know that I still loved him, the plan was to loosen him up before tossing around a couple of questions. I needed to know how he got his hands on a gun, and whether or not he was capable of getting his hands on another one.

As I approached Kenyatta's bedroom door, I could tell that he was still crying. It struck me to the core to know that my baby was hurting, but at the same time I knew it was a necessary pain. I mean, shit, life is hard enough as it already is. But it's even harder for a young black man who's susceptible of making bone headed mistakes. Statistics show that their mishaps and stumbles are less likely to be forgiven by society. So, hopefully, by experiencing his first real ass whipping, it instilled in Kenyatta a healthy fear and made him realize that for every action there's a reaction, whether positive or negative.

"Yatta?" I spoke in a soft voice, as I gently pushed his door open. "I brought you a bowl of ice cream. It's your favorite, butter pecan."

I held up the bowl, but he rolled over and gave me his back.

"Baby, I know you're hurting, but you left me no other choice," I told him as I sat down on the edge of his bed. I placed the bowl of ice cream on his nightstand, then I gently caressed his back. "Can you turn around and talk to me?"

"I don't wanna talk," Kenyatta sniffled. "You lied to me. You promised you wouldn't beat me, but you did it anyway. So, that makes you a liar."

I started to pop his ass for talking slick, but I let it slide. I, too, was a child once and was more than familiar with effects of a superstar ass whipping. Aside from the welts on his ass and back, his pride was hurt, and he was dealing with the misplaced feelings of being betrayed. He probably called me a thousand bitches between now and then, and had wished death on me ten times over. I used to say the same exact things about Big Mama, but under my breath of course.

Still caressing Kenyatta's back, I said, "Baby, if nothing else, just know that I love you, and that I'm willing to do whatever necessary to keep you safe."

"So, what'chu spank me for?"

"Giving you a spanking was never my intention. But when you told me you had a gun, I just—I just lost it. Do you even realize how serious this is? A gun is not a toy, Kenyatta. It's a deadly weapon, and the aftermath of playing with one is far from a goddamned video game. So many things can and *do* go wrong with a child having access to a gun. Countless black men are losing their lives every day, all at the squeeze of a trigger; your daddy being one of them."

At the mentioning of Big Jabby, Kenyatta rolled over to face me. His wet eyes were puffy and red. "My daddy?" He looked at me skeptically. "But you said that he died in a car accident."

"Well, technically, he *did* die in a car."

"So, which one is it?" Kenyatta asked me. "Did he get shot, or did he die in a car accident?"

I sucked in a deep breath and exhaled slowly. I knew the day would eventually come when I had to tell him the truth about his father's murder. I just never assumed it would be under such circumstances.

"Come on, Ma, are you gonna tell me the real story or not? Whatever the case, I'm big enough to handle it. I'm not a baby anymore."

I quit smoking a few years back, but damn I needed a cigarette. Maybe even a nice fat Blunt. I was so not ready to have this conversation.

"Alright," I spoke slowly, trying to figure out the best way to tell him what happened. "Your daddy was— Your daddy was murdered, and..."

"And what? My daddy was murdered, and what?"

I lowered my head and sucked in another deep breath.

"Come on, Ma. My daddy was murdered, and what?"

"And you were there when it happened," I managed to say. "He was murdered right in front of you."

It seemed as though the earth stopped spinning. Silence filled the room, and it felt like all of the air had been sucked out.

"I was there when it happened?" Kenyatta asked me in a slow, cracked voice. His glossy, wet eyes were locked on mines looking for confirmation.

"Yes, baby, you were there when it happened. You were sitting in the back of his car, strapped down in your car seat."

"Yo, that's crazy." Kenyatta replied, then he slowly shook his head. "So, who killed him, and why?"

"I really can't say for sure. But the guy who ordered the hit, his name was Mook. Him and your daddy had a heated argument, then a week later your daddy was murdered."

"So, if I was there, then why is it that I don't remember?"

"You don't remember because you were only two years old when it happened. As you already know, he died on the morning of your second birthday. He was actually taking you to get your first haircut. I told him that it was safer to take you to a barbershop down in Delaware, where we were living at the time, but he simply wasn't having it. He insisted that his personal barber be the first one to cut your hair, so that's the reason he drove back to the Philly. His barber was the only one who knew he was coming, so I'm assuming he's the one who set him up to be killed."

"And what barbershop was this?" Kenyatta asked me. "And who was his barber?"

"I forget his barber's name, but the barbershop was Cutting It Up on Woodstock and Susquehanna."

"Oh yeah?" Kenyatta nodded his head. "I know that barbershop, it's a few blocks away from the playground."

"And that's the corner where your daddy was killed. The two of you were just leaving the barbershop, when three gunmen ran up from behind. They shot him a total of nineteen times, as he was strapping you down in your car seat. According to the police report, there were bullet holes all around you. But because your daddy was big, his body absorbed all the bullets. He died trying to protect you from the gunfire."

Kenyatta had tears in his eyes, but he didn't cry. He just laid there in silence staring up at the ceiling. I could literally feel the heat oozing from his body.

"So, now do you understand why I reacted the way I did? Our family's been devastated by gun violence in the worst way possible. Not only was your daddy murdered, but I also lost my father to gun violence. He's serving a Life Sentence for killing the man who murdered my mother. This revolving cycle of gun violence has affected our family for two generations, and the buck stops here. So, if it takes for me to whip your ass a thousand times just to keep you from playing with guns, then I'll kick your ass all over this fucking house.

"This shit is not a game, and I need you to know that. What if you would have hurt yourself? Or even worse, what if someone else would have hurt you because they saw a gun in your hand and considered you a threat? Just look at what happened to that baby in Cleveland, Ohio, Tamir Rice. That baby," my voice cracked and my bottom lip quivered, "that beautiful baby, may God bless his soul. He was playing with a BB gun, and the police killed him. Those bastards didn't even take the time to figure out the gun wasn't real. Now, what if something like that would have happened to you? Can you imagine how that would have made me feel?"

244

I broke down crying, and Kenyatta cried, too. He sat up and wrapped his arms around me, begging me to stop crying because I was making him cry.

"Yatta," I leaned into him and sobbed against his shoulder, "I would fucking die if something like that were to happen to you. I wouldn't have been able to take it. You gotta promise me. ..Promise me that you'll never touch another gun. *Promise me.*"

"I promise, Ma. The last thing I ever wanna do is hurt you. I love you, and I never wanna be the reason you're crying. So, can you please stop?"

I pulled away and grasped his face with both hands. Looking him square in the eyes, I said, "Yatta, you need to tell me where you got it."

"Got what?"

"*The gun,*" I raised my voice. "Where did you get it?"

He looked away, and I could sense that he didn't want to tell me. I didn't say it, but I was beginning to suspect he got the gun from Jabari. Not to say that my oldest would give his little brother a gun, but what if he had onesecretly stashed away and somehow Kenyatta managed to find it?

"Listen, Yatta, you already got a spanking, so there's no reason to give you another one. I just need to know where you got it, so I can see to it that you can't get another one."

Kenyatta lowered his head and nervously began biting down on his thumb knuckle. He was clearly debating on whether or not he should tell me.

"Boy, you better spit it out!" I demanded, quickly losing my cool. "'Cause if you don't," I looked at him with a raised brow, giving him his final warning, "you know what it is."

"Alright, Ma, dang." He raised his hands in defeat. "I stole it."

"You stole it?" I shot back, praying that he didn't say Jabari. The last thing I needed was for both of my sons to be carrying a goddamned gun. "From where, Kenyatta? Where did you steal it from?"

"Earlier today, at Auntie Erica's house."

"*Erica's house?*" My octave escalated.

"Umm-hmm." Kenyatta nodded his head. "She stepped out for a while, and that's when I stole it from her bedroom closet. Don't be mad at Auntie Erica, because it's not her fault. She told me to stay out of her bedroom, but I didn't listen."

That goddamned Uzi! I thought to myself, as my eyelids became slits. *I should have known his ass had something to do with this shit!*

"Ma, *please* don't say anything to Auntie Erica?" Kenyatta begged me. "I don't want her to be mad at me for stealing out of her house. She told me to stay out of her bedroom, but I did it anyway. And even worse, I betrayed her trust. So, please don't tell her?"

I sat there anxiously biting down on my bottom lip, as Kenyatta's words went in one ear and out the other. Everything inside of me wanted to drive back to the city and slap the piss out of Erica *and* Uzi. But what good would that have done? Because even though Erica knew better than to be having guns around my son, Kenyatta's little bad ass shouldn't have been snooping around and stealing from her house. So, basically, either way the situation was a loss.

"Come on, Ma, I see you getting all mad." Kenyatta pointed out. "Please don't tell Auntie Erica what I did? She's my favorite auntie, and if she finds out that I stole from her house she's gonna look at me different."

"No, I'm not going to tell her," I finally replied after silently weighing my options. "But from now on, you're not allowed to go over there anymore. That shit is a wrap. Now, lay down and go to sleep. You still have to get up in the morning."

"But who's gonna watch me if I can't go back to Auntie Erica's house?"

"That's for me to worry about, and not you. I'll probably just call your Uncle Tony. He's usually home during the day, so hopefully I can get him to watch you for a few days."

After kissing Kenyatta's forehead, I returned to my bedroom and cried like a baby. My children were rapidly spinning out of control, and it seemed as though there was nothing I could do about it. I thought about calling Zion, but what was I supposed to say: *"I'm in dire need of a husband, and my boys need a strong black man to show them how it's done?"* I would have sound so crazy, and surely that would have scared him away. So, essentially, in the most critical time of my boy's life, I was forced to figure it out on my own. I just prayed that I didn't fail, and that I could somehow find a way to steer them back on the right track. Especially, since the feeling in my heart was that something terrible was about to happen.

Please, Lord, give me strength.

Askari

CHAPTER FORTY-NINE

DOMINIQUE

10:49 pm

"Nique-Nique, wake up," I heard Giovanni's voice. I was laying on my bed spread eagle, and could feel the warmth of his words tickling my earlobe.

"Wake up," he whispered in my ear some more. His breathing was hot and heavy, and I could feel my body catching fire. He kissed the nape of my neck, and then slid his fingers down the crack of my ass to play with my coochie from the back.

"Your Mommy's knocked out in the other room, and Daddy Dick wanna come out and play with his baby. Especially after everything that happened earlier. You had Daddy Dick scared. He thought you was running away and that he wouldn't be able to dip in his honey no more. You know that shit wasn't right."

"Uhn-uhn," I shut him down, but was loving the feel of his touch. He was rubbing my clit in a circular motion, and sucking on the right side of my neck. "I already told you, I'm not messing with you like this anymore. My mommy's gonna find out."

"She's not gonna find out, trust me." He nibbled on my earlobe and then slipped his fingers deep inside of me. "She's knocked out from the pills I gave her. And besides...she hasn't found out yet, and we've been doing this for over two years now. I told you from the beginning, I promise not to tell if you won't. It'll be our little secret. Remember?"

"Ummmm," I released a soft moan. He was fucking me so good with his fingers that I began winding my hips, making sure that he caressed me in all the right places.

"But—But you promised you would leave her, and you didn't. And on top of that, I'm still mad at you."

"Mad at me?" He slipped in a third finger, causing me to cream on his hand. "Mad at me for what?"

"I—I already told you," I panted. "It's D'Lovely. I saw the way you were looking at him. So, don't even lie. I know you been creeping with him behind Mommy's back."

"Yo, Nique-Nique, cut it the fuck out. You know me better than that. You know I don't be rocking wit' none of that funny shit." He quickened his pace, and my coochie became so juicy that I could feel the shit dripping between my thighs. "All I want is you, Nique-Nique. And you already know that. The only reason I didn't leave your mom is because I wanted to stay here so I could be close to you."

Giovanni turned my head sideways and began kissing me passionately. I knew what we were doing was wrong, but I can't lie, this nigga had me addicted. He showed me what it felt like to truly be a woman, and to keep it real, fucking Mommy's man was the best way to extract my revenge on her. Since she wanted to be a bitch and deprive me of the man in my life, that man being my daddy, I decided to take *her* man and make him my *big* daddy.

Me and Giovanni's situationship started off innocent. He would always tell me how pretty I was, and would go out of his way to spend his time and money on me. He's been in my life since I was twelve years old, when he and Mommy first got together. But a couple of years ago, on my fourteenth birthday, the dynamics of our relationship changed forever. I had come a long way from the skinny little girl that Mommy introduced him to. My titties were fuller, my thighs were thicker, and my ass was phatter.

Giovanni noticed, and little by little he became more touchy feely. Whether it was brushing against my titties while squeezing past me in the hallway, or brushing against my ass while I was standing at the sink washing the dishes, he just *had* to get him a feel of this body. I'm not gonna lie and say it wasn't awkward at first, because it was. But for some strange reason, I found myself loving the attention.

Then, on the night of my fourteen birthday, my curiosity got the best of me. Mommy was knocked out as usual, probably high on Xanax, and Giovanni was downstairs in the living room watching Monday Night Football. I slipped on a mid-drift T-shirt and a pair of thongs, and then went downstairs and stood in front of the television. I was nervous as hell, afraid that Giovanni would reject me and rat me out to Mommy. But when he licked his lips and motioned for me to come over and have a seat on his lap, I knew he was under my spell. That was the night I became a woman, and since then nobody could make my body feel as good as Giovanni did, not even Tone Boy.

"Come on, Nique-Nique, Daddy Dick needs you," Giovanni panted. He sank his teeth into my bottom lip, and then flicked his tongue against mines. After that, he positioned himself on top of me and softly kissed the back of my neck.

"Stop playing, girl. You know Daddy loves you."

"And I love you, too, Daddy."

I reached back and grabbed his manhood, and then slowly eased it inside of me. It stretched me out and gave me some pain, but then my pain became pleasure. The pleasure was bliss, and the bliss was knowing that I'd taken from Mommy what she'd taken from me. *Her daddy.*

Askari

CHAPTER FIFTY

TONYA

11:16 pm

When I tell you that my boo, Jabari, popped up at my front door unexpected, bent me over the couch and dicked me down something vicious, please believe it! This lil' juice box had him going crazy, too. Had his ass "*oohing*" and "*ahhing*," and telling me how much he loved me and couldn't live without me. And best of all, he came nice and hard, deep down inside of my pussy just the way I needed him to. Hopefully, one of his lil' soldiers came with a million-dollar signing bonus. Because I'm tired of being broke and stuck in the projects. I need Giuseppe's on my feet, diamonds on my neck, a house on the hill, and a brand-new Bentley. But most of all, I wanna be the star on my own reality show—*Basketball Wives Philly*. The show doesn't even exist yet, but I'ma set that motherfucker off. So, that way I can come back to jects, pull up in my baby-blue Bentley, hop out dripping in my full-length mink, and then stretch my arms out screaming at the top of my lungs, "*I'm rich, bitch!*"

Umm mmm mmm, now wouldn't that be something? Well that's the plan, anyway. But lately, there's something about Jabari that's been rubbing me the wrong way. Usually, whenever we have sex, it's all about him. But a few hours ago, when was getting our freak on, he was acting all affectionate and shit, rubbing on my stomach and kissing me all over. He even had the nerve to go down-town and eat the booty like groceries, and he *never* did that.

Now, I never claimed to be the brightest bitch in the bunch, but I'm smart enough to pick up on the fact that his sneaky-ass is up to something. Exactly what? I can't say. But he's definitely up to something.

About thirty minutes ago, I woke his ass up and demanded that he take me to get a pint of ice cream and a chili-cheese hotdog. He was bitching and moaning, and complaining about how tired he was. But being the good lil' puppy dog that I trained him to be, he got his ass up and attended to his *"pregnant"* girlfriend. I didn't even want the shit, but every now and then I had to play the pregnancy card. And what better way than to fake a craving for strawberry ice cream and a chili-cheese hotdog? I probably should have told his ass to get me a jar of pickles to go along with it. Maybe even a bag of marshmallows.

So, anyway, there I was, sitting in Jabari's car, parked outside of the A Plus gas station on Broad and Girard. I was nodding my head to the sounds of Chief Keef, and looking at Jabari through the front glass window. His too-tall ass was standing at the cash register paying for my food. He must have felt me staring because he looked back at me and smiled. He licked his lips and mouthed the words "*I love you,*" and then just like that, I was right back to being suspicious.

His sneaky ass was up to something, and I was determined to find out what. So, after turning down the music, I popped open his glove compartment. Lo and behold, guess what the fuck I found. Yup. A goddamned party-sized box of condoms. Trojan Magnums, extra-large, ribbed for the next bitch's pleasure. I knew they weren't for me, because me and Jabari never used them. He was probably using them on the light-skinned bright who caught these hands the other night, with her smutt ass. Ol' side-chick-fa-life, bucket head bitch. She probably had the bumps or sum'n, looking all stank and whatnot.

Ol' sneaky motherfucker! I rolled my eyes at Jabari through the window.

After stealing two of Jabari's condoms, I stuffed the box back inside of his glove compartment. Still suspicious, I reached down and pulled back the lid on his center console. Jabari's cell phone was laying inside. I snatched it up quick and thumbed in the digits to the password he gave me on the first day he bought it. And wouldn't you know it, his stupid-ass never even changed the motherfucker.

Niggas are so stupid!

Never in a million years would I give Jabari the *real* password to my phone, even though that's the deal we made. Between our cell phones, Facebook, Instagram and Twitter, we had to hand over the password to at least one of them. We settled on the passwords to our cell phones. But unlike Jabari's stupid ass, I changed mines the same day I gave it to him.

Niggas are so stupid!

Jabari's cell phone came to life, and I noticed he had an unread text from a person who was only listed as *Meek*. Initially, I assumed it was the rapper bul, Meek Mill from 24th and Berks, which is a few blocks over and a few blocks down from my projects.

The reason I assumed it was him, was because rappers and ball players be kicking it like that, especially when they both be reppin' the same city. Plus, I heard on the radio that Meek Mill was back in Philly. I haven't seen him since he blew up in the rap game, and according to my girlfriend, Shonda, now that he's rich and famous and be fucking all these superstar bitches like Nicki Minaj, he doesn't fuck with the hoodstar bitches like us anymore. But maybe, just maybe, and I'm going out on a limb, if I text him back and tell him who I am, I could persuade him to change his mind. At least that way, if things didn't work out with me and Jabari, I would still have a backup plan.

Love & Hip Hop Philly? Humph, sounds good to me.

Unfortunately, when I pressed down on the unread text, I realized this was a whole different *Meek*. The text message read:

11:48 pm: Meek: *I know you're mad at me for throwing you under the bus, but I had no other choice. My parents made me do it. It was either tell them who you were, or be kicked out of the house. It was never my intention to hurt you, and I meant to cause you any trouble. I know what you said about me having an abortion, but I just can't do it. Try to understand, please. I love you.*

I was madder than a motherfucker scrolling through their past messages. Apparently, this so-called *Meek* was the same bitch from a few nights earlier. The worst part, and what hurt me the most, was that the bitch had somehow managed to get pregnant before I did. I'd been trying like hell for Jabari to get me pregnant, but instead of me this nigga done knocked up the next bitch?

Oh, helllllllllll nawl! This motherfucker got me chopped!

255

I looked out of the window and saw Jabari was walking back to the car. He moved around the back and then climbed in on the driver's side. He settled back in his seat, then he looked down at his cell phone clutched in my hand. If looks could kill, his fucking ass would have been stretched out leaking.

This bitch-made motherfucker!

CHAPTER FIFTY-ONE

JABARI

"Nigga, what the fuck is this?" Tonya snapped at me, pushing my phone so close to my face that I could barely see the screen. "Ya triflin' ass ain't shit!"

"Yo, Shameeka, what the fuck is you talking 'bout?"

"*What?*" Tonya screamed at me like a woman possessed. "*Not only did you get this bitch pregnant, you got the nerve to be calling me by her fucking name? Is you fucking stupid?*"

Whack!

She banged my phone against the bridge of my nose, and my vision became blurred. I tried to restrain her, but shorty was going straight up crazy—punching me in the face and clawing at the right side of my neck.

"*Jabari, I'ma fucking kill you!*" She growled like a beast, and then leaned in to bite me. She almost got me, but I reached out and pushed her ass back. I wasn't trying to hurt her, but what else could I do to stop her from hitting me?

"Calm ya ass down! What the fuck is wrong wit'chu?"

"Motherfucker, ya ass gon' die!"

She raked her fingernails across my face, and then reached up and poked me in the eye. I slammed her ass back against the door, but the bitch kept coming. She grabbed the front of my hoody and somehow managed to pull it up over my head. I couldn't see a god-damned thing, but could definitely feel the cell phone banging against the top of my shit.

Whack! Whack! Whack! Whack!

Flaming mad, I slipped out of my hoody and cocked my fist back. The only thing that stopped me from swinging, was that a cop car was parked in front of my whip. I was so caught up in the bull-shit with Tonya, that I failed to notice the police officer when he pulled into the gas station and saw that we were fighting.

"Show me your fucking hands!" the police officer shouted. He was already out of his squad car and moving around to my driver's side door. His service pistol was aimed at me through the window.

"Your hands!" the police officer continued shouting. "Show me your fucking hands! *Now!*"

I was just about to comply with his order, but another blow from my cell phone sent me into a frenzy. I smacked the shit out of Tonya, then I reached down and snatched my phone from her hand. I spun back around to face the officer, and that's when it happened.

Bang!

A loud blast lit up the night, and my driver's side window shattered to pieces. A devastating force slammed into my shoulder, and I spun back around facing Tonya.

Bang! Bang!

Two more left me slumped over the console. My body was on fire, and it felt like my breastbone had been cracked in half. I heard another *Bang!* Then another *Bang!* And another *Bang!* I could hear Tonya screaming, but then the piercing sound was cut short.

Bang!

My eyelids closed and everything went black. It's crazy, though, because amidst the darkness I could see Ma' Dukes. She was smiling at me, but crying at the same time. I reached out to touch her face, but then her beautiful face became a distant blur. It seemed as though she was slipping away, but really it was me. I was crossing over to the other side.

"Ma, please?" I cried out for her in a voice so low, that it fell short of a whisper. "Don't—leave me. I can't—I can't—*breathe.*"

To Be Continued...
Coming Soon
Shadows of the Game 2

DISCUSSION QUESTIONS

1) Do you agree with the way Ebony chose to punish Kenyatta when he was suspended from school?

2) Would you consider Kenyatta to be a bad kid, or just a little adventurous and mischievous?

3) Why do you think the police were so aggressive when they arrested Reeko?

4) Do you think Jabari had a legitimate reason to carrying a gun?

5) What so you think about Zion's efforts to have a positive impact on the youth in his community?

6) Do you think Felicia was wrong for the way she treated Zion?

7) Do you think Erica overreacted when she saw what the police did to Reeko?

8) Do you think Zion should have felt responsible for Raekwon killing Shyheem?

9) Do you think Jabari was wrong for his treatment of Shameeka?

10) Why do you think Jabari chose Tonya over Shameeka?

11) Do you think Felicia was responsible for the relationship between Dominique and Giovanni?

12) Do you think the police officer was justified in the way he handled the situation with Jabari and Tonya?

About the Author

My pen name is ASKARI, but I'm known throughout the city of Philadelphia as S-CLASS. Prior to writing books, I was one of the hottest rappers in the city. This was in the early 2000' s before social media, but I still had a strong buzz, blazing mixtapes and rocking clubs from Jersey to New York City.

In October 2001, my homie, Peedi Crack, was signed to Roca-fella Records, and like the real nigga he is, he took our crew along for the ride. Our sole mission was to lock down the rap game and get our families out of the hood. Unfortunately, in February 2003, just as my career was beginning to take off, I was arrested and charged for a murder that I absolutely did not commit. Aside from the fact there was no physical evidence linking me to this crime. (No Gun. No Fingerprints. No DNA. No video surveillance. Nothing!) Immediately after the crime, the shooter was described as a DARK-SKINNED BLACK MAN WITH A SUNNI MUSLIM BEARD. As you can see from my pictures, I'm light brown-skinned and at the time I had a baby's face.

When I was kidnapped by the system, I had just turned 20 years old, a father of three beautiful children, I was working two jobs and busting my ass in the studio, primed to be the next Jay Z. I didn't have a criminal record and in my spare time, I was working with the youth in my community as a coach on our little league's football team. At my trial, the district attorney's case relied exclusively on one eyewitness. This witness was a convicted felon and serving time for an unrelated matter. (He admitted the district attorney gave him a deal to testify against me.) He testified that at the time of this incident, he was a fugitive of justice, standing on the corner selling crack cocaine. He admitted that he was under the influence of alcohol and drugs and he only had a partial view of the shooter's face because the shooter was wearing a hoody and because the scene was not well lit.

He also testified that another individual TOLD him that I was the shooter. SMH!!! Typical jealousy and hate!!! In the end, after a TWO DAY TRIAL, I was convicted of first degree murder and given a life sentence. SMFH!!!! I was crushed to say the least. I couldn't believe it. I couldn't understand How the fuck could I be convicted of some shit that I never even did? Excuse my language, but I'm angry as hell!!! In the midst of the bullshit, I knew that I had to remain focused. I knew that I had to maintain and work hard to prove my innocence, while at the same time conduct myself as a man, standing firm on the principles that my mother and father taught me as a child. I have not waivered and I never will. I shall and must continue to fight for my freedom, that just my nature.

You know, it's funny to me, thinking about this book game. I thought that I'd be triple platinum by now, captivating audiences with my creativity and word play. I guess I still am, but instead of a microphone, I'm using a pen. Still focused on using my creativity to open the doors that confine me. Whether they be the doors that kept a young nigga locked in the hood, or the doors that kept a young nigga locked behind bars. Either way, I will be free!

To my family and friends, fans and supporters, I love y'all from the bottom of my heart. Words could never express my gratitude.

Submission Guideline

Submit the first three chapters of your completed manuscript to <u>ldpsubmissions@gmail.com</u>, subject line: Your book's title. The manuscript must be in a .doc file and sent as an attachment. Document should be in Times New Roman, double spaced and in size 12 font. Also, provide your synopsis and full contact information. If sending multiple submissions, they must each be in a separate email.

Have a story but no way to send it electronically? You can still submit to LDP/Ca$h Presents. Send in the first three chapters, written or typed, of your completed manuscript to:

LDP: Submissions Dept
Po Box 870494
Mesquite, Tx 75187

DO NOT send original manuscript. Must be a duplicate.

Provide your synopsis and a cover letter containing your full contact information.

Thanks for considering LDP and Ca$h Presents.

Shadows of the Game

<u>Coming Soon from Lock Down Publications/Ca$h Presents</u>

BOW DOWN TO MY GANGSTA
By **Ca$h**
TORN BETWEEN TWO
By **Coffee**
BLOOD STAINS OF A SHOTTA **III**
By **Jamaica**
STEADY MOBBIN **III**
By **Marcellus Allen**
BLOOD OF A BOSS **VI**
SHADOWS OF THE GAME II
By **Askari**
LOYAL TO THE GAME **IV**
LIFE OF SIN **III**
By **T.J. & Jelissa**
A DOPEBOY'S PRAYER **II**
By **Eddie "Wolf" Lee**
IF LOVING YOU IS WRONG... **III**
By **Jelissa**
TRUE SAVAGE **VII**
By **Chris Green**
BLAST FOR ME **III**
DUFFLE BAG CARTEL **IV**
HEARTLESS GOON
By **Ghost**
ADDICTIED TO THE DRAMA **III**
By **Jamila Mathis**
A HUSTLER'S DECEIT III
KILL ZONE **II**

Askari

BAE BELONGS TO ME III

SOUL OF A MONSTER II

By **Aryanna**

THE COST OF LOYALTY **III**

By **Kweli**

RENEGADE BOYS **III**

By **Meesha**

A GANGSTER'S SYN II

By **J-Blunt**

KING OF NEW YORK V

RISE TO POWER III

COKE KINGS III

By **T.J. Edwards**

GORILLAZ IN THE BAY IV

De'Kari

THE STREETS ARE CALLING II

Duquie Wilson

KINGPIN KILLAZ IV

STREET KINGS III

PAID IN BLOOD II

Hood Rich

SINS OF A HUSTLA II

ASAD

TRIGGADALE III

Elijah R. Freeman

MARRIED TO A BOSS III

By Destiny Skai & Chris Green

KINGZ OF THE GAME IV

Playa Ray

SLAUGHTER GANG III

BORN HEARTLESS

By Willie Slaughter

THE HEART OF A SAVAGE II

By Jibril Williams

FUK SHYT II

By Blakk Diamond

THE DOPEMAN'S BODYGAURD II

By Tranay Adams

TRAP GOD

By Troublesome

YAYO

By S. Allen

GHOST MOB

Stilloan Robinson

KINGPIN DREAMS

By Paper Boi Rari

Available Now

RESTRAINING ORDER **I & II**

By **CA$H & Coffee**

LOVE KNOWS NO BOUNDARIES **I II & III**

By **Coffee**

RAISED AS A GOON I, II, III & IV

BRED BY THE SLUMS I, II, III

BLAST FOR ME I & II

ROTTEN TO THE CORE I II III

A BRONX TALE I, II, III

DUFFEL BAG CARTEL I II III

Askari

Shadows of the Game

BLOOD OF A BOSS **I, II, III, IV, V**

SHADOWS OF THE GAME

By **Askari**

THE STREETS BLEED MURDER **I, II & III**

THE HEART OF A GANGSTA I II& III

By **Jerry Jackson**

CUM FOR ME

CUM FOR ME 2

CUM FOR ME 3

CUM FOR ME 4

CUM FOR ME 5

An **LDP Erotica Collaboration**

BRIDE OF A HUSTLA **I II & II**

THE FETTI GIRLS **I, II& III**

CORRUPTED BY A GANGSTA I, II III, IV

BLINDED BY HIS LOVE

By **Destiny Skai**

WHEN A GOOD GIRL GOES BAD

By **Adrienne**

THE COST OF LOYALTY I II

By Kweli

A GANGSTER'S REVENGE **I II III & IV**

THE BOSS MAN'S DAUGHTERS

THE BOSS MAN'S DAUGHTERS II

THE BOSSMAN'S DAUGHTERS III

THE BOSSMAN'S DAUGHTERS IV

THE BOSS MAN'S DAUGHTERS **V**

A SAVAGE LOVE **I & II**

BAE BELONGS TO ME I II

A HUSTLER'S DECEIT I, II, III

Askari

WHAT BAD BITCHES DO I, II, III

SOUL OF A MONSTER

KILL ZONE

By **Aryanna**

A KINGPIN'S AMBITON

A KINGPIN'S AMBITION **II**

I MURDER FOR THE DOUGH

By **Ambitious**

TRUE SAVAGE

TRUE SAVAGE II

TRUE SAVAGE **III**

TRUE SAVAGE **IV**

TRUE SAVAGE **V**

TRUE SAVAGE **VI**

By **Chris Green**

A DOPEBOY'S PRAYER

By **Eddie "Wolf" Lee**

THE KING CARTEL **I, II & III**

By **Frank Gresham**

THESE NIGGAS AIN'T LOYAL **I, II & III**

By **Nikki Tee**

GANGSTA SHYT **I II &III**

By **CATO**

THE ULTIMATE BETRAYAL

By **Phoenix**

BOSS'N UP **I , II & III**

By **Royal Nicole**

I LOVE YOU TO DEATH

By **Destiny J**

I RIDE FOR MY HITTA

Shadows of the Game

I STILL RIDE FOR MY HITTA

By **Misty Holt**

LOVE & CHASIN' PAPER

By **Qay Crockett**

TO DIE IN VAIN

SINS OF A HUSTLA

By **ASAD**

BROOKLYN HUSTLAZ

By **Boogsy Morina**

BROOKLYN ON LOCK I & II

By **Sonovia**

GANGSTA CITY

By **Teddy Duke**

A DRUG KING AND HIS DIAMOND I & II III

A DOPEMAN'S RICHES

HER MAN, MINE'S TOO I, II

CASH MONEY HO'S

By Nicole Goosby

TRAPHOUSE KING **I II & III**

KINGPIN KILLAZ I II III

STREET KINGS I II

PAID IN BLOOD

By **Hood Rich**

LIPSTICK KILLAH **I, II, III**

CRIME OF PASSION I & II

By **Mimi**

STEADY MOBBN' **I, II, III**

By **Marcellus Allen**

WHO SHOT YA **I, II, III**

Renta

GORILLAZ IN THE BAY **I II III**

DE'KARI

TRIGGADALE I II

Elijah R. Freeman

GOD BLESS THE TRAPPERS I, II, III

THESE SCANDALOUS STREETS I, II, III

FEAR MY GANGSTA I, II, III

THESE STREETS DON'T LOVE NOBODY I, II

BURY ME A G I, II, III, IV, V

A GANGSTA'S EMPIRE I, II, III, IV

THE DOPEMAN'S BODYGAURD

Tranay Adams

THE STREETS ARE CALLING

Duquie Wilson

MARRIED TO A BOSS... I II

By Destiny Skai & Chris Green

KINGZ OF THE GAME I II III

Playa Ray

SLAUGHTER GANG I II

By Willie Slaughter

THE HEART OF A SAVAGE

By Jibril Williams

FUK SHYT

By Blakk Diamond

DON'T F#CK WITH MY HEART I II

By Linnea

ADDICTED TO THE DRAMA I II

By Jamila

<u>BOOKS BY LDP'S CEO, CA$H</u>

<u>TRUST IN NO MAN</u>
<u>TRUST IN NO MAN 2</u>
<u>TRUST IN NO MAN 3</u>
<u>BONDED BY BLOOD</u>
<u>SHORTY GOT A THUG</u>
<u>THUGS CRY</u>
<u>THUGS CRY 2</u>
<u>THUGS CRY 3</u>
<u>TRUST NO BITCH</u>
<u>TRUST NO BITCH 2</u>
<u>TRUST NO BITCH 3</u>
<u>TIL MY CASKET DROPS</u>
<u>RESTRAINING ORDER</u>
<u>RESTRAINING ORDER 2</u>
<u>IN LOVE WITH A CONVICT</u>

<u>Coming Soon</u>
BONDED BY BLOOD 2
BOW DOWN TO MY GANGSTA

Askari

Printed in the USA
CPSIA information can be obtained
at www.ICGtesting.com
LVHW050317141123
763862LV00011B/18